A cluster of grenades came from the Reds. Millett went into his dancing and dodging act again. Eight detonations nicked the terrain around him—then a ninth exploded behind him and some of its steel found a target in his back and legs. He could feel the blood coursing down his back, drenching his shirt and jacket.

Abandoning his plan for a straight-up assault, he circled to his right, passing by a series of empty fox holes as he moved.

"Let's go!" he screamed. "Use grenades and cold steel! Kill 'em with the bayonet!" As the men hesitated, for an instant, he cursed them bitterly, and howling unprintable epithets—some of them in Chinese—he raced alone into the gun position. Stunned at first by his display of temper the men took up his cry as they followed.

But he was yards ahead of them. He tossed three hand grenades rapidly, and then, all alone, he rushed the V-shaped gun position, bayonet gleaming in the glare of ice and sun.

HEROES
OF THE ARMY

THE MEDAL OF HONOR AND ITS WINNERS

BRUCE JACOBS

JOVE BOOKS, NEW YORK

This Jove book contains the complete
text of the original hardcover edition.

HEROES OF THE ARMY

A Jove Book / published by arrangement with
W. W. Norton and Company

PRINTING HISTORY
W. W. Norton and Company edition published 1956
Jove edition / July 1987

ISBN: 0-515-09136-7

Jove Books are published by The Berkley Publishing Group,
200 Madison Avenue, New York, New York 10016.
The name "JOVE" and the "J" logo
are trademarks belonging to Jove Publications, Inc.

PRINTED IN THE UNITED STATES OF AMERICA

10   9   8   7   6   5   4   3   2   1

. . . to the brave American soldiers who won a proud nation's highest award for valor on the field of honor, this book is humbly dedicated.

CONTENTS

꙳꙳꙳ ꙳꙳꙳

FOREWORD

⋙ ⋙ ⋙ ⋘ ⋘ ⋘

SEVERAL years ago during a party at an Army post in the South, one of the celebrants climbed up on the shoulders of a brawny companion and made a futile pass at one of the bright-colored balloons that dangled from the ceiling. Presently he lost his balance, tumbled from his perch, and landed at the feet of an irate lieutenant colonel, who growled, "What are *you* trying to do? Win the Medal of Honor?"

"Oh no, sir!" replied the crestfallen warrior, as he ruefully brushed the dust from his clothing. "I've *got* that; I was just trying to snag a balloon for one of the kids!"

It is a matter of record that the lieutenant colonel gasped, muttered an apology, and disappeared hastily, as he saw the star-flecked blue ribbon over the left breast pocket of the young man's uniform.

On another occasion a Pentagon group was preparing to welcome Audie Murphy, who was an outstanding personality in Hollywood, but who is best known among military men as a Medal of Honor hero of World War II. Prior to Murphy's arrival at Army Headquarters, a one-star general and a full colonel argued at length whether or not they should salute the hero (a former second lieutenant) when he put in his appearance.

The colonel finally declared that he could find nothing in the regulations about saluting winners of the Medal.

"Well," exclaimed the general, "I don't give a hoot what you say. He's a Medal of Honor man and, by the Gods, he rates a salute in my book!"

In an era when military uniforms fairly glisten with colorful snips of ribbon and highly-polished bits of metal, an aura of the extraordinary still surrounds the few (less than 350, all services, still living) who have earned the right to wear their nation's highest award for gallantry and intrepidity in combat.

There are many myths and fables attached to the Medal that have little or no basis in reality. Take the matter of the salute, for instance. Many people, in and out of the Army, believe that a Medal of Honor man is entitled to the salute of his superiors. There is no basis for this belief in the regulations. Nor may a Medal winner use the Medal to avoid subsequent hazardous duty, to gain promotion, or demand special consideration in future duty assignments.

He *may* travel free of charge in military aircraft on a "space available" basis (the military version of first come, first served); his son may get a presidential assist to an appointment to West Point or Annapolis; if he is an enlisted man an extra two dollars is tacked on to his pay each month (which is also true for those who hold the Distinguished Service Medal and the Soldier's Medal, neither of which is a combat award); and when he has reached the age of 65, a former serviceman who has earned the Medal may, if he wishes to apply, receive a pension of $120 a year.

A good deal of research necessarily went into the preparation of this manuscript. For access to records official and unofficial, for personal recollections and anecdotes, for kindly words and excellent ideas, I am indebted to many. To all who helped me, I wish to express my sincere gratitude.

I wish, especially, to thank Major Vernon Pizer, formerly

of the Public Information Division, Department of the Army, and at this writing on the staff at Headquarters, SHAPE, Paris, France, who made many valuable suggestions that have been incorporated in this manuscript.

My grateful thanks, too, to Major General Guy S. Meloy, Jr., the Chief of Information and Education; and to Major General John H. Stokes, the Chief of Military History, Department of the Army.

My sincere appreciation goes also to Lieutenant Colonel James G. Chesnutt, Chief, Magazine and Book Branch, Department of the Army—and to Colonel Chesnutt's efficient and hard-working staff, Majors Robert F. Prentiss and Victor Walker, and Mrs. Barbara Gore.

Of the many military and semi-military agencies which I haunted during the days when this project was in the research stage, none did I trouble more, and none was more kind and helpful, than the Office of the Adjutant General. My thanks are due to Major General John A. Klein, The Adjutant General; and to Colonel Keith O. Dicken, of The Adjutant General's Office.

For their kindly assistance I am indebted to Miss Laurie Jones of The Infantry School Library, Fort Benning, Georgia; Mrs. Pauline Snyder and Fanny C. Howe, of Troy, New York; Mrs. E. C. Taggart of Harrisburg, Pennsylvania. Also, Miss Alice Coyne of the *Newark* (Ohio) *Advocate*, Mr. Norris F. Schneider of Zanesville, Ohio, Mr. John Weatherford of the Ohio Historical Society, Mr. James R. Gouffer of the Carlisle, Pennsylvania, *Evening Sentinel*, and Mr. Myron Kandel.

For helpful thoughts and advice I am deeply grateful to Dr. Stewart F. Alexander (Colonel, MC-USAR, Ret.) of Park Ridge, New Jersey; to Messrs. Orville Splitt and Matthew Portz of the Department of Defense; to Dr. Louis B. Morton of the Office of the Chief of Military History; and to Dr. Sidney Forman, Archivist of the United States Military Academy at West Point.

Also, Colonels Orrin C. Krueger, Edwin W. Richardson, Herbert V. Mitchell, Paul H. Mahoney (Ret.), and Homer H. Bowman; Captains Perry H. Davis II and Walter L. Frankland; Lieutenant Colonel James B. Deerin of the National Guard Bureau, Colonel Roy W. Hogan of the Georgia National Guard, Lieutenant Fred B. Hays of Mansfield, Georgia, and Lieutenant Colonel Robert B. Phelps, and Lieutenant Colonels Jack R. Melton and Charles Cawthon.

I wish to thank Mrs. Mildred Halsey of Park Ridge, New Jersey, who typed the manuscript.

And for assistance that was truly "above and beyond the call of duty," thanks are due to my wife, Shirley K. Jacobs, and to Louisa, Martha, and Philip for their forbearance in detouring around the place they gloomily refer to as "the typewriting room."

To all whom I have mentioned by name, and to those whose names must be omitted because of limited space, my sincere thanks. I hope that the publication of this book will, in some small way, contribute to the further recognition of those men who bore arms when their country needed them.

Bruce Jacobs

Park Ridge, New Jersey

HEROES
OF THE ARMY

ONE

❯❯❯ ❮❮❮

A CIVIL WAR ADVENTURE
The Mitchel Raiders

❯❯❯ ❮❮❮

IT WAS fitting that this strange adventure should begin on a bleak and stormy night. Out of the gloom came twenty-one silent men who were to keep an important date with destiny out on the old War Trace Road, about a mile east of the camp at Shelbyville, Tennessee.

All of them knew that something mighty unusual was in the wind; but none suspected that they were about to embark upon an expedition that was to be called, "the deepest laid scheme, and on the grandest scale, that ever emanated from the brains of any number of Yankees combined."

They gathered in a small knot around the tall thin man who was to lead them on this mission, and they looked speculatively at one another—as well they might. There was nothing they resembled less than soldiers of the Union Army. They were clothed in ill-fitting suits of cheap homespun cloth, or in plaid shirts and baggy jeans. If they were armed there was no outward evidence of the fact.

Their leader swiftly outlined their first objective—to re-assemble inside enemy-held Chattanooga. Meanwhile, it was to be over the mountains, every man for himself.

When General Don Carlos Buell moved out of Tennessee en route to Shiloh, he left behind him his 3d Division under the command of Major General Ormsby M. Mitchel, who had in civilian life been an astronomer of some note, and, incidentally, an 1829 West Point graduate and classmate of Confederate Generals Robert E. Lee and Joseph E. Johnston. Mitchel had decided upon a bold movement into northern Alabama, with the town of Huntsville as his initial target, and in conjunction with this drive he dispatched his "Raiders" under James J. Andrews.

Andrews was not a soldier, but a "civilian scout," as spies were euphemistically termed in those days. He had just returned from a trip into Central Georgia, and he sketched a plan that immediately caught Mitchel's fancy.

For little skinny Jacob Parrott of Company K of the 33d Ohio Volunteer Infantry Regiment the weird adventure began when his company commander called him out of his tent. When they were out of earshot of any others, the officer turned to Parrott and asked him if he would volunteer for a secret mission which meant going behind the enemy's lines.

"More than that I cannot tell you, because I do not know," the captain explained in a grave voice. "You do not have to tell me your decision now—but if you agree to go, please come to my tent in thirty minutes."

Parrott, an orphan who had never learned to read or write, needed only a few minutes by himself to make up his mind. When he presented himself at the captain's tent, that officer merely looked up and said, "Well, come along now, I've got to take you to the colonel."

Colonel Oscar F. Moore was able to throw little additional light on the subject. He told Parrott of the rendezvous that had been arranged on the War Trace Road and instructed him to dress in civilian clothing.

The 33d Ohio was brigaded with two other Ohio outfits and a Wisconsin regiment under Brigadier General Joshua W. Sill's command. When the Raiders assembled outside the camp that night, they found men from each of the Ohio regiments in the little band.

There were seven from Parrott's regiment, four from the 2d Ohio, and nine from the 21st Ohio. Beside Andrews, another civilian was present. Identified by the Army later only as William Campbell, a citizen of Kentucky, he remains a man of mystery. One report states that he was visiting friends at the camp of the 2d Ohio and volunteered to accompany the Raiders in the place of a friend who had volunteered but who had fallen ill. Another version has it that he was a correspondent for an Ohio newspaper. Campbell identified himself only as a private in Company K when he was later court-martialed.

At any rate, the detachment of Raiders at the outset included twenty Ohio soldiers and two civilians.

Traveling singly or in pairs, the Raiders drifted through the mountains toward Chattanooga. When questioned by curious hill folk, they identified themselves as Kentucky boys who were on their way to join the Confederate Army. They forded flood-swollen streams, negotiated tricky mountain passes, and finally reached their first destination.

It was here that they got an inkling of the daring plan at hand. Andrews distributed several hundred dollars worth of Confederate scrip among them and coolly said that the next meeting would take place in his room at the hotel in Marietta, Georgia—deep in the heart of the Confederacy.

Pretending to be ordinary passengers for the South the Raiders boarded the morning train for Marietta—a town a few miles northwest of Atlanta. Their cover story went over. So convincing were the Raiders that two of them, Privates Martin J. Hawkins and John R. Porter, were actually mustered into a Georgia volunteer battalion.

In the early morning hours of April 12, 1862—twenty-four hours behind schedule—the Raiders (less Hawkins and

Porter) assembled in Andrews' room at the Marietta Hotel to learn at last the full details of the fantastic scheme that had brought them to the State of Georgia.

According to the old reports that now repose in the National Archives in Washington—the writings of William Pittinger in particular—Andrews spoke softly but tersely. Every man in the room strained to catch his words.

"General Mitchel," he explained, "is on his way into Alabama. His target is Huntsville."

"We," he then said slowly, "are going to capture a Confederate train called *The General*, and run it north. We'll tear tracks, burn bridges, and disrupt communications between Atlanta and Chattanooga. If all goes well, by this time tomorrow we'll be back in Mitchel's camp."

His plan, swiftly outlined, was to seize the morning express when it reached the Big Shanty (now Kennesaw) stop, a few miles to the north of Marietta. One possible complication lay in the fact that the railroad yard at Big Shanty had been turned into a Confederate Army camp since Andrews' last reconnaissance.

"We ain't got a chance," someone said.

"Anyone who wants to can walk right out that door," Andrews offered. "As for me—I'm going through with it."

No one moved.

The leader of the Raiders looked at his watch and said it was time to move out. The men drifted casually up to the ticket booth to purchase tickets on the express for various stations along the way—Cartersville . . . Kingston . . . Adairsville . . . Calhoun . . . Resaca . . . Ringgold. . . .

The first rays of daylight found them on the train sweating out the short ride to Big Shanty, the spot Andrews had chosen because it was a breakfast stop and because there was no telegraph station there.

The train braked to a crawl as it entered Big Shanty, and

through steaming windows the Raiders could see the outlines of the tents of the Confederate Army camp. The conductor's hoarse bellow shattered the morning air.

"Big Shanty! Twenty minutes for breakfast!"

The passengers and trainmen got off on the right side of the train. Andrews and his Raiders exited from the left, then moved swiftly to the head of the train. Andrews and Private Wilson Brown, a locomotive engineer in civilian life, checked the track in front of the engine to make sure the switch was open.

"Looks perfectly all right," Brown muttered.

"Can you handle her?" Andrews asked anxiously.

Brown looked at the engine, an 1855 eight-wheeled wood-burning locomotive with wagon-top boiler, balloon type smoke stack, and oversize cow-catcher.

"I can ride her away," he replied laconically.

"Well then, let's get started."

Andrews, Brown, Knight (another engineer), and Alf Wilson, the fireman, uncoupled a section of the train that was to be left behind to block the track while the Raiders made their getaway in a section of train including the locomotive, tender, and three boxcars. Andrews, Brown, Knight, and Wilson leaped into the cab, and the rest of the Raiders took refuge in the last boxcar.

They had neglected to sever the emergency bell cord, however; and as Brown eased the locomotive gently up the track to get it started, there was a loud clanging alarm. The crew raced to the track in time to see their train heading north without them.

Thus the chase was organized minutes earlier than Andrews had anticipated. A further complication, which didn't seem too important at first, but which gained a significance as the day developed, was that the Raiders had seized the train twenty-four hours later than originally planned. Had the scheme gone off as scheduled, they would have had a clear sunny day; as it was, the rain came down incessantly and was to prove a serious enemy. Andrews' plan was to conform as closely as possible at first to the train's scheduled run to allay suspicion, and then to tear open the throttle once they passed a slow local freight that would be encountered on the way.

The Raiders were in high spirits over the ease with which they had commandeered *The General*. They were particularly tickled over the fact that a Confederate sentry had watched curiously, musket in hand, as Andrews and his accomplices uncoupled the passenger cars. Their first objective had been taken in grand style.

They stopped a few miles up the track to cut the telegraph wires and to load a boxcar with crossties that would make ideal kindling on the bridges that were to be burned. At one station they stopped for water and wood and aroused the suspicions of William Russell, the railroad agent. Andrews airily explained that he was an agent of General P. G. T. Beauregard and was taking an important powder train through to Corinth. To cap the story, he asked Russell for a current timetable.

"I'd send my shirt to Beauregard if he wanted it," Russell declared warmly; he produced the timetable and gratuitously pointed out to Andrews that as a result of the rainy weather, the entire road was in disorder. Every train was running far behind schedule and, in addition, two "extras" were coming down from the north.

Andrews thanked Russell and *The General* again chugged off.

"There was a wonderful exhilaration," Corporal William Pittinger later declared, "in passing swiftly by towns and stations through the heart of an enemy's country. It possessed just enough spice of danger—in this part of the run—to render it thoroughly enjoyable."

At Etowah Station they passed the old locomotive *Yonah*, with its steam up, but decided it would only alert the local authorities if they attacked it. Leaving it there proved to be one of the steps in their downfall.

Nearly two hours after their departure from Big Shanty, the Raiders rolled into Kingston, 30 miles up the line. They were sidelined as a freight rumbled southward and one of the Raiders pointed out to Andrews that it carried a red flag, which meant that another train was close behind.

Andrews leaped from the cab and angrily hailed one of the crew of the slow freight.

"What's the meaning of this?" he demanded. "I have orders to take this powder to Beauregard without delay!"

He got no answer; and when the second train arrived, it too carried a red flag. Still another train was coming. The Raiders in the cab and those in the boxcar ("where we were impersonating Beauregard's ammunition," according to Pittinger) began to sweat in earnest.

In addition, their presence had, by this time, aroused lively curiosity. The trainmen in the yard area had recognized *The General* as the locomotive that was supposed to bring the morning mailtrain; for on a branch siding, a Rome, Georgia, train was waiting for that mail. The romance of the train capture and of the exciting dash through Georgia began to evaporate, as the men began to realize that at any moment they might be unmasked as Union agents.

Andrews sent a terse message to the last boxcar as he saw the curious stares directed at *The General*.

"*Be ready to fight in case the crowd starts to make any investigation.*"

The Raiders, who had armed themselves with Navy Colt pistols, drew their weapons and prepared for action.

After sixty-five minutes of waiting, some of the Raiders would have welcomed a fight, but Andrews managed to reassure their questioners. An instant after the third train cleared the siding, *The General* darted out and resumed its trip north on the main line.

But pursuit was closer at hand than Andrews or any of the Raiders dreamed it could be. Led by William A. Fuller, conductor on the train at Big Shanty, the pursuers had seized the *Yonah*, and had reached Kingston, where they expected to fight it out with the train thieves. By this time, however, the extra trains blocked the track in front of Fuller.

But Fuller knew about the Rome train on the siding, and decided on a bold maneuver. He left the *Yonah*, and dashed past Kingston on foot to the branch half a mile away where the Rome train was waiting for the mailtrain. He uncoupled the locomotive and tender from the rest of the train, chugged out on to the main line, and set off in pursuit. Now there was nothing on the rails between the Raiders and their pursuers.

The Raiders, considerably buoyed up by the manner in which they had come through the train jam at Kingston, had paused to tear up tracks. Suddenly someone heard the noise of an approaching engine, and shots rang out, leaving no doubt that pursuers were close on their trail.

The hour that followed saw a nip-and-tuck chase. Whenever the Raiders stopped to try to tear up the tracks in front of the relentless Fuller, the pursuers came within rifle range and the Raiders were forced to move on again.

At Adairsville there was a freight and passenger train standing by, waiting for a southbound express to pass. There being no time to waste, Engineer Wilson raced through the station hoping to reach Calhoun Station and a siding before the arrival of the express.

Nine miles were covered in nine minutes as *The General* flew over the rails. Then the express loomed ahead of them. Luckily it heard *The General's* frantic whistle and was able to back up to allow the Raiders to reach the siding.

But the Beauregard powder train story wouldn't work any more—for, as the Raiders learned to their astonishment, Mitchel had already taken Huntsville and all Confederate equipment was being moved southward, away from the Yankees. No one on the express could understand why Andrews was carrying powder north to a hopeless cause.

When the Raiders finally regained the main line, they were aware that Mitchel's successful movement into Alabama had caused unusually heavy southbound train travel, which explained the extra traffic that had been encountered at Kingston. They hardly knew what to expect as they neared Chattanooga.

Blocked by a well-placed crosstie, meanwhile, Fuller had left the Rome train and raced to the head of *The Texas*, the train the Raiders had passed at Adairsville. He commandeered it and again renewed his pursuit of *The General*.

Once again he caught up with the Raiders as they were attempting to tear up tracks. Foiled within a few minutes of success, the Raiders leaped back on board *The General* and raced for the Oostenaula Bridge, a long covered bridge they hoped to burn and thus escape pursuit.

To delay the Confederates following in *The Texas*, two boxcars were detached near Resaca and left on the rails. But Fuller eased on his throttle and "picked them up," pushing them easily ahead of him until he could dump them.

The Oostenaula Bridge was crossed in such a hurry there was no time to fire it, but the Raiders readied themselves for an all out effort to destroy the Chickamauga Bridge. But time and the elements conspired to defeat them. On a dry day, they would have had no problem. But in the pelting rain it was impossible to set a fire and keep it going.

Their mission was clearly doomed, and their only hope of escape lay in derailing Fuller. They tore around curves, speeding ever closer to Chattanooga. Every time they disappeared from Fuller's sight they prayed it was for good—but then on the straightaway he would appear again, relentlessly running after them.

At one place they put a rail on a curve so that Fuller couldn't see it until he had run on it at full speed. There was a fearful jolt, and the Confederates' train seemed to leave the track. But then, somehow, it returned to the rails again!

The Raiders, meanwhile, hatched a plan that would let them shoot it out with the Confederates on fairly even terms. They urged Andrews to lay an ambush to enable them to attack at close quarters, so that their revolvers might have a chance against Fuller's rifles. Their plea was ignored.

Now, with fuel getting low and Fuller dogging them—they had reached their last chance.

They sped through the long tunnel north of Dalton, leaving it untouched. Fuller anticipated an obstruction of some sort at the tunnel, however, and momentarily slowed down when he reached it. Andrews and his band of Raiders ran unmolested past a Confederate regiment encamped at Dalton. Then, to slow the pursuers in *The Texas*, the last of the crossties were dropped on the rails. Engineer Wilson pushed *The General* to the utmost of its capacity, coaxing a better than a mile a minute speed out of its weary boiler, and the Raiders cheered as this spurt opened a wider gap between them and Fuller.

Meanwhile, Andrews ordered the side and end boards of the last remaining boxcar to be smashed, heaped on the floor of the car, and set afire by blazing brands from the engine.

They were by this time approaching the long covered Chickamauga Bridge, and every one of the Raiders knew that it was now or never. As the flames shot up and engulfed the car, all of the Ohioans climbed into the cab of *The General*. The burning car was uncoupled and left in the middle of the bridge.

Andrews issued terse orders to go into effect if Fuller were delayed. They would stop at the next town to take on fuel and water—at pistol point, if necessary—and then continue on to the Tennessee border, only a few miles away at most. Once near Chattanooga they could easily slip into the city, obtain new disguises, and set out to rejoin Mitchel.

Once more, however, their plans were foiled.

Fuller drove *The Texas* through the smoke, pushed into the burning car, and rolled it ahead of him until he was clear of the bridge. Then willing hands tipped it off the rails—and the chase was resumed.

Near Graysville, after 90 miles of flight, *The General* ran out of fuel, coughed, choked, and slowed to a halt.

"Throw 'er in reverse so's she'll smash those rebs," someone shouted. But *The General* only rolled weakly into the oncoming *Texas* as the Raiders spilled from the locomotive and crashed into the woods, scattering as they ran.

The great train chase had come to an end. In a few days all of the Raiders had been hunted down by Confederate cavalry patrols, and imprisoned.

The imprisonment of the Raiders constitutes one of the blackest pages in Civil War history. Jailed at first in a rathole prison in Chattanooga, the Raiders were reunited there with Porter and Hawkins who had been denounced just as they were being mustered into the Confederate Army.

On comparing notes they learned that Parrott had been taken with Samuel Robinson in the woods near Ringgold—and from Robinson the Raiders heard of the torture that had been inflicted on Parrott in an effort to make him disclose the details of the plot.

An officer and four men had stripped him, bent him over a stone, and whipped him. They said if he didn't talk, they'd shoot him. A Confederate Army lieutenant gave him more than 100 lashes with a rawhide whip, stopping three times during this beating to ask if he would tell who was the engineer. Then they got a rope and were threatening to hang him, when a colonel came along and took both men into custody. Parrott by this time was more dead than alive.

Last of the Raiders to reach the jail were Alf Wilson, the erstwhile fireman, and Corporal Mark Wood, a frail Englishman who had settled in the midwest and volunteered to fight for the Union.

They regaled their fellow prisoners with their experiences in a strange Georgia town where they had coolly walked into a bookstore and bought a school atlas to provide themselves with a map of the area. They had noted with a grim sort of satisfaction that the author of the volume was their own General Mitchel.

They had finally been captured by Snow's Company of Cavalry just a few miles from the Union lines in Tennessee, and had promptly been taken before Brigadier General Danville Leadbetter, Confederate commander of the Chattanooga garrison.

Wilson and Wood later related the details of their interview with General Leadbetter in a deposition taken by Colonel Morgan of the Union Army at Key West, Florida, on November 10, 1862. They told how Leadbetter sneered as he looked them over.

"I suppose," he declared, "Old Mitchel picked and culled over the whole Yankee Army to find the most reckless, hardened men he could—and I'll be damned if I don't hang every last one of you!"

Lending weight to Leadbetter's words, twelve of the Raiders were suddenly taken from Swims' infamous jailhouse to Knoxville for courts-martial proceedings.

Andrews and John Wollam managed to cut their way out of prison in a vain bid for freedom. They were caught, however, brought back battered and bruised, and put into ankle chains.

One morning the executioners came for Andrews—the Raiders by this time had been removed to a prison in Atlanta. Then without warning, the Confederates suddenly executed seven other Raiders. Without any advance word, the seven were taken out and hanged in the prison courtyard.

There was young Campbell who insisted to the last he was a member of Company K of the 2d Ohio. There was John Scott who had been married only three days when he joined the Army; big Marion A. Ross, Sergeant Major of the 21st Ohio; Robinson, who had to be dragged from a sickbed; Perry Shadrach; George D. Wilson; and Samuel Slavens, a huge, athletic fellow who gasped to his friend Robert Buffum, "Wife . . . children . . . tell . . . them . . ."

The rest of the Raiders, unable to convince Confederate officials that theirs had been a legitimate military assignment given by their commanding officer, languished in jail in Atlanta under the most horrible conditions, never knowing when they would be called for by the ominous cavalry escort.

In October, they heard a rumor that Jefferson Davis had refused to approve clemency for them, and that they were to be hanged. Carefully, the survivors readied a last-gasp effort to escape, mending their clothes so their ragged appearance wouldn't give them away, and cutting out pieces of blanket to stuff inside torn worn-out shoes.

They gathered up sticks, bottles, cans—anything they could fashion into weapons—and after praying for help, they readied themselves to attack their jailer when he returned to collect their empty food bucket. The jailer was seized and hit from behind as he entered. As he crumpled, Buffum sprang forward and snatched his keys. Led by Alf Wilson, they sped for the frontyard gate.

"Alf!" called Wood, "Company of guards coming!"

They bolted over the fence as musket fire crashed around them. Knight and Brown made it safely to the woods, and a month later rejoined their regiment. Porter and Wollam reached the Union lines at Corinth. Hawkins and Daniel Dorsey reached Union friends in the Cumberland Mountains and rejoined the federal forces in Kentucky.

Alf Wilson and Mark Wood escaped down the Chattahoochee, hid out near Columbus, Georgia, and then made their way to Florida, where they were picked up by a U.S. gunboat and taken to Key West. From there they got transportation north.

William Bensinger, Robert Buffum, Elihu Mason, Jacob Parrott, William Pittinger, and William Reddick, however, were recaptured and clapped into irons to prevent any further attempts at escape. In December, 1862, the six were transferred to Libby Prison where they were kept briefly. Then they were shuttled to the misery of the criminal prison, Castle Thunder, where they were locked in a tiny, dark room which had no provisions for fire. Finally, on March 18, 1863, the last six of Mitchel's Raiders were exchanged by the Confederate commissioners at City Point, Virginia.

The emaciated, sickly group reached Washington, D.C., on March 25. They picked their way through the streets of the crowded capital and reported to the Judge Advocate General, who questioned them on their mission and asked for a report on the treatment they had received as prisoners of war.

Secretary of War Stanton sent for them, and, according to a contemporary newspaper account, the six were swept through the waiting room, leaving behind "numbers of military and civil dignitaries who were anxiously awaiting outside to see Mr. Stanton, but who were required to wait until these soldiers had been commended."

Stanton shook hands with each of them and introduced them to the others in his office—Salmon P. Chase, the Secretary of the Treasury, and Andrew Johnson, the Governor of Tennessee, who was to become President of the United States two years later.

Stanton seemed to take a particular fancy to Jacob Parrott, the youngest of the group. He talked at considerable length to him, and his visage grew stern as he heard of the beatings the boy had endured during his long imprisonment.

In a quiet voice the War Secretary told the six Raiders of his and the nation's appreciation for their devotion to duty. He gave them each one hundred dollars to spend in Washington and turned to James C. Whetmore, State Agent for Ohio, to ask that each of the six be appointed by the Governor to first lieutenancies in Ohio regiments. He added that if there were no vacancies in these regiments, he would himself brevet them first lieutenants in the regular army.

Then he opened a drawer, took out six small leather cases and placed them before him on the desk. The account that appeared in the Washington *Chronicle* the following day, March 26, 1863, described the Secretary of War's emotion as he picked up one of the small boxes and turned once again to Parrott.

"None of these," he said to Parrott, "has yet been awarded to any soldier. I now present you with the first one to be issued. . . ."

Stanton then handed a similar case to each of the others. The six soldiers stammered their thanks and inspected the glittering treasure inside each box. They had been awarded the first Medals of Honor in the history of the United States Army.

TWO

➤➤➤➤ ◄◄◄◄

ROAD TO GLORY

➤➤➤➤ ◄◄◄◄

A RELATIVELY unknown general named Ulysses S. Grant, soon to be nicknamed "Unconditional Surrender" Grant, had seized the Confederate stronghold at Fort Donelson, Tennessee. He had confounded the military experts by using the river as his line of operations, as no military commander had ever done successfully before in the history of what was then modern warfare. The capture of Donelson marked the most significant incursion of Union arms into territory controlled by the Confederacy. The North was electrified and emboldened by the news that this man had refused to parlay with the Confederate garrison commander, but had made his terms "unconditional surrender."

This was the background against which Senator Harry Wilson of Massachusetts arose to introduce in the Senate a resolution to provide for "medals of honor" to be awarded soldiers of the army and voluntary forces who should "most distinguish themselves by their gallantry in action, and other soldier-like qualities."

But uniforms of the United States Army had gone unadorned for so many years that there was, even in military circles, strong opposition to the suggestion that a medal for valor be created. Winfield Scott, General-in-Chief of the Army, a hero of the War of 1812 and the Mexican War, was, like many Americans of that era, opposed to medals, medallions, decorations, or any of the trappings of the European armies. Scott's own adjutant, Colonel Edward D. Townsend, later Adjutant General of the Army, had noted, however, that a goodly number of Union soldiers took a lively interest in the colorful decorations worn by foreign officers who came to visit Scott to offer or attempt to sell their services.

In the summer of 1782 General Washington had created the Badge of Merit (revised in 1932 as the Order of the Purple Heart) "to have retrospect to the earliest days of the war, and to be considered a permanent one." But the heart-shaped, purple cloth Badge had been issued only to three soldiers of the Continental Army before it was lost from sight.

In the years between the end of the War for Independence and 1862, when the Army Medal of Honor was finally authorized, there was no way to reward combat bravery except by the "brevet system," which generally meant a promotion to temporary higher rank with no commensurate increase in pay.

Although a small number of Medals had been struck by the federal government during those 80 years, they were always awards given to specific individuals by congressional enactment. Thus, the militiamen who apprehended Major John André were rewarded by medals; and medals for important contributions to the nation were also authorized for Generals Washington, Horatio Gates, and "Light-Horse Harry" Lee— father of General Robert E. Lee.

Despite all the tradition in America against the trappings of foreign armies, however, the Medal of Honor rapidly earned a place of honor on the American scene. Americans, who so heartily detested practically everything and anything that reeked of "old world militarism," took the Medal of Honor to their hearts because, in the words with which General Washington established the long-forgotten Badge of Merit: *"The road to glory in a patriot army and a free country is thus opened to all."*

A private was as apt to win it as the captain who commanded the company. A general could scarcely win it unless he took leave of his headquarters and hied himself into the field at the head of his troops. This wasn't a medal for members of any privileged class or group—it was to be given to the bravest of men from all walks of life and the only thing necessary for winning it would be . . . courage.

President Abraham Lincoln put his signature on the Army Medal of Honor bill on July 12, 1862—shortly after the fight at Malvern Hill and the Seven Day's Battles. Nonetheless, the Medal seems to have been forgotten until March, 1863, when Secretary Stanton reached into his desk drawer and bestowed the first six Medals of Honor of the United States Army upon the Mitchel Raiders. Apart from the Raiders, only four other Union Army soldiers received the Medal during 1863.

But in 1864 nearly 100 Medals were awarded, and in 1865 more than 300 Medals were issued.

Fears that a Medal would prove unpopular were unfounded. If anything, the Medal became too popular—or so it seems now in retrospect. What neither the Congress nor the Army realized in the beginning was that the Medal's very eminence as the only U.S. decoration for extraordinary gallantry in action was also its greatest weakness. For example, there was no suitable way to reward an entire unit that had acted in an outstanding manner during battle. As a result, there was actually an instance where an entire regiment had been cited and every man in the regiment awarded the Medal of Honor (revoked in later years).

There was, of course, the case of the Mitchel Raiders, whose activities were described in Chapter One. Nineteen of the 21 members of the original detachment eventually received the Medal, although no man's citation specified any outstanding *individual accomplishment*. The citation simply states vaguely: "For special services under General Mitchel."

In the spring of 1863, Grant was pounding at Vicksburg; and before settling down to the siege that eventually licked Confederate General John C. Pemberton, he decided upon one last massive assault. To spearhead the movement of Major General William T. Sherman's corps, he called for a volunteer storming party of 150 men to move out in the van of the attack.

A deadly fire met the volunteers, who nevertheless pushed up the heights toward the Confederate works. That night, when the blue-clad forces pulled back, there was talk of little else but the way this brave band had gone about its self-imposed task. Practically every one of the survivors, about 83 in all, earned the Medal of Honor that day.

Today, of course, action by an entire unit may be recognized by the presentation of a Distinguished Unit Citation. But a regulated system of awards for combat valor was nonexistent in the middle of the 19th Century, and so the official list of the Medal of Honor winners swelled to immense proportions. Counting the Medals that were later revoked, approximately 2,100 were awarded in the Civil War era.

Once the Civil War was over, the small regular army was sent to the plains of the west, where it engaged in bitter conflict with the hostile Indian tribes that still resisted the white man's encroachment. In 1869 a considerable number of Medals were awarded to soldiers of the 8th Cavalry Regiment, who had been recommended for the honor as a result of valorous combat "from August to October, 1868." No locale was specified other than "Arizona," and no details were given as to the nature of the gallantry other than "bravery in scouts and actions against Indians."

The awarding of these Medals brought a dispute about whether the Medal ought properly to be awarded for a series of actions extending over a considerable period of time, or if it ought to be confined to outstanding climactic instances of combat. To some degree this argument has not yet been fully resolved.

However, these *en masse* recommendations for the nation's highest award for gallantry in action did provoke considerable controversy. The matter came to a head after Custer's ill-fated fight on the Little Big Horn, June 25, 1876, when the company commanders who had attempted to relieve Custer's detachment recommended great numbers of men for the award.

To Brigadier General Alfred A. Terry, the Department Commander, it appeared that "company commanders have recommended every man . . . that behaved *ordinarily well* during the action. . . ." Terry therefore rejected the entire list and sent it back to Colonel Samuel F. Sturgis, commander of the 7th Cavalry, with a note directing him to convene a board which would review the recommendations and forward to him for approval only those which clearly indicated outstanding combat heroism *beyond that normally expected of a soldier*.

What General Terry said, in effect, was that the Medal of Honor was not to become a good conduct medal or an attendance award.

Since he was the commander of only one military department, Terry's action did not carry Army-wide weight; but at least his action provided field commanders with a "rule of thumb" in determining which members of their units rated the Medal.

The 7th Cavalry review board finally forwarded a list of 22 names; and these were in turn approved by Colonel Sturgis, General Terry, and Lieutenant General Phil Sheridan. Two years and two months after the disastrous action these Medals were issued—but the story does not end there. A glance at the official Medal of Honor list today shows that there are 24 heroes of the 7th Cavalry action known to schoolboys as "Custer's Last Stand." The two additional Medals were awarded as a result of a number of applications received by the War Department in the 1890's, when several old troopers suddenly put in claims for the Medal.

In 1890, 22 Medals of Honor for Civil War actions were approved; the number jumped to 40 in 1891, and 66 in 1892. In 1894, a year in which 16 soldiers earned the Medal for fighting the Indians in the west, no less than 127 veterans of the Civil War were similarly honored.

At the direction of President William McKinley, the Army revised the vague regulations covering the award of the Medal, and for the first time a set of requirements were drawn up.

It was decided that, effective June 26, 1897, all applications for the Medal of Honor would have to fit into one of these three categories: (1) For military service from outbreak of Civil War to December 21, 1889; or (2) for services between January 1, 1890, and date of the new regulation; or (3) for cases "that may arise for service performed hereafter." In addition, for the first time eye-witness supporting accounts were made mandatory. For actions subsequent to January 1, 1890, the application could not be made by the candidate for honor, but had to be made by his commanding officer or by some other individual who had personally seen his gallantry in action.

The regulation also stated that, in the future, recommendations would have to be made within one year after "performance of the act for which the award is claimed."

These are, in essence, the basic modern requirements: a time limit for applying for the Medal, and the affidavits of eye-witnesses.

But these reforms still created no bar to the further submission of claims for Medals arising out of Civil War heroism and consequently 120 were awarded in 1896, 118 in 1897, and 61 in 1898. The Army men who believed in the Medal and wished to keep its reputation untarnished were seriously concerned.

They got action soon after Elihu Root became Secretary of War in 1899. By his order the War Department convened a board to submit recommendations in connection with the award of the Medal.

This was the beginning of the modern era of the Medal; slowly but surely the Army had come to realize that it had to find a way to safeguard the Medal if its meaning was to be perpetuated.

The need for continual concern about the Medal was clear as late as 1906, when Medals of Honor were issued for the War with Spain (1), and the Philippine Insurrection (13). At the same time two venerable citizens, who had soldiered in the Civil War, were also awarded Medals. One of these was James M. Seitzinger, who had fought at Cold Harbor in 1864; the other was John C. Sagelhurst, a volunteer cavalryman from New Jersey who had fought at Hatchers Run in 1865. Their Medals, in other words, were bestowed 40 and 41 years after the actual fighting had taken place. Whatever the merits of the individual cases, here was a situation that cried out for clarification.

It was about this time, too, that the War Department became concerned with a number of imitations of the Medal which were in evidence. "With few exceptions," noted Brevet Brigadier General Theophile F. Rodenbough, "these have no national, official significance."

It was high time, the Army decided, to settle upon a new and distinctive design—and to take steps to prevent it from becoming a medallion that could be adopted by social and athletic clubs.

Brigadier General George L. Gillespie, then Chief of Engineers, came up with the best of the new designs submitted to the Department. Gillespie had himself earned the nation's highest award for bravery as a young officer in the Civil War when he had been trapped inside enemy lines while carrying dispatches for General Sheridan. He had escaped only after a running gun fight at point-blank range.

It was Gillespie also who furnished the War Department with the way to protect the Medal against imitators and jewelry manufacturers. Gillespie's design for a medal was granted a patent; and on December 19, 1904, he transferred the patent "to W. H. Taft and his successor or successors as Secretary of War of the United States of America."

This put control of the Medal squarely into the hands of the Secretary of War for the first time.

The next full-scale discussion of the Medal was by Congress in 1914—by which time many more medals had been issued: the last half-dozen or so awarded for the Civil War; 30 for the War with Spain, 70 for the Philippine Insurrection, 4 in the Boxer Rebellion, and 1 for the Mexican Punitive Expedition.

The discussions developed into an act of April 27, 1916, which provided for the creation of a Medal of Honor Roll. Intended to give Medal of Honor winners a "special status," the act stated when a Medal of Honor winner reached age 65, he would have his name recorded on the Honor Roll and be entitled to a special pension of $10 a month for the rest of his life. The act also stated that the applicant's Medal of Honor must have been won by an action involving *actual conflict with the enemy, distinguished by conspicuous gallantry or intrepidity at the risk of life above and beyond the call of duty.*

Accordingly, an Army Board was convened to review all instances of the award of the Medal of Honor since 1863, to determine whether or not any Medals of Honor had been awarded or issued "for any cause other than distinguished conduct . . . involving actual conflict with the enemy."

Between October 16, 1916, and January 17, 1917, this Board

reviewed all of the papers pertaining to the 2,625 Medals that had been awarded up to that time. On February 15, 1917, it struck 911 names from the official Medal of Honor list. This included all of the 864 members of one Civil War regiment, and 47 other cases in which the Board decided that the Medal had not been properly awarded.

The Board noted that in some cases the reward was greater "than would now be given for the same act"; but it also pointed out that there were "few instances where the Medal has not been awarded for distinguished service."

To enhance the importance of the Medal, lesser decorations were created for deeds other than those involving the highest degrees of intrepidity above and beyond the call of duty. An ancient award known as the Certificate of Merit was done away with, and the Distinguished Service Medal was created to replace it for exceptionally meritorious noncombat service in a duty of great responsibility. Congress, in approving this, noted that "it is believed if a secondary medal had been authorized in the past the award of the . . . Medal of Honor would have been more jealously guarded." To provide "secondary medals" for combat heroism, the act of July 9, 1918, created the Distinguished Service Cross and the Silver Star. Other medals were added to the list in later years, and the Purple Heart which George Washington had created in 1782 was revived in 1932.

The so-called Pyramid of Honor now consists of the following:

1. Medal of Honor. For gallantry and intrepidity at the risk of life above and beyond the call of duty.
2. Distinguished Service Cross. For extraordinary heroism in military operations against an armed enemy.
3. Silver Star. For gallantry in action.
4. Distinguished Flying Cross. For heroism and extraordinary achievement while participating in aerial flight.

5. Soldier's Medal. For heroism not involving actual conflict with an enemy.
6. Bronze Star Medal. For heroic or meritorious achievement or service against an enemy not involving aerial flight.
7. Purple Heart. For wounds received in action against an enemy of the United States.

※ ※ ※ ⋘ ⋘ ⋘

OVER THERE!

Thomas A. Pope

※ ※ ※ ⋘ ⋘ ⋘

ON THE morning of June 5, 1917—draft registration day for ten million young Americans—Tom Pope left his Edison Park home in the outskirts of Chicago, and put civilian life behind him.

As he traveled downtown to register at the draft board, he was indistinguishable among the ten million except for two things. For one thing he had already decided that he wasn't going to wait to be drafted. Secondly, he had made up his mind to enlist at once in the 1st Illinois Infantry of the National Guard. He did not know, however, that he was destined to be the Army's first Medal of Honor winner in France.

He was sworn in that afternoon at the big armory on the corner of Sixteenth and Michigan, as a private in Company E, 1st Illinois Infantry. Although the regiment had been called out by the Governor in March and had been mustered into the federal service in April, it was stall quartered at its armory awaiting orders to proceed to Camp Logan, Texas.

On the Armory's highly-polished drill floor, and on guard posts near Chicago's outlying power plants and railroad bridges, Tom Pope began to learn the soldier's trade in Captain Hamlet C. Ridgway's company. From the very start he was in Lieutenant Arthur N. Clissold's 1st Platoon, and he remained in Clissold's Platoon during the entire span of his active duty in the Army.

As a member of Company E he would, so he reckoned, get to stay with his younger brother, Joe, and the other men from Edison Park who were his boyhood friends—John Fox, Ed Krum, Waldo Campbell, Lester Whitson, Paul Kendrick, and Victor Moe. Although Joe was Tom's junior by two years, he considered himself an old soldier by virtue of having served with the regiment at Camp Wilson on the Mexican Border the previous year.

Toward the end of the summer, having had more than its fill of guard duty, the regiment started on the long trek to Camp Logan. First, there was a dusty march from Lockport to Camp Cicero, covering 46 miles in two days, and from there the regiment moved to Camp Grant. It was here that the Guardsmen met, with ill-concealed contempt, the draftees of the 86th Infantry Division—not knowing, of course, that nearly 5,000 of these men were to join them in Texas and were destined to fight with them in France.

Before leaving for Texas, the regiment was visited by Teddy Roosevelt—a former volunteer soldier who had made quite a name for himself in the Spanish-American War. Roosevelt warmly greeted Colonel Joseph B. Sanford, a Spanish-American War veteran who was in command of the Illinois guardsmen.

By October the regiment was assembled in Texas where, as Pope and his buddies learned, the nights and some of the days were as raw and cold as in the Windy City. Those men who had expected a pleasant winter in the sunny south were bitterly disappointed.

At midnight on October 10, 1917, the regiment was renamed the 131st infantry. It was formed with the 132d Infantry, formerly the 2d Illinois, into the 66th Infantry Brigade under Brigadier General Paul A. Wolf, an Illinois-bred West

Pointer. The 65th and 66th Infantry Brigades and the 58th Artillery Brigade were designated the major components of the new 33d Infantry Division under the command of Major General George Bell, Jr.

All that the Illinois men knew about General Bell was that he was said to be an old-timer. Later they learned that his father had been a general officer in the Civil War, and that he had followed in his father's footsteps and had graduated from West Point in 1880. He had been soldiering for 37 years at the time he was given command of the Illinois National Guard division at Camp Logan.

During November the regiment was visited by Governor Frank O. Lowden, who presented to the Chicagoans a stand of handsome new silk flags—national and regimental colors —to replace those of the old 1st Illinois.

It was not without regret that Pope and his fellow soldiers watched the old regiment pass into history. It had been formed under Frank Sherman back in 1874, and had become one of the outstanding Guard organizations in the midwest. It had put down the Stockyard Riots of 1879, had escorted President Grover Cleveland at the World Columbian Exposition in 1893, had served in Cuba, had been escort for President William Howard Taft in 1911, had drilled at the California Exposition in 1915, and had served on the Mexican Border under Pershing.

A rugged training grind began. Under the watchful eyes of French and British officers who were fresh from the trenches of the battle line, the Illinois men dug and manned trenches and perfected their marksmanship on the firing ranges at Camp Logan.

General Bell, meanwhile, went to France for a tour of the battle zone, then returned to watch his Division wind up its stateside training. Tough competition was devised to select a model company in each regiment, and Captain Ridgway's

Company E marched off with the prize. Then the model companies of the four infantry regiments competed, and Company E once again scored highest. Division Special Orders No. 24, dated January 24, 1918, designated Company E as the No. 1 company in the entire 33d Division; Hamlet was promoted to major, and the company came under the command of Captain James W. Luke.

A Division Review was made in April, and although it went off without a hitch, it showed that, after nearly a year of routine training and drilling, the troops were getting stale. Colonel Sanford found a remedy for the 131st. He marched the regiment to Morgan Point, where the old 1st Illinois camped on the historic San Jacinto battlefield.

After nearly a week in the field and on the march the regiment returned to Logan tired and dust-stained, but revitalized. At Logan it learned that the "fillers" had arrived, the men to fill the understrength ranks of the Guard outfit, mostly draftees from Camp Grant.

Although practically all of the Edison Park crowd were still in the company, two faces were missing as the regiment readied itself for overseas. One of the no-longer-present-and-accounted-for of the Company E old-timers was Private First Class Joseph J. Pope—the younger brother Tom Pope had enlisted to serve with. The Camp Logan medics had decided he had varicose veins, and he had been discharged and sent packing for home, much to his, and Tom's, disgust.

However, a few weeks later "E" Company was astounded to learn that upon his return to Chicago, Joe had been drafted into the army, and sent to an engineer outfit that was just about to leave for overseas. Consequently, he reached France months before his buddies of the old 1st Illinois!

In May the regiment moved to Camp Upton, New York, and from there to the port of embarkation and the U.S.S. *Leviathan*. In early June the Illinois men were at last in France, assigned for training with the British Army. From the looks of things, the men figured it would be many weeks before they would hear a shot fired in anger.

An unusual combination of circumstances, however, were destined to thrust elements of the 33d Division into the fight at the village of Hamel, France, exactly 34 days after their arrival in the war zone. It is doubtful that any other U.S. unit got into the thick of things that soon after stepping off the boat.

On the first day of spring in 1918, the Germans had un-leashed a great offensive designed to wreak destruction on the French and British before the U.S. Army could arrive on the scene in force.

The Germans' attack, which was initially successful, drove a deep salient into the Allies' lines, threatening the key rail junction at Amiens. Then, while the Allies' attention was focused on Amiens, the Germans launched a second offensive to the north. When they were confident that British reserves had been lured north, they again assailed Amiens. The Allies fought desperately to check the German advance, but the enemy won the so-called Marne salient—a cancer in the Allied lines bounded by Reims, Chateau-Thierry, and Soissons.

Large-scale attacks failed to enlarge this salient; but the Germans did accomplish one objective, in that they forced General Pershing to postpone his demand for authority to put an American army in the field. The 33d Division was reassembled under British command at Abbeville in mid-June, and on June 21 it moved toward Amiens, into the sector held by the British 3 Corps. Here the 66th Infantry Brigade temporarily took over the secondary defense line which the Illinois Division would be required to man in the event of new enemy attacks.

While in this sector on a defensive training mission, the

American infantry brigade learned that the Australian Brigade to which it was attached had been ordered to make a sweep into the Bois de Vaire and to seize the town of Hamel. The British commander asked that U.S. units be attached to him for the attack, and subsequently four companies of the 33d Division were ordered to report to the Aussies—although this was clearly in opposition to General Pershing's expressed wishes.

Captain Luke, commanding Company E, was ordered to the Australian 43rd Infantry Battalion. There were two days of vigorous rehearsals; each of Luke's platoons was attached to an Aussie company for the assault. Art Clissold's 1st Platoon was to attack with the Aussies' Company A.

The American officers sat in on the Aussies' council of war, and returned to their platoons to tell the men that the attack was to be launched a little after 3 a.m. on July Fourth. Their battalion was to make the assault on a 2,600 yard front, extending from the Somme to the left of the Vaire woods.

"We were anxious to show them that we were pretty good, too," Tom Pope was to recall later. "After all, they had been in combat before; we were pretty green, and, I guess, not smart enough to realize it."

Clissold checked his men and whispered last minute instructions in the dark. Corporal Tom Pope inspected the bayonet affixed to his rifle, and made sure his cartridge belt carried a full supply of ammunition. Mentally he reviewed the lieutenant's orders to carry rations for two days and two canteens of water.

Then someone whispered, "Hey, we're movin' out."

A bit after midnight the assault platoons started moving into the jumping-off places about 300 yards in front of the trenches. It took nearly an hour to get everyone in position. Then there was an interminable wait as they listened anxiously for the promised artillery barrage. Suddenly—there it was.

Shell after shell screamed overhead, roaring toward the enemy lines.

"We learned later," relates Tom Pope, "that there were 161 guns firing to support us."

"Here we go!" ordered Clissold, and the 1st Platoon bolted forward as the Aussie battalion began its attack.

Their objective was Hamel, and a triangular-shaped piece of terrain which included an important ridge east of the village. Their attack carried 300 yards before they encountered resistance. Then the infantry found themselves in a bitter fight. Tanks pushed through toward the enemy, but were driven back by artillery and trench mortar fire.

The infantry doggedly tried to overcome this resistance, but were repeatedly driven back by concentrated machine gun fire coming from one particular enemy strong point. No one seemed able to spot the gun that was holding up the advance.

Then Pope yelled, "I see it!" He sprinted out in advance of the Aussies, and ran across an open patch of ground, ducking the enemy's pot shots.

A few men had started to follow Pope, but fell back in the face of the rain of fire being concentrated on Pope as he sped toward the enemy machine gun emplacement. The gun crew swung the gun on him, but before they could pull off a burst he had charged into their midst.

Pope had no time to use his rifle. He waded into the Germans with his bayonet, and wiped out the entire crew.

A nearby enemy squad mounted a furious charge toward him, but Pope, standing astride the machine gun, leveled his rifle and calmly picked them off. More Germans surged in toward him, but the Chicagoan coolly reloaded and fought them off, still standing over the gun.

Finally the rest of the attack caught up with him, and Pope's captured machine gun and a number of prisoners were sent back to the rear. The attack swept on and the battalion smashed its way into Hamel, blasting through machine gun nests, houses, barns, factories, stores, and trenches.

Hamel was seized—and a major step toward the elimination of the Marne salient had been accomplished.

The four American companies were ordered to rejoin the 33d Division at once, but they were not able to move out of the lines until July 6. They fought off numerous counterattacks; the company's most serious casualties were inflicted on July 5, when the Germans launched a gas attack that cost Company E 34 men. Among the seriously gassed was Corporal Tom Pope, who was invalided back to a hospital in England. The triumphant company, led by Luke, left the Aussies at Corbie and returned to Moliens-au-Bois to present General Bell with the first enemy rifle captured by the Division in France.

Company E, the model company of Camp Logan days, had proved itself a model company in combat too. It had taken its first combat objective with dash and vigor, had captured 3 trench mortars, 25 machine guns, and taken 293 prisoners.

This was but the beginning of the road for the 33d Division in combat—but none of the veterans of the Hamel fight ever forgot Tom Pope's unbelievable dash across that field of fire to storm the enemy machine gun. He was recommended for the nation's highest award.

In 1919, while the Division was on occupation duty, Corporal Thomas A. Pope was among those who received the Medal of Honor from General Pershing in a ceremony at Chaumont, France.

The British recognized his valor by awarding him their Distinguished Conduct Medal, and the French bestowed both the *Medaille Militaire* and the *Croix de Guerre* upon him.

Pope was discharged from federal service on June 6, 1919—two years and a day from the date he had walked into the Armory to enlist in the old 1st Illinois.

TOM POPE was the first Army man to participate in a Medal of Honor action, but his fight at Hamel on July 4, 1918, actually followed one involving two members of the Marine Corps. The Leathernecks were Sergeant Charles F. Hoffman (real name, Ernest A. Janson) and Gunnery Sergeant Fred W. Stockham. Both were members of the Marine Brigade of the Army's 2d Infantry Division, which helped stop the Germans at Chateau-Thierry on June 6, and then took part in the Division's great counterattack in the Belleau Woods. Eventually a total of six Marines were awarded the Army's Medal of Honor for service in the A.E.F.; all these men later received the Navy Medal of Honor as well.

It was several weeks after the capture of Hamel that the 3d Infantry Division became engaged in the holding action that earned it the "Rock of the Marne" nickname that it bears to this day. An important artillery observation post was under attack by a German artillery bombardment and its lines of communication were knocked out. A young artillery lieutenant named George Price Hays (later lieutenant general) turned messenger in an effort to maintain liaison with the firing batteries. Making his hazardous rounds under heavy enemy fire, he was eventually wounded after having seven horses shot from under him.

Private George Dilboy, a New Englander of the 26th (Yankee) Division, was reconnoitering in advance of the lines with an officer from his company when they were fired on by a machine gun. Dilboy routed the enemy with his bayonet despite painful wounds in both legs. And Dan Edwards, a 1st Division infantryman with something of a reputation as a colorful character in his company of tough hardened regulars, smashed his way toward Soissons as a member of Company C, 3d Machine Gun Battalion. He had been seriously wounded in an earlier action and, although his C. O. didn't know it, he was AWOL from a hospital cot.

In the advance toward Soissons on July 18, he was seriously and painfully wounded by a burst of machine gun fire which shattered one of his arms. When the pain became so intense he could no longer walk, he crawled into an enemy trench and demanded the surrender of its eight occupants. The Germans had little intention of giving in to this blood-spattered apparition and moved to disarm him. Edwards calmly shot four of them—and the remaining four surrendered without a murmur.

He motioned them to start moving toward the rear. Dragging himself laboriously, Edwards had nearly reached his outfit's lines when an artillery shell which exploded nearly at his side blew off one of his legs, and killed one of his prisoners.

During this same action, Second Lieutenant Sam Parker started off as a platoon leader of Company K, 28th Infantry regiment—but by the time the vicious fight had passed into a second day, he was the only one left to command the handful of survivors of what had been two infantry battalions.

Late in the summer of 1918, General Pershing was at last authorized to organize the United States First Army as a field command. One of First Army's initial successes was the reduction of the St. Mihiel salient in September, 1918. During this fight, Second Lieutenant J. Hunter Wickersham of the 89th Division, Captain L. Wardlaw Miles of the 77th Division, and Lieutenant Colonel Emory J. Pike of the 82d Infantry Division took part in courageous attacks which gained them Medal of Honor citations.

Then, on September 26, the A.E.F., 600,000 men with 2,700 big guns to support them, moved into the great, dank, Argonne Forest—and it was here that the U.S. soldiers engaged in their bloodiest and most gallant fighting of the war. In the Argonne, 79 soldiers in 41 days of combat earned immortality as Medal of Honor men.

Among them were Captain George H. Mallon, who commanded Company E, 132d Infantry, 33d Division, and his

First Sergeant, Sydney G. Gumpertz. These two stormed enemy lines and captured 110 prisoners of war, 4 machine guns, and 4 155-mm. howitzers.

There was the tough old regular, Sergeant Mike Ellis of the 1st Division, who had already earned a DSC at Soissons.

"He didn't know what the word 'afraid' meant, or even how you spelled it," an A.E.F. buddy once commented of Ellis.

In the Argonne he fought as a one-man assault force in front of his company's advance, seeking out and then destroying German machine gun nests which had been placed to deliver a withering flanking fire. During the particular action for which he received the Medal, Ellis captured 6 machine guns and 27 prisoners.

Most of the heroes were footslogging infantry soldiers— but there were also members of the fledgling air force, then called the Army Air Service. There was the fabulous ace, Captain Eddie Rickenbacker, and the colorful Lieutenants Frank ("Balloon Buster") Luke, and Erwin R. Bleckley and Harold E. Goettler, who died in an effort to supply the beleaguered "Lost Battalion."

There were tank soldiers, too, forerunners of the men of the armored forces that were to sweep across the battlefields of France nearly three decades later. One tank battalion was commanded by a young colonel named George S. Patton, Jr. In his hard-fighting battalion, Patton had soldiers like Corporals Donald M. Call and Harold W. Roberts, both of them Medal of Honor men.

Donald Call and one of the officers of his company were in a tank attacking a line of enemy machine gun nests, when part of their turret was blasted off by the direct hit of a high-explosive artillery shell. Call leaped out and sprinted toward a shell hole 30 yards away.

When he reached the shell hole, however, he realized that his officer hadn't followed. Call braved the enemy fire to return to the stricken tank, located the unconscious officer, and saw that he was still breathing. He lifted him on his back and carried the wounded man to safety—a distance of more than a mile—over fields and through woods, constantly being peppered by sniper fire.

A few days later, in the Montrebeau Woods, a tank being driven by Corporal Roberts slithered into a ten-foot deep, rain-filled shell hole, as he was maneuvering to screen a disabled tank. With his tank under water, Roberts realized that there was time for only one man to escape. He turned to his gunner, and said, "Well, only one of us can get out, so out you go." He shoved the other man through the door to safety, and was himself drowned.

Other A.E.F. heroes of the Army were men like Lieutenant Deming Bronson of the 91st Division and Captain Edward C. Allworth of the fighting 5th; Sergeant Reider Waaler of New York's 27th Division, Sergeant Joseph B. Adkison of Tennessee's 30th "Old Hickory" Division, Corporal Sam Sampler of the 36th (Texas) Division, and Colonel W. J. (Wild Bill) Donovan of the Fighting Irish of the famed Rainbow Division.

FOUR

※→ →※ →※ ※← ※← ※←

THE LOST BATTALION

Charles W. Whittlesey

※→ →※ →※ ※← ※← ※←

NOTHING stirs the imagination so strongly as a bold strike into the enemy's lines, or a magnificent stand in the face of overwhelming odds.

This is the story of U.S. soldiers who did both.

In the beginning, they made a great and successful attack which tore a mighty hole in the enemy's lines. But then the men found themselves far in front of their division's advance, surrounded on all sides by the enemy. Commanded by a brave and inspiring leader, this group of soldiers held its ground during five terrible days during which it was cut off from the rest of the A.E.F.

Under constant gunfire, assaulted by waves of enemy who screamed like 10,000 devils as they attacked, the Lost Battalion made a stand that remains without parallel in the history of American arms.

The story of these men is completely entwined with that of their leader, Charles W. Whittlesey, a lawyer turned soldier. It was he who commanded them, who breathed fire into them to give them the will to resist, who calmed them when it seemed that they would be overwhelmed, who kept their hopes from flagging, who gave them courage by showing his own contempt for the enemy.

To his friends and associates in New England, where he

had grown to manhood, and in New York City, where he was a successful lawyer, Whittlesey seemed a rather unlikely candidate for the role of a fighting man. But then, so were a vast majority of the city-bred soldiers of the 77th Infantry Division, who turned the 77th into one of the finest divisions in the A.E.F. Its slashing campaign in the Argonne is one of the most brilliant pages in the history of the U.S. Army.

Of all the U.S. divisions that entered the Argonne fight, as a matter of fact, the 77th was the only one that pushed through the entire length of the forest, and didn't stop fighting until it emerged at the northern extremity of the Argonne on the road toward Sedan.

No incident of valor during the division's fight in the ancient forest outshines that of Major (later Colonel) Whittlesey's "Lost Battalion" which was neither "lost," nor a battalion.

Normally a battalion is a tactical grouping of four companies. But Whittlesey commanded his own 1st Battalion of the 308th Infantry, along with most of the 2d Battalion commanded by Captain (later Major) George McMurtry. This force of six rifle companies was supplemented with sections from Companies C and D of the 306th Machine Gun Battalion —and on the morning of the second day of the operation it was joined by Company K of the sister 307th Infantry, led by Captain Nelson M. Holderman.

Whittlesey's detachment, therefore, which would probably be called a "task force" today, was considerably nearer *two* battalions at the outset.

The action in the pocket near the Charlevaux Mill came about as the result of an attack that got under way shortly after noon on October 2, 1918. The forward movement of the Allied force was satisfactory until the French were hurled back on the left. At the same time, the division's right was unable to make any progress. But the left portion of the division, spearheaded by six companies of the 308th Infantry Regiment, cracked the German defenses and slashed forward to secure the regiment's principal objective.

In the Army publication, *77th Division, Summary of Operations in the World War*, there appears this concise statement of the facts:

During the afternoon [October 2] a composite group of infantry and machine-gun units [Whittlesey's command] broke through the German defenses east of the ravine south of Moulin de Charlevaux. This group advanced to the Apremont-Moulin de Charlevaux road and took up an isolated position. From October 3 to 6 the remainder of the division was unsuccessful in numerous efforts to move up abreast of the surrounded force, which succeeded in beating off frequent attempts of the Germans to destroy it. On October 7 the Argonne Forest was enveloped in the east by other American divisions and the Germans began to withdraw. This enabled the 77th Division to begin a general advance about noon that reached the isolated force about seven p.m.

That is the story in the terse language of a military document. In this description nothing is said of the terror of knowing an enemy was lurking behind every bush, the strain of constant mortar and artillery shelling, or of the horror of the moment when it became apparent to Whittlesey that his command was not only far in advance of the division line, but in an isolated ravine where it was a sitting duck for an enemy closing in from all sides.

Before dawn on October 3, Whittlesey sent a company to seize a nearby hill which gave the Germans a bird's-eye view of the battalion's position. Soon afterward he heard the rattle of gunfire off to his left.

This turned out to be Holderman's company, and when it was safely inside his perimeter Whittlesey knew that he could count on no assistance from that flank. Later in the morning he located Germans on his other flank; then when he lost contact with the runner outposts he had left behind in the wake of his advance, he knew that he had to expect the worst.

In mid-morning a platoon returned, reporting that the men of the company who had attacked the hill were cut off.

This was the crusher. It was definite now that the enemy was in force on all sides. Whittlesey assembled his officers and read a grim statement to them. Their mission, he emphasized, was to hold the position at all costs.

Rifle pits were improved and crude bunkers thrown up, as Whittlesey's command readied itself for the siege. Since they were assault troops, they were ill-prepared for a fight of this sort. Overcoats and blankets had been left behind, so as not to hinder their movements. But the freezing drenching rain which poured down on them was only the beginning of their misery. The Germans began their screaming attacks, and were thrown back time and time again. Whittlesey's men, as well as the Germans, suffered casualties. The stench of dead bodies and the moans of the maimed and the dying filled the ravine with a horror beyond description.

No rations were left by the end of the second day, and for food the men chewed leaves. Their canteens soon ran dry, but luckily someone found a clear spring. Each trip to get water was a hazardous venture; it meant running a gauntlet of fire in clear view of the enemy. Nevertheless, there were always volunteers for this detail.

There was no surgeon; but the two medical corps privates worked like Trojans. Whittlesey never ceased to marvel at their energy. When relief finally came, the pair collapsed and had to be carried off in stretchers with the wounded.

They had the anguish of seeing planes that were searching for them shot down, and of seeing sorely-needed supplies dropped into the hands of the enemy.

McMurtry was severely wounded in the knees by shell

fragments, but he hobbled among his men as though nothing were wrong. During one attack he was struck in the shoulder by an enemy grenade. His wounds were painful, but he stayed in the thick of the fight.

Holderman also was wounded four or five times, but he never gave his injuries a thought. One day he dragged himself, under heavy machine gun fire, into an area where two of his wounded men were pinned down. Despite his own hurts, he carried them both to safety.

Runners volunteered to attempt to reach the division lines —but none was able to penetrate more than a few yards beyond the perimeter without being cut down.

Through the thick of the battle Whittlesey moved quietly among the men, counseling them to keep cool. He checked their positions and looked at their weapons. And he watched the ever-dwindling ammunition supply, by no word or gesture did he ever communicate his worries and fears to the men.

Meanwhile, for the division's part, there were, as the *Summary of Operations* states, numerous attempts made to reach the isolated force. On the third day of the siege a mighty effort was made by the 2d Battalion of the 307th Infantry. They attempted to storm the German lines, but were greeted with tremendous massed artillery and mortar fire. The battalion commander fell; he sent for the captain in command of "H" Company, and ordered him to take over.

Captain Eddie Grant, former second baseman of the New York Giants and an ex-Harvard athlete, organized the survivors of the battalion for another thrust.

"We've got to get to those people," he told the men. When the attack was launched, he ran to his own company to lead them into the fight, and was struck by an exploding shell. He died a few days later.

"The real story is not here," Whittlesey was to say to the

correspondents who later interviewed the survivors of the
Lost Battalion. "It is with the men who day and night fought
their way to our relief."

At 4 p.m. on the afternoon of October 7, when the misery
in the ravine was at its very worst, a figure carrying a white
flag was seen scurrying toward the perimeter. The men recognized him as a private named Lowell R. Hollingshead who,
with seven others, had made an unauthorized break on the
morning of the second day. They learned from Hollingshead
that the group had come under fire an instant after leaving the
dugout. Four of the men had been killed outright, and four
wounded and taken prisoner. He, as the least hurt of the
wounded, had been selected to carry a message to the major.

Whittlesey without a word took the paper, which contained
a badly typewritten note. As he scanned it he told Hollingshead to get back to his position.

Sir:

The Bearer of the present, Lowell R. Hollingshead, has been
taken prisoner on October —. He refused to the German Intelligence Office every answer to his questions and is quite an
honourable fellow, doing honor to his fatherland in the strictest
sense of the word.

He has been charged against his will, believing he is doing
wrong to his country, in carrying forward this present letter to
the Officer in charge of the 2nd Batl. J.R. 308 of the 77th Div.
with the purpose to recommend this Commander to surrender
with his forces as it would be quite useless to resist any more
in view of the present conditions.

The suffering of your wounded men can be heard over here
in the German lines and we are appealing to your human senti-
ments.

A white flag shown by one of your men will tell us that you
agree with these conditions. Please treat the Lowell R. Hollingshead as an honorable man. He is quite a soldier we envy you.

                    The German Commanding Officer

There is a legend that Whittlesey, aroused, wrote "Go to Hell!" on this note, wrapped it around a rock, and hurled it back into the German lines. Actually, he sent no reply. After studying it carefully, he passed it to McMurtry and then to Holderman. McMurtry was of the opinion that the note was a good sign, that it meant the Germans were worried and getting edgy.

Having spurned the surrender demand (Whittlesey never even acknowledged its receipt), the battered command trapped in the pocket knew it must face an all out attack at any moment. To make certain that the Germans did not mistake his silence for anything but defiance and contempt, Whittlesey ordered the removal of white aircraft identification panels that had been spread on the ground. He wanted no white showing on the battalion's position.

The German commander, enraged that his offer had been spurned, dispatched the heaviest assault that Whittlesey's command had yet seen, using machine guns, grenades, and flame throwers. To his astonishment, he was hurled back after suffering savage casualties. Holderman, holding down the right flank, was out in front, waving his pistol and firing point-blank into the attacking waves of enemy infantry. He was wounded once again, but stayed on his feet [1] and inspired the brilliant defense that repulsed the Germans. Even the sick and the wounded dragged themselves painfully to the firing line to help stem the attack. The Germans' surrender demand had given the weary command a new and fierce sort of determination.

But even with their new-found hope, Whittlesey was scarcely prepared for the surprise he got around 7 o'clock that evening when a soldier stuck his head in the dugout and said

[1] Nelson M. Holderman was awarded the Medal of Honor in General Orders No. 21, War Department, 1921.

that a patrol was on the road and that an officer was asking for him by name.

Whittlesey's orderly looked at him questioningly and wondered aloud, "Do you suppose it's safe on the road?"

Whittlesey didn't answer right away—and then it hit him! The soldier had said "on the road." He dashed out and in a matter of seconds the wonderful, unbelievable news made the rounds of the watery dugouts. They had been relieved at last.

Everyone whooped for joy as the newcomers passed around cans of corned willie. McMurtry [2] saw a lieutenant munching on a thick sandwich and happily accepted half. In a few minutes' time the survivors of the outfit that the correspondents were already calling the "Lost Battalion" marched in orderly fashion toward the rear. Behind them they left 69 dead and nearly 200 wounded, casualties who would have to be carried out on stretchers to the aid station set up in a medieval abbey on the edge of the forest.

In the days and years that followed Major General Robert Alexander, the division commander, became enraged at any suggestion that the battalion had been lost. "Colonel Whittlesey's command was neither lost nor was it rescued," he stated in an official report to the War Department.

The historian, Frederick L. Paxson, has noted, "The battalion was never lost. It knew only too well just where it was, and its division knew."

In effect, in a general advance that had not succeeded, Whittlesey's command was the only unit that gained its objective.

Whittlesey was awarded the Medal of Honor in General Orders No. 118, War Department, 1918. The presentation took place on the Boston Commons on Christmas Day, 1918.

The full measure of the tragedy in the Argonne did not

[2] George G. McMurtry was awarded the Medal of Honor in General Orders No. 118, War Department, 1918.

take place until long after the regiment left France, however. The deaths that had been suffered during the ordeal weighed terribly on Whittlesey's soul. Even the words of his commanding general and the commendation of General Pershing failed to convince the lawyer of the important role that his command had played in the Argonne campaign. In the late fall of 1921 he left New York City, ostensibly to see the Army-Navy game. Instead he boarded a steamer for Cuba. On the first night out he disappeared over the rail, and his body was never recovered.

FIVE

➤➤➤ ➤➤➤ ➤➤➤ ⊰⊰⊰ ⊰⊰⊰ ⊰⊰⊰

MOUNTAIN MAN IN THE ARGONNE

Alvin C. York

➤➤➤ ➤➤➤ ➤➤➤ ⊰⊰⊰ ⊰⊰⊰ ⊰⊰⊰

B Y NIGHTFALL on October 8, 1918, the legend had already begun to snowball. The tall soldier became aware of this when he reported to the brigade commander in the woods near Chatel-Chehery, France.

"Well, York," the general said amiably, "I hear tell you've captured the whole German Army!"

The big, red-haired mountaineer from Tennessee mumbled, embarrassed at having been singled out. At that moment Corporal Alvin Cullem York of Pall Mall, Tennessee, a turkey-shooting marksman who was a lineal descendant of frontiersman Davy Crockett, wished desperately he was any place but in a general's command post.

Even in later years, when he had become accustomed to the acclaim the nation bestowed upon "Sergeant York," it always seemed somewhat incredible to him that his exploit should have been called by Marshal Foch of the French Army "the greatest thing accomplished by any soldier of all the armies." Or that it should have been referred to by Major General George B. Duncan, commander of the 82d Infantry Division in which York soldiered as "the most remarkable incident in the whole war."

An action near Hill 223 in the Chatel-Chehery sector brought York the Medal of Honor. He was promoted to sergeant several days after the incident, and was thereafter known as "Sergeant York" to countless millions of Americans.

But the true measure of York's greatness lay not in what he had accomplished in the physical sense; not in the astonishing revelation that he had singlehandedly outfought an entire German machine gun battalion; not in the fact that his keen eye and steady hand had cut down 22 German gunners; not in the boldness that had enabled him to take 35 enemy machine guns; nor even in the courage that enabled him to bluff 132 armed enemy soldiers into surrendering.

Far more difficult for Alvin York than storming the line of enemy machine guns was the inner battle he had been forced to fight. This was a terrible conflict of moral values that had precipitated a period of mental turmoil and anguish for York from the moment that he entered the military service as a drafted soldier in the United States Army.

York, in the beginning, was a conscientious objector. The first time he had received a notice that he was required to register for the draft, he scrawled "I don't want to fight" on the card, and returned it to the county draft board. Later on he formally listed himself as a conscientious objector by virtue of his membership in the Church of Christ in the Christian Union.

But the board ruled that this was not, in their opinion, "a well organized religious sect," and they declined Alvin's request to be excused from military service. He was ordered to report for induction into the Army. He appealed this decision, but again his petition was denied. He wrote to President Woodrow Wilson explaining his position. Wilson turned the letter over to the army and it got lost in the shuffle of wartime Washington. There was nothing for York to do but report for induction or be classified a draft-dodger.

Fear had nothing to do with York's dislike of fighting. Fear, as a matter of fact, was an emotion the mountaineer scarcely knew. Bearing arms in battle seemed to Alvin to be a violation of the principles of his church; and it was this sincere and deep-rooted belief that plagued York as he stripped off his civilian clothes and buttoned up the tunic of his olive-drab army uniform.

To some of his old acquaintances in Fentress County, York's stand as a conscientious objector seemed odd. Alvin's early background was not exactly of a God-fearing, church-going sort. As a young man, he had been quite a gay blade, with a considerable hankering for the powerful moonshine native to the section in which he grew up.

But those who knew him well had no doubts about York's sincerity. He had made a complete break with his old life, and had quit drinking, smoking, and running around. He studied the Bible for long hours, and he was determined to live the rest of his life by the rules of the Good Book. He became a leader in the Church of Christ in the Christian Union, a small sect with a considerable following among the mountain folk.

Alvin York, 6 feet tall, weighing 180 pounds, 29 years old, was at the prime of his life when he embarked upon his army career at Camp Gordon, Georgia. The 82d Infantry Division, to which York was assigned, was composed mostly of drafted men from Alabama, Georgia, and Tennessee. Before it was sent overseas, its ranks were filled with recruits from the New England and Middle Atlantic States—hence its nickname, the "All American Division." York was assigned to the company with which he was destined to spend all of his eighteen months as a soldier—Company G, 328th Infantry Regiment.

The mountaineer, his body and muscles hardened from years of hunting, ploughing, and blacksmithing, was one of the most striking men in Captain E. C. B. Danforth's company. But the captain, a former Augusta, Georgia school-teacher, was sorely troubled by York's steadfast conviction that he was "doing wrong" by being in the Army. Yet at the same time he had to admit that York was easily the outstanding recruit in the outfit. He could shoot, he carried himself well, he responded intelligently to orders, and, as a matter of fact, were it not for his conscientious objector's views, Danforth would have made him a noncom. But Danforth had questioned York repeatedly about his beliefs, and he knew that the Tennessean was convinced that in going to war he was breaking his faith.

One of their conversations concluded with York pouring out a torrent of words that troubled Danforth considerably. York told Danforth that he would go to France, he would continue to be a good soldier, he would continue to obey the orders that were given to him—and when the time came he would go into the trenches and shoot to kill. But, he gravely warned Danforth, *he would hold the captain responsible for the lives he had taken when he appeared before God in Heaven on Judgment Day.*

Danforth's own feelings had become involved; but instead of simply attempting to get York out of his hair, he put the case before his battalion commander, Major George E. Buxton, a New Englander who, it turned out, knew the Bible as well as York did.

As Buxton listened to Danforth's account, he sensed that York was a man well worth salvaging if he could be made to listen. He felt that for all of the mountaineer's dedication to the principles of the sect to which he belonged, there was some nagging thought in back of the man's mind which would not let him play the passive role of a conscientious objector.

"Bring him to my hut tonight," he told Danforth. That night the three talked for a long time together. Danforth found himself mostly listening as Buxton and York warmly debated the moral issue, each quoting from the Scriptures to prove his point.

Buxton cited Matthew in the New Testament and Ezekiel in the Old. York replied in kind.

When Buxton drew upon, "He that killeth with the sword must be killed with the sword," (Rev. 13:10) the private answered, "Nation shall not lift up sword against nation, neither shall they learn war any more" (Is. 2:4). Finally, the Major arose. He turned to Danforth. "I want you to send him home on furlough for two weeks." To York he said, "That will give you time to do some thinking and praying. If you then can find it in your heart to return with a free conscience, we will take you with us. If you cannot . . . I will see that you are let out."

York's torment continued during his two weeks back in the hills in the forks of the Wolf River. There was no one he could turn to, no one from whom to seek advice. It was something he had to solve by himself—and solve it he did, on the last day of his leave.

The next day he rejoined Company G, and told Captain Danforth that he had become convinced he could fight for his country without violating the precepts of his faith. From that day on York marched in the ranks with a light heart and clear mind, as the division traveled north to Camp Mills and Camp Upton in New York, and thence to the ports of embarkation.

The division fought that summer in Lorraine, where the lanky York earned corporal's stripes and command of an automatic rifle team. He had always been known as a good man on a squirrel or turkey shoot in his native Fentress County, and his phenomenal marksmanship on the front lines was soon the talk of his regiment. Then, in the fall, the 82d Division took part in the Meuse-Argonne offensive.

On October 7, 1918, the 82d, which had been held in re-

serve, was slipped into the I Corps (Liggett) line between the
1st and 28th Divisions. It was Pershing's intent that the three
divisions should increase the pressure down the Aire Valley
toward St. Juvin to pinch the Germans out of the northern
extremity of the Argonne.

In conjunction with the 28th Division, the 82d slashed at
the east flank of the Forest near the communications center
of Chatel-Chehery. Meeting determined enemy resistance,
it was only able to push its line forward one mile by nightfall.

General Pershing then planned to cut the vital road and rail
lines by a co-ordinated infantry and artillery assault. During
the night of October 7–8, the 2d Battalion of the 328th Infantry, including Company G in which Corporal York was
a squad leader, pushed across the Aire River, passed through
the 1st Battalion which had taken Hill 223, and launched its
attack at precisely 6 a.m. behind a rolling artillery barrage.
The artillery was timed to creep ahead of the doughboys at
the rate of 100 yards every three minutes until the troops were
on the objective—the railroad.

Its initial thrust carried the battalion in which York was
fighting about one mile west of the line of departure—but
here the Americans locked horns with a determined enemy
who was comfortably situated in the high ground.

Out in front of the battalion advance was part of a platoon
belonging to Company G. When this force came under a
violent hail of machine gun fire, the men raced for the cover
of trees and bushes in a pell-mell scramble.

The terrible enemy fire took its toll. Three noncoms and
all but seven of the men in the group fell in those first minutes
after the German machine guns opened fire. York, the only
surviving noncom, was left in command. He called for the
others to move forward. They advanced and succeeded in
overcoming the first machine gun nest and taking its crew

prisoner. York told someone to see to getting the prisoners to the rear; then he moved out in advance of his tiny command to see what lay ahead of them. He had gone forward only a few yards when a line of 35 machine guns opened up and pinned him down.

The Tennessean found himself trapped and under fire within 25 yards of the enemy's machine gun pits—and he coolly decided to do something about the situation. He began firing into the nearest enemy position, aware that the Germans would have to expose themselves to get an aimed shot at him. His estimate of the situation proved correct. The Germans did have to rear up a little to get a shot off. And every time a German head showed over the parapet, York drilled a bullet into it!

After he had shot down more than a dozen enemy gunners in this fashion, he was charged by six German soldiers who came at him with fixed bayonets. York thereupon used a shooting trick that has been unofficial doctrine in the army ever since. With six men headed his way, he realized that if he dropped the first one the others would take cover behind their fallen comrade's body and be in a position to fire a volley at him.

York therefore drew a bead on the *sixth* man, and then on the fifth. He worked his way down the line, and practically before he knew it, the first man in line was charging the eagle-eyed American sharpshooter all by himself. York dropped him with a dead-center shot.

With the attack on his position disposed of, York again turned his attention on the machine gun pits. Every time he fired, another enemy soldier fell. As a captured German officer later observed, "Such marksmanship is bound to have a most demoralizing effect on the men who are the targets. . . ."

In between shots York called for the Germans to surrender.

At first it may have seemed funny to the well-entrenched enemy; but the joke had become rather hollow by the time the Tennessean had killed his twenty-second victim. Shortly afterward a German officer (he turned out to be a major) advanced under a white flag and offered to surrender if York would stop shooting at his men.

The tall American agreed that it would be best to put an end to the bloodshed. He called his seven men forward, and with his pistol in hand followed the German officer back to the line of machine gun positions where 35 guns now stood silent.

York and his soldiers disarmed 90 Germans and prepared to move them to the rear. Then they realized that to do so would involve getting the entire detachment through a line of occupied German trenches. They were now inside enemy lines!

There was only one way to play it—boldly—York decided; and he resolved to march the whole kit and caboodle right through a trench filled with German riflemen. He jabbed his pistol in the enemy major's back, and through an interpreter warned that one false move would cost the officer his life. The officer quickly realized that the tall American wasn't bluffing.

They brazenly marched up to the front line trench, where York demanded—and received!—the surrender of the remaining Germans. Having taken a total of 132 prisoners, and knocked 35 machine guns out of action, York finally returned to his regiment's lines and found himself in a neighboring battalion's sector. He left the prisoners with this battalion and headed back to his own outfit. Captain Danforth was puzzled at seeing York, and asked why he didn't come from the direction of the front. For the first time in their relationship he found the mountaineer apprehensive and vague.

"If it was anyone but you, York," Danforth said, "I'd

figure he'd ducked out during the shooting. But I know you too well. I suppose you've got your reasons, but I'll be dog-goned if I know what they are!"

But then, as the day wore on, rumors of Corporal York's amazing feat began to circulate throughout the regiment. Danforth got the story then, and nearly exploded in rage because York hadn't reported the affair to him.

"It all fits in," he told the battalion commander. "This morning after things quieted down we took 80 prisoners who said they were all that was left of a German machine gun battalion. I guess it was the rest of the battalion that York got!"

Intelligence officers questioned the prisoners and learned from their testimony the incredible story of how a fighting battalion was destroyed by one determined soldier armed only with a rifle and pistol.

What's more, it was learned that York had destroyed this battalion at a moment when it was supposed to support a German counterattack against the Americans on Hill 223. As a result of the battalion's demise, the counterattack was never made.

As word of York's exploit filtered to the rear, it was greeted first by disbelief, then by utter astonishment. All doubts were dispelled by a message from First Lieutenant Joseph A. Woods, Assistant Division Inspector.

The lieutenant's report stated, "I personally counted the prisoners reported by Corporal Alvin C. York, Company G, 328th Infantry, on October 8, 1918, and found them to be one hundred and thirty-two in number."

The combat accomplishments of the soldier from Pall Mall, Tennessee caught the fancy of a generation of Americans. More than thirty years later, rifle marksmen would still be trying to pattern themselves after Sergeant York of the A.E.F.

SIX

REGULAR ARMY SOLDIER
Samuel Woodfill

SAMUEL Woodfill, a big, backwoods country boy from Jefferson County, Indiana, typified the old army, and those dependable, rough-and-ready sergeants who were its backbone.

The summer of 1918 found Sam Woodfill overseas with the 5th (Red Diamond) Infantry Division, as a "temporary" wartime officer assigned to Company M, 60th Infantry Regiment. Woodfill was a good deal older and considerably more experienced than his fellow lieutenants. At the age of 35 he was a veteran of more than 17 years' service in the army. By contrast, his battalion commander, Major Lee Davis, had not even entered high school when Sam was already fighting the *insurrectos* in the Philippines.

The rugged beauty of the Ohio River valley in which he grew up held no allure for young Woodfill; and he had determined to join up at the earliest possible moment. He was turned down for being too young for service during the war with Spain; but three years later, at 17, he made the grade as a soldier in the regular army, when there was a call for recruits to fight Aguinaldo in the Philippine Insurrection.

Sam soldiered in the 11th Infantry, in Captain Robert Alexander's company. Three years were spent smoking *in-*

surrectos out of the *barrios* on Mindanao, but Sam saw few pitched battles, since the Moros were old hands at guerrilla warfare. After three years of bush skirmishes and jungle patrols, the 11th returned to the United States; and Woodfill, after a brief visit home, enlisted in Company G, 3d United States Infantry.

Thus he found himself a member of "The Old Guard," the oldest regiment in the Army, which dated back to the days of General Mad Anthony Wayne and the battle of Fallen Timbers. As a soldier in the 3d, Woodfill, who was fresh from the tropics, found himself headed for the remote interior of Alaska.

The regiment arrived at Skagway, negotiated the Yukon in an overloaded paddle steamer, and then found itself deep in the Arctic at America's northern frontier post, Fort Egbert.

Woodfill grew to love this bleak land. He remained north of the Arctic Circle for more than eight years, and when he left it was with the intention of returning on his next reenlistment.

Back in the States, however, he found himself forced to pay the price exacted of a soldier who requested transfer— for in those days enlisted men were rarely transferred in grade. After nearly 12 years of military life, Sam was once more a buck private.

He was ordered to the 9th Infantry Regiment at Fort Thomas, Kentucky. Here his new company commander took one look at the ramrod-straight soldier, examined his service record, and promoted him to sergeant on the spot.

The 9th Infantry was a proud and colorful regiment. It had served in the army since the Indian Wars. It had fought in the Civil War, in the war with Spain, the Insurrection, and in the Boxer Rebellion. It was not destined to remain long in peaceful Kentucky, either; for as trouble developed along the

Mexican Border, the 9th was sent to the Rio Grande country to skirmish with Carranza.

In the spring of 1917 the United States declared war on Germany. Woodfill and the other regulars confidently anticipated early orders rushing them to France for a crack at "Kaiser Bill." Instead, he and other superior-rated noncoms were ordered to an Officers' Training School, and in July, 1917, Sam Woodfill was commissioned a second lieutenant. Although he tried hard to get back to his old regiment, he was ordered to a new outfit, the 60th Infantry Regiment, 5th Infantry Division.

Upon reporting to the 60th Infantry, which had been organized with the 61st Infantry in the 9th Infantry Brigade, Woodfill learned that his new regiment had been formed around a nucleus of officers and noncoms from the 11th Infantry—the regiment with which he had served on Mindanao in his recruit days. He also learned that the division's line-up included the 11th Infantry, which was formed with the 6th Infantry in the 10th Brigade.

The 5th Division was, in time, to become a regular army outfit—but as it readied itself for combat in the first World War, it was strictly a cross-section of volunteers and draftees with a thin leavening of regulars.

At Gettysburg, Pennsylvania, where the 60th was assembled, Woodfill was assigned to Company M under Captain George E. Ventress. When Ventress was ordered overseas with the Division's advance party, it was left to Woodfill to finish organizing the company. This posed no problem for a crackerjack regular like Sam Woodfill. Sergeants had been running infantry companies for years.

During the Christmas holidays Sam took some leave, went home to Indiana, and married his boyhood sweetheart. There was precious little time for a honeymoon before he had to report back to the regiment, which by this time was at Camp Greene, North Carolina.

Finally, the regiment was on its way to France. After leaving New York, they stopped first at Liverpool. Then they crossed the channel, and boarded cattlecars for the trip to the front.

Upon reaching its sector, the division found the advance party waiting. Captain Ventress again took command of Company M, and Woodfill, now a first lieutenant, resumed normal company officer duties.

Billeted near Bruyeres, the 60th Infantry was attached for training first to the French 70th Division and then to the French 62d. When it went into battle for the first time, it was with the 64th French territorials. During a session in the battle line in June, 1918, the Red Diamond soldiers were introduced to the horrors of mustard and phosgene gas.

Finally, the entire 9th Brigade, under Brigadier General J. C. ("Uncle Joe") Castner, was moved into the St. Dié area where, for the first time, it was completely responsible for the defense of a segment of the line. The regiment remained there until it was relieved in August to rejoin its sister brigade. The 5th Division was scheduled to take part in the first all-U.S. action by the newly formed American First Army—the reduction of the St. Mihiel salient.

Early in September the 5th Division moved out on a 30-mile march from the Moselle District—a miserable forced march in a drenching downpour that turned the roads to quagmires and brought traffic nearly to a standstill.

After reaching its assigned sector on September 10, the 60th, led by Colonel Frank B. Hawkins, sliced up the St. Jean-St. Jacques road north of Martincourt in the shock action that helped drive the Germans out of the St. Mihiel salient.

After a short rest in the Souilly area, southeast of Verdun, the Division thrust into the Argonne and relieved the 80th Infantry Division. As the Red Diamond Division took over the front line positions, officers from each regiment went out to make a reconnaissance of the terrain between them and the enemy.

Woodfill was now in command of Company M—Captain Ventress had transferred to the engineers. He set out to scout the terrain, but was fired on by the enemy, and quickly became the target for a number of German marksmen. As he darted for cover, Woodfill thought that this time his number was surely up.

He inched his way toward a shellhole which offered him some measure of protection. It was shallow—but better than nothing. He flattened himself against the earth, fully expecting that at any moment the searching bullets would find him.

As flying lead whined around him, he pulled the stub of a pencil from his shirt pocket and took his wife's picture out of his wallet. There wasn't much time. As the war raged around him, Woodfill wrote in an amazingly steady hand: "In case of accident or death it is my last and fondest desire that the finder of my remains shall please do me a last and everlasting favor, to forward this picture to my darling wife. Tell her I have fallen on the field of honor. . . ."

But Sam Woodfill was spared that afternoon. Possibly it was because he had a date with destiny the very next morning. The 5th Division was getting set to launch an attack in the brutal Argonne offensive, and Lee Davis's 3d Battalion of the 60th Infantry was ordered to advance up the rail line east of Cunel. The battalion's mission was a combat reconnaissance of the Bois de la Pultiere, the woods beyond Cunel. The purpose was to learn the location of the German defense line.

October 12, 1918, was a bleak and foggy morning. Davis's battalion began moving out shortly before 6 a.m. All of his companies of riflemen came under ferocious enemy fire almost simultaneously from a series of machine gun outposts on the edge of the town.

To Woodfill, who was at the head of the advance, it seemed that the heaviest fire was coming from three directions —from the front; from the upper floor of a stable off to his right; and from a church steeple about 200 yards to his left. Sam picked up a Springfield rifle, and quickly satisfied himself that his eye had lost none of its keenness. He fired five rounds through a little window in the church tower. The gun inside stopped firing. Reloading quickly, he let go another clip which he aimed at a gap—just about the right size for the snout of a machine gun barrel—under the roof of the stable. That one, too, went out of action.

Then Woodfill began to advance toward the chatter of the machine guns in front of him. Plunging from one shell hole to another, he ran across the flat terrain. In one hole where he had taken momentary refuge from the hail of bullets, he gagged and nearly choked to death. With horror he realized that he had blundered into a lingering patch of phosgene gas, and he coughed and sputtered and struggled to clear his lungs of the searing chemical. For a moment he considered the gas mask that hung in its container at his hip, but discarded the idea because wearing it might hinder his shooting.

Two Company M men, who had followed him at a distance of about 25 yards, caught up with him, and Sam posted them to fire at a machine gun nest as he flanked it. He stealthily worked around to the German emplacement, moving on his belly with his rifle cradled in his arms. When he was less than ten yards from his objective, the gun stopped firing, and four German soldiers bolted out into the open—headed straight for him. Woodfill fired furiously and dropped three of them. There wasn't time to reload his rifle before the fourth German charged him. Woodfill seized his rifle by the barrel and tried to club his opponent, but the rifle was wrested away from him and the two men grappled at close quarters. The savage struggle ended when Sam managed to work his pistol out of its holster.

Picking up his rifle, Woodfill waved for Company M to start moving; but once again they advanced only a few yards before coming under fierce machine gun fire. Sam hit the dirt just as a stream of bullets kicked up the earth at his feet, rolled over behind a clump of bushes, and lay still. The enemy gunner apparently thought he had killed Sam, for he altered his range and switched to a different target.

Sam propped himself up on an elbow and studied the terrain. He saw that the heaviest fire was coming from a gun emplaced in a clump of thistle bushes about 40 feet ahead of him. He crawled over behind a mound of gravel and readied himself once again for action. He took his pistol from its holster and placed it in front of him, along with an extra clip of bullets for the rifle. Then he cautiously slid the Springfield over the gravel heap and painstakingly adjusted himself behind the sights. Sighting the rifle was a painful task for his gas-clouded eyes. He thought he saw the glimmer of an enemy helmet and slowly squeezed off his first shot. There was a rustle in the bushes, and Sam was unable to see any further sign of the helmet that had been his target.

Then the Indiana sharpshooter saw that a second German had pushed the first aside and was getting himself settled behind the gun. Sam fired a second shot—and a second man slumped over the gun. A third—and then a fourth—tried. Woodfill fired twice more and each time a would-be gunner became a casualty. The fifth man in the machine gun nest tried to get away, and Sam dropped him also.

Then another enemy soldier appeared in the gun position. Woodfill was ready even though there wasn't time to reload the Springfield. The German leaped out, and Sam cut him down with a blast from his .45.

Tensely waiting and watching, Sam reloaded the Springfield without taking his eyes off the enemy position. It seemed to be deserted—but he wasn't taking chances. He thrust the reloaded pistol back in his belt and charged with his rifle at the ready into the machine gun nest which was apparently littered with dead—although one was only pretending to be a casualty.

As Sam stepped over him the man who was lying doggo reached up and pulled the rifle from Woodfill's hands. But Sam drew his pistol and shot him before he could do any damage.

Determined to seek out the remainder of the enemy in this area, Woodfill headed for another machine gun nest. He was nearly felled by a sniper's bullet, which missed him by less than the length of a trench knife, but Sam's runner flushed the sniper and killed him.

Sam then attacked and wiped out this third machine gun nest. He was inspecting the gun he had taken, when a trio of German ammunition carriers appeared on the scene. They took one look at the body-littered emplacement, stared at Sam as though he were the Devil, dropped the ammunition belts, and threw their hands in the air.

Sam impatiently disarmed them and motioned them to the rear, where his men would take them prisoner. He then continued his incredible fight—even though it was obvious that he had already adequately carried out the battalion mission of learning the location of the German line of resistance.

Sheltered behind a tree he searched diligently for the telltale muzzle blast that would enable him to locate the enemy machine gun which was pouring lead into the ravine his company had to cross to catch up with him.

Crouching, creeping, and crawling, Woodfill moved in

on the gun, ploughing through a sea of mud and slime until he had found its position and come to a vantage point from which he could bring aimed rifle fire to bear.

Again—five shots, five enemy victims.

That gun was silenced, and once again Sam ran for the gun emplacement to inspect the damage. Suddenly another gun, off to his flank, turned on him. He reached the trench that was his objective unscathed, leaped in, and found himself face to face with a German who was attempting to get the silenced gun back into action.

Sam had his pistol in his hand this time, and shot the enemy gunner. But another German rounded the corner of the trench, and this time Woodfill's .45 jammed. Fortunately, he spotted an enemy pick stuck in the side of the trench, yanked it free, and prepared to wield it as the German attacked. His adversary had drawn a Luger and fired at Sam at point-blank range—but his shots went wild as Woodfill slammed into him with the pick and beat him to death.

Meanwhile, the curtain of fire across the ravine had lifted, and Company M charged across the woods to rejoin its hard-fighting lieutenant. The rest of the battalion wheeled into line as the Germans drew back into the woods beyond Cunel —retreating from their defense positions, thanks to the tenacity of one man.

━➤➤ ➤➤ ➤➤ ⧫⧫ ⧫⧫ ⧫⧫

IN THE NAME OF THE CONGRESS

━➤➤ ➤➤ ➤➤ ⧫⧫ ⧫⧫ ⧫⧫

TODAY we think of the award of a Medal of Honor in terms of a colorful military pageant or a solemn White House ceremony. But for many years the presentation of the nation's highest award involved only so much pomp and ceremony as is generally involved in signing one's name on the postal card which comes with a piece of registered mail.

Aside from the six Mitchel Raiders discussed in Chapter One, awards of the Medal of Honor were made as quietly and inconspicuously as possible.

There were occasions during the Civil War when winners of the Medal received it in full view of their comrades; and two Civil War heroes were awarded the Medal by President U. S. Grant in a White House ceremony. But for the most part, the master of ceremonies was the letter carrier who brought the Medal in a registered parcel. More often than not, by the time his Medal had been approved and forwarded from the Adjutant General, the winner had died in subsequent fighting or had transferred to another outfit.

In the early years there was often a considerable span of time between the date of the action in which a soldier won the Medal and the actual issuance of a Medal. And so it was only infrequently that the rest of the nation had occasion to take notice when one of its heroes was honored. It seems singularly appropriate that this rather indifferent attitude should have come to an end during the presidential administration of

Theodore Roosevelt. The colorful former commander of the "Rough Riders," the volunteer cavalrymen who had earned immortality in the fight at San Juan Hill in the war with Spain, was well aware of the value of *esprit de corps*. As an old soldier, "T.R." listened with keen interest when Major William E. Birkhimer, artilleryman and Medal of Honor hero himself in the war with Spain, suggested that considerably more attention should be given to presenting a Medal of Honor to a man who had earned it.

Eventually Roosevelt signed an Executive Order outlining the basic policy still in force; his order stated that awards are to be made with formal and impressive ceremonial, and that the recipient "will, when practicable, be ordered to Washington, D.C., and the presentation will be made by the President, as Commander-in-Chief, or by such representative as the President may designate." To Roosevelt's immense delight, the very first ceremony scheduled for the White House, on January 10, 1906, was the presentation of the Medal of Honor to one of his "old boys"—Assistant Surgeon James Robb Church, who had served in Teddy's famous 1st U.S. Volunteer Cavalry. The Military Aide gravely intoned the citation: *"In addition to performing gallantly the duties pertaining to his position, he voluntarily and unaided carried several seriously wounded men from the firing line to a secure position in the rear, in each instance being subjected to a very heavy fire and great exposure and danger."*

It is interesting to note the frequency with which men who earned the Medal crossed T.R.'s path, although he himself never received the coveted combat decoration. General Leonard Wood, who preceded him as commander of the Rough Riders, earned the Medal in the Indian Wars as an assistant surgeon in the Apache campaign during the summer of 1886. T.R. personally appointed two special military observers to the 1905 Russo-Japanese War—Lieutenant General Arthur

MacArthur and Lieutenant Douglas MacArthur—both of whom also won Medals. And Teddy's own son, Theodore Roosevelt, Jr., who earned the D.S.C. in the first World War and served as a Brigadier General in World War II, earned the Medal of Honor in the heat and fury of combat on D-Day at Utah Beach.

Ninety-five members of the American Expeditionary Force in World War I ultimately qualified for the Medal. General Pershing created a board to screen every recommendation; but up to the time of the Armistice, commanders had recommended only 24 men in the A.E.F. for the Medal, and of these, only four were approved.

Not a single World War I Medal of Honor was actually *awarded* while the fighting was going on. With the advent of the second World War, however, General George Marshall declared, "We cannot do too much in the way of prompt recognition of the men who carry the fight and live under the conditions that exist at the fighting front." The Army Chief of Staff was equally determined that nothing should tarnish the value and high esteem placed on the Medal. He therefore formed a War Department Decorations Board which kept two cardinal principles in mind:

1. To fail to recognize valor promptly would defeat the purpose of the decorations system.

2. To make unmerited awards of the Medal of Honor would depreciate its value.

From every active theater of operation this Board received hundreds of recommendations from unit commanders on behalf of combat soldiers who, they thought, had performed deeds which rated the Nation's No. 1 award for gallantry in action. Every recommendation was substantiated by at least two eyewitness accounts; no secondhand evidence was admissible. Even recommendations that were disapproved in the field had to be forwarded to Washington for final action by the Board.

As early as February 5, 1942—only 64 days after Pearl Harbor—General Orders No. 9 announced the award of the first Medal of Honor for World War II, a posthumous award to Lieutenant Alexander R. Nininger, Jr.

In the years of war that followed, an additional 291 members of the United States Army earned the Medal of Honor, although in deference to wartime conditions few of the presentations were made with much pomp and pageantry.

President Franklin Delano Roosevelt presented the Medal to General James A. Doolittle at the White House on May 20, 1942, upon that flier's safe return from the first air raid on Tokyo. January, 1943, found the President in Casablanca, North Africa, where he made a presentation to Brigadier General William H. Wilbur, who had led a small party on to the beaches well in advance of the landings, to attempt to parlay with the French.

President Roosevelt bestowed the priceless Medal on 42 soldiers. From the steaming jungles of the Pacific and from the rubble-strewn cities of Europe they came—men like Staff Sergeant Jessie R. Drowley of the Americal Division; Technical Sergeant Forrest L. Vosler of the Army Air Corps; Private First Class William J. Johnston of the 45th Division, who fought in the campaign in Italy; and Lieutenant Arnold L. Bjorklund of the 36th Infantry Division.

And there were the other heroes . . . the ones who could not appear. Their Medals were presented to grieving fathers and mothers and widows, or to bewildered children who didn't quite know what all the fuss was about.

During World War II, it was not uncommon for the actual presentation of the Medal to be made by field commanders. Sometimes these presentations were made only a few hundred yards from the fighting front.

Van T. Barfoot, a soldier in the 45th Infantry Division (now an officer of the regular army), who earned a battlefield commission, received his Medal from Lieutenant General Alexander M. Patch, with his division commander, Major General William W. Eagles and his own company witnessing the occasion. When the simple ceremony was over, Second Lieutenant Barfoot, Major General Eagles, and Lieutenant General Patch sat down to a luncheon of canned rations in an open field that was near enough to the front for them to be able to hear the booming of the guns.

In the spring of 1945, before the end of the fighting in the E.T.O., General George S. Patton, Jr. visited the 5th Infantry Division to confer the Medal upon Private First Class Harold A. Garman, a member of the 5th Medical Battalion. Patton noted that Garman's award was for an action during a crossing of the Moselle; he swam through a hail of heavy enemy machine gun fire to save three wounded men in a bullet-riddled assault boat that was sinking fast.

"Why did you do it?" Patton asked the young soldier from Albion, Illinois.

"Well," replied Garman, in a tone which clearly indicated he thought it was a stupid question, "someone had to do it."

When Harry Truman, who had served as a captain of field artillery in World War I, became President, he well understood the meaning and value of the Medal. He often said that of all his duties as President of the United States, awarding the Medal of Honor was the one from which he derived the greatest pleasure.

By the end of World War II, the Medal had clearly achieved a new and indestructible status. During two world wars it had been earned only by the most extraordinary combat action; no longer was it awarded for "soldier-like qualities." It had become strictly a Medal for fighting men.

The suggestion was made at one time that the Medal be

bestowed upon General of the Army Dwight D. Eisenhower in recognition of his leadership during the campaigns in Europe. But when "Ike" learned of this, he refused to consider the idea.

"This," he declared, "has got to remain a Medal for the soldier who comes to grips with the enemy at close quarters."

Many years later, the former Supreme Commander of Europe told a young war hero upon whom he had just bestowed the Medal, "Son, I would rather have the right to wear this than be President of the United States."

❯❯❯ ❯❯❯ ❯❯❯ ❮❮❮ ❮❮❮ ❮❮❮

INFANTRY SOLDIER, BATAAN

Alexander R. Nininger, Jr.

❯❯❯ ❯❯❯ ❯❯❯ ❮❮❮ ❮❮❮ ❮❮❮

THE ARMY into which Sandy Nininger and his class-mates graduated as brand new second lieutenants was rapidly expanding in size, and was anything but "peace-time," although the nation was not yet at war. Pearl Harbor was only 175 days away as Nininger and his classmates joined the long gray line of graduated cadets on June 11, 1941, and entered active duty.

As a cadet, Alexander Ramsey Nininger, Jr., had been something of a puzzle to his fellow West Pointers. Devoted to music, art, and the drama, he appeared to some of them an unlikely candidate for a regular army officer. Born in Georgia, raised mostly in Florida, Sandy had spent several of the early years of his life with his mother in Central Valley, New York—a small community just over the rolling hills from West Point—and had decided then that he wanted to be-come a West Point man and an Army officer. He had gained admittance to the Military Academy by the tough competitive examination route.

After completing the infantry officers' basic course at Fort Benning, Georgia, Sandy headed home to Fort Lauderdale, Florida. He had scarcely unpacked, when new orders from the War Department cut short his leave and sent him hurry-ing to the West Coast to catch a troop transport headed for

Manila. As it turned out, it was one of the last ships to reach the Philippines—but even in late October of 1941, few people suspected that war was only weeks away.

Upon his arrival in "P. I.," Second Lieutenant Nininger was posted to the 57th Infantry Regiment, Philippine Scouts, one of the best Filipino-American units in the army. By law, membership in the Scouts was limited to 12,000 Filipinos. Standards for selection were high, and many would-be recruits who couldn't make the grade were turned away. Consequently the Scouts had a very high *esprit de corps*. The regiment was officered by Americans, most of them regular army officers.

War descended upon the Philippines with the news that Pearl Harbor had been smashed by a Japanese air attack. There was little that could be done to defend the 11,500 miles of coast line. General Douglas MacArthur, who had been recalled to active duty in the U.S. Army only the previous summer, had but meager forces at his command.

Nininger had become a platoon leader in Company A of the 1st Battalion. His battalion commander was Captain Royal Reynolds, Jr., a 31-year-old West Pointer. The company was commanded by Lieutenant Fred Yeager, who had graduated from the Academy one year before Nininger.

The Scouts of the 57th were ordered out of Fort McKinley into the field. Nininger and his men found themselves guarding positions near an army cemetery. Jumpy gunners bagged two aircraft the very first day—both low-flying U.S. planes. The pilots and observers bailed out of both craft safely. One of the observers was Lieutenant Al Fangman, a former officer of the 57th Regiment, who had recently transferred to the Air Corps. He was wounded just seriously enough to rate a bunk in the last hospital ship to leave Manila.

The Japanese landed on the beaches, smashed rapidly in-

land, and began a pincers movement toward Manila. The 57th
Infantry was held in mobile reserve under its commander,
Colonel George S. Clarke, a veteran of World War I. Clarke
was ordered to move the regiment to an area near Camp
Murphy. Before the move could be completed, the order was
countermanded when a report came in that Japanese paratroopers had dropped in the Mt. Arrayat-Pampangas sector.
Nininger and his men raced off to do battle—in gaily-colored
Pambusco buses—but the road was jammed and they didn't
reach the scene of the supposed air drop until nearly midnight. Then they learned it was just a false alarm.

The regiment was then ordered to hide out in the Parac-
Guagua sector pending further developments. Christmas
passed and Manila was declared an open city to spare its
civilian population. The 57th was ordered to move once again
—this time to outpost Highway No. 3, to cover the Southern
Luzon Force withdrawal into Bataan. Nininger and his men
patrolled the southern approaches to Fort Stotsenberg until
it was their turn to join the trek to the Bataan Peninsula.

By New Year's Day, 1942, the regiment was established in
the new main line of resistance that was to become known as
the Abucay Line. It was familiar terrain to Nininger and most
of the other officers, as they had held maneuvers there not
long before.

Defensive works were rushed as the inadequate U.S. and
Filipino forces prepared for the grim business that lay ahead
of them whenever Homma, the Japanese commanding general,
chose to attack. On January 4 the regiment went on half
rations; the officers had to inform the men that there would
be only two meals a day from then on—one before daylight,
the other after dark.

The sector on the extreme right was being defended by
the 57th. Clarke deployed his regiment with the 1st Battalion

on the right and the 3d Battalion on the left. In the 1st Battalion sector, Company A manned the left flank where it adjoined Company K.

The front line battalion sectors were totally dissimilar. The 1st Battalion was on dikes where the water was so deep and where the walls of the fish ponds so steep that it would be impossible for any but foot troops to attack. The battalion's extreme right flank actually extended out over Manila Bay.

The 3d Battalion's zone of action, however, held a serious threat. To the front was an open field—a perfect approach for tanks. And one of its flanks was a hard-surface road leading from Jap territory into Bataan.

The regiment's officers knew from experience and battle reports that the Japanese liked to stick to the roads wherever possible, and that when their attacks failed they were likely to slide off to the flanks and make repeated probing attacks until they found a weak spot.

So, for four days the men labored to deny this sector to the enemy. They cut trees and bushes to improve their field of fire. Wires were strung out in front of the main line of resistance. There was no steel for poles, so they improvised and used bamboo. In front of the wires they placed a triple line of land mines. And then they waited.

On the afternoon of January 9, 1942, the battle for Bataan was joined as the Japanese, confident of quick victory, unleashed unusually heavy artillery concentrations into the eastern sector, where the 57th Infantry was manning the front. During that day also, a Scouts' reconnaissance patrol encountered a heavily-armed Japanese patrol south of Hermosa, a town well beyond the U.S. outpost line. There was a brief fight, and then the Scouts headed back to their command post to report the size and nature of the enemy force.

Exultantly, a Japanese commander reported to General

Homma that the Scouts had "made a general withdrawal and fled into the jungle without putting up a fight."

On the afternoon of January 10, another Japanese force smashed at the regiment's outpost line on the coastal road. The Filipinos fought doggedly, but were overwhelmed and driven back as the enemy surged down to the Calaguiman River near the point where it empties into Manila Bay north of Abucay. The main enemy movement against the U.S. battle line began on January 11, when the Japanese pushed a battalion across the Calaguiman into a cane field less than 200 yards from the main line of resistance. This put the Japanese force opposite the Scouts' 3d Battalion. The sun went down, and in the darkness, enemy soldiers smashed at Company I.

Artillery pounded at them, barbed wire entanglements snared them—but still they came, wave after wave. Their dead formed human bridges for the living to use in breaching the barbed-wire entanglements.

The Japanese overcame Company I and started to engulf Company K. The battalion commander threw his reserve, Company L, into the fight; but the Japanese refused to be stalled, and finally it was necessary for Colonel Clarke to rush in a company from his reserve battalion.

This seemed to slow down the enemy assault; when daylight came the Scouts rallied to counterattack—and their drive enabled them to regain nearly all of the ground that had been lost on the night before.

But serious damage had been done. Large numbers of Japanese had infiltrated the 3d Battalion area, and, operating as snipers, they seriously threatened the Scouts' rear. Sniper parties were organized to track them down.

Fred Yeager, commanding Company A, was puzzling over the relative quiet in his company's sector when Sandy Nininger sat down beside him. Nininger reminded Yeager that he knew the terrain where Company K was having its troubles, since he had organized the defenses in that area when they had been on maneuvers.

"Fred," he said, "I know a good approach—an irrigation ditch—into the area. Give me ten good men and I'll try to pick up enough information so that we can figure out some kind of counterattack."

Yeager agreed at once and let Nininger take ten men from the company. The sturdy Filipinos moved behind Nininger as he headed for the ditch armed with an M-1, a load of hand grenades, and a pistol.

His plan was to work down the ditch into the area where the Japs had infiltrated Company K, which would enable him to come into their midst undetected. His surprise strategy worked; then, as he leaped from cover, he spotted a Jap sniper crouching in a tree.

His M-1 flew up to his shoulder. A shot cracked out, and the Jap toppled from his perch. After that first shot, the action became fast and furious.

Sandy twice led his anti-sniper patrol into the midst of the enemy. Each time he relentlessly stormed in front, smoking out snipers and shooting them down. His little group was hit hard, however, and just when Sandy was readying them for a third attack, Major Reynolds, his battalion commander, ordered him out of the area.

Nininger considered the order carefully for a moment, then turned to his remaining men and ordered them to remain where they were. He sent a brief message back to the battalion commander, and then set out by himself. With his pistol and hand grenades, he attacked the Japanese who were left in the shrinking salient.

Company K, meanwhile, had rallied, and began to surge back into the area where Nininger was waging his one-man war.

"There he is!" someone yelled, pointing to Nininger who, though badly shot up, was still staggering in pursuit of the enemy. Out of a clump of bushes came three Japanese soldiers, charging at him from behind.

Fear-crazed, or out of ammunition, not a one of the trio fired. Instead, they charged with their bayonets. Sandy whirled to meet their attack. Weak from loss of blood from three wounds suffered earlier in the action, he blasted away at them with his pistol until his flagging strength deserted him and he sprawled in the *cogon* grass, surrounded by the bodies of the three who had made that final attack upon him.

At posts the world around, West Point classmates mourned the passing of the first '41 man to die in action. Sandy Nininger's mortal years had been pitifully few; but he had earned the special immortality that is reserved for the gallant Americans who have, over the years, given their lives so that their nation might endure.

NINE

≫≫ ≫≫ ≫≫ ≪≪ ≪≪ ≪≪

ACTION AT GALLOPING HORSE
Charles W. Davis

≫≫ ≫≫ ≫≫ ≪≪ ≪≪ ≪≪

PERHAPS somewhere in the vastness of Oceania, there really exists an island paradise that lives up to the song-writers' imaginations. But it certainly was not Guadal-canal in the British Solomons in January, 1943, when the 27th (Wolfhound) Infantry Regiment of the 25th Division was slugging its way into the oddly-arranged hill area called Galloping Horse.

On the eastern side of a high ridge whose northern slope had been partially wrested from the enemy, Captain Charles W. Davis and two other officers inched their way behind a waist-high shelf that offered them a covered approach toward an enemy stronghold. Two rifle companies of an attacking battalion were pinned down by deadly machine gun and rifle fire within yards of the enemy they could not see.

Davis, who was executive officer of the 2d Battalion, 27th Infantry Regiment, had gone up forward, carrying orders from the battalion commander. Then, with two companions, he had begun to work his way down the slope toward the enemy's guns, looking for an opening that might be exploited. There was none. One of the officers was killed by machine gun bullets; Davis nearly had his head taken off by chunks of rocks and dirt, and fragments of shells that showered on him as he tried to bring effective mortar fire to bear on an enemy who was well-hidden in the shadowy jungle.

Lieutenant Colonel Herbert V. Mitchell, the battalion commander, reached the ridge just before dark and listened soberly to the younger man's account of what it had been like out on the exposed slope of the ridge. Then he issued his orders—allround perimeter defense and dig in for the night. He and Davis remained in the advance position on the hostile ridge all that night. Weary, thirsty infantrymen huddled in fox holes around them and took turns at trying to get a few hours of sleep.

Because he was a big-framed, slow-talking Southerner, Chuck Davis sometimes gave people the idea he was lazy. Those who worked with him soon learned otherwise. He had an air of nonchalance, but when something had to be done, he did it. He was a 24-year-old second lieutenant when he first joined the regiment in June, 1941, and was assigned as a platoon leader in Company A, 1st Battalion. The regiment then belonged to the old Hawaiian Division posted at Schofield Barracks. Behind the young officer was little more than a year of active-duty soldiering. Before he received his commission, by way of ROTC, he had been a law student at the University of Alabama and had done some part-time soldiering as a member of an Alabama National Guard infantry regiment.

Early fall, 1941, found the Hawaiian Division in the throes of reorganization. The old division was to be dissolved and two new divisions organized. The 27th Infantry was assigned to the brand new 25th Infantry Division. Davis, by then a first lieutenant, became a member of the 2d Battalion, 27th Infantry.

First as battalion motor officer, then as the commander of Company G, Davis earned a reputation as one of the regiment's outstanding young officers. When there was a difficult or boring subject on the training schedule, it was standard operating procedure to send for Davis. He had the knack of making people sit up, listen, and learn.

His men found out he wasn't the sort of officer who was content to sit back and issue orders when there was a job to be done. Davis would tell them, "This is what's got to be done—let's do it." And then he would pitch in to help.

He had been made executive officer of the battalion over the heads of several senior captains, who were mildly outraged by his rapid promotion. His battalion commander had hand-picked him for the job because, he said, "Davis is the man we need in there when this battalion gets into the fight."

Mitchell, who had relieved Davis's old battalion commander on the eve of the regiment's departure for the South Pacific, wisely decided he would keep Davis as his exec. They had been in the fight only a few hours when he knew that his judgment had been eminently correct.

By New Year's Day, 1943, the 25th Division was ashore at Guadalcanal. Ten days later the Tropic Lightning Division was called upon by Major General Alexander M. Patch, XIV Corps Commander, to lead the most extensive U.S. ground assault made on the island since the previous August, when the initial landings had been made. The Division, under Major General J. Lawton Collins, was to open the final drive against strongly fortified enemy positions guarding the approaches to the island's north coast.

The most prominent terrain feature of the corps objective was a hill mass known as the Galloping Horse because of its appearance in an aerial photograph. It stretched about 2,000 yards in a northeasterly direction from its tail (Hill 50) to its head (Hill 53).

The Wolfhound Regiment (a nickname dating back to the time when the 27th Infantry was stationed in Siberia after World War I) was ordered into battle by its commander,

Colonel William A. McCulloch, an old professional soldier who had commanded a machine gun battalion in the A.E.F. in the first world war. A West Point classmate of General Patch, the Corps Commander, McCulloch neither smoked nor drank ("He doesn't even like his coffee strong," an irreverent junior officer once remarked), and he soldiered sternly and by the book. He was a crack regimental commander, and later became assistant commanding general of the Americal Division. For the assault upon the Horse he hurled his 1st and 3d Battalions forward, and held his 2d Battalion in reserve in an assembly area at the base of Hill 55.

The assault began at precisely 0635 on January 10, 1943. For two days the 3d Battalion fought a bruising engagement that left it spent. And so, for the third day of the drive, McCulloch ordered Mitchell's 2d Battalion, 27th Infantry, to take over the assault against the ridges that lay before the key corps objective of Hill 53.

Mitchell launched his attack on January 12, after an air strike and a heavy artillery barrage. He dispatched his companies to the attack at 0630. Captain Alan M. Strock's Company G and Captain Harvey Blatt's Company F moved out abreast. Mitchell held Browning (Company E) in reserve, and ordered Robertson to displace his heavy machine guns and 81-mm. mortars (Company H—the battalion heavy weapons company) to Hill 52 to support the advance.

"Dave—you'd better stay with me for the time being," he told his executive officer. Strock's company (Davis's former command) moved out on the right, fought its way through scattered rifle and machine gun fire, and reached its objective, Hill 57, by noon.

But Blatt had his hands full. His company came under the guns of Japanese holding a network of positions on two key ridges. Between these ridges (later named Exton and Sims Ridges), there was a shallow dip. It was marvelous terrain for defensive warfare—and the Japanese exploited it to the fullest.

Company F, slashed at by enemy fire from these ridges. veered too far to its right and exposed the battalion's left flank. Instantly seizing an opportunity to hurt the attackers by luring them on, the Japanese pulled off Exton Ridge and bulwarked the other ridge with more machine guns and rifles. Mitchell countered by thrusting Company E in on the left of Company F to protect the battalion's south flank. Company F, meanwhile, overran Exton Ridge and then attempted to move on Sims Ridge.

They were met with rifle and machine gun fire. It was effective, deadly fire that stunned them and forced them to seek cover. They tried to move, but were stymied at every turn.

At the command post, where Mitchell was receiving only the scantiest information from the hard-pressed company commanders fighting at the ridge, Davis begged to be sent forward to see what was happening.

"Not yet, not yet," Mitchell answered.

Then, a few minutes later, he turned to Davis and told him to go up there and give new instructions to the company commanders. Company F was to pull off Exton Ridge, and move to its right to attack from the north. Company E was to continue forward, so that the enemy position could be enveloped from two sides.

"When you get up forward," Mitchell finished, "stay up there and take whatever action seems best."

Davis nodded and ran out.

Company F pulled off Exton Ridge and began the envelopment. Meanwhile Company H displaced its machine guns to Exton Ridge to support the attack.

Company E moved out, but was pinned down on the approaches to Sims Ridge. Company F attacked southward and swarmed over the north slope of the ridge. Halfway toward the top, however, its attack was stopped cold by ferocious machine gun fire from an enemy gun emplacement situated on the west slope.

The infantry couldn't pinpoint the location of the enemy position. It was covered by machine guns on all four sides, and no one was able to get close enough to spot it.

Davis, who was with the lead elements of the assault, decided to make a personal reconnaissance of the lower slope. Accompanying him were Captain Paul K. Mellichamp, an aide to General Collins, and First Lieutenant Weldon Sims, the battalion communications officer. Sims was hit by machine gun fire, and Davis continued alone while Mellichamp pulled Sims' body back down the ridge. The young battalion exec officer picked up Sims' radio and used it to call for fire from the 81-mm. mortars.

High explosive shells came hurtling through the air to pound at the Japanese—and the enemy was so close that Davis, out on the exposed slope, was showered and cut by clods of dirt, hunks of rock, and shell fragments. Mortar fire, however, failed to silence the Japanese machine guns, and the enemy stronghold on Sims Ridge was still holding both Companies E and F at bay as Colonel Mitchell reached the forward positions shortly before dark.

Mitchell and his executive officer remained on Sims Ridge through the long night that followed. In the morning the 2d Battalion (actually Companies E and F, since Company G was "on" its objective) was to attack according to its prearranged plan. Company F was to pull off the Ridge and strike between the jungle and the Horse's neck, to attack the north end of Hill 53. Meanwhile Company E would continue to attack Sims Ridge from the north.

Company E attacked, but once again was halted in its tracks. Blatt sent six volunteers from Company F out to try to learn the precise location of the enemy stronghold; they were within 25 yards of it when a Japanese machine gun opened up. Two men were instantly killed and the others withdrew.

It was a critical moment, and nothing seemed to be breaking their way. Then Mitchell and Davis hastily improvised a course of action. Neither of them knew that Lieutenant Colonel Donald Suggs, the regimental exec who had spent the night at the 2d Battalion command post, had been joined by Colonel McCulloch, the regimental commander, and General Collins, the division commander; and that all three were watching the action.

Davis rounded up the four Company F soldiers who had survived the earlier reconnaissance mission. The four—Sergeant William P. Curran, Corporal Russell A. Ward, Private First Class Joseph D. Stec, and Private Oran L. Woodard—all agreed that they were ready to give it another try.

"Good," said Davis. "Then come on with me."

The five of them, armed with rifles and loaded down with grenades, set off toward the enemy strong point. They edged their way down the west slope, and successfully passed the spot where the six-man group had been fired on.

Colonel Mitchell, meanwhile, was leading part of Company E down Sims Ridge. They crept down the east slope, hugging the waist-high shelf. Mitchell halted when he figured that he was just due east of the enemy stronghold. His orders were simple: "We'll charge over the slope in a line when we hear Davis whistle."

On the western slope Davis and the others were within ten yards of the enemy position when they were spotted by the Japanese, who promptly started hurling grenades. The enemy's aim was good. One grenade hit the ground, rolled a little, and came to rest about one yard away from both Curran's and Davis's heads. Fortunately it was defective, and failed to go off. A few more Jap grenades landed in their midst, but they also were duds.

Davis pulled the pin out of a grenade and let it fly. The others followed suit. After about eight grenades had been thrown, Davis called out, "All right! Let's go and get them!"

He leaped forward to lead the attack, brought his rifle up to his hip, and fired. But after the first round, the M-1 jammed. He tossed it away angrily, drew his pistol, and led the way into the enemy position. A few of the Japanese fled, but most of them stood their ground.

"Come on! Come on!" called Davis. "We've been here long enough. Let's show these birds what happens when we mean business."

As he and his four companions slugged their way into the enemy strongpoint and destroyed it, something very like an electric shock swept over the men on the ridge.

Mitchell's group came up over the eastern slope in time to see Davis and his men finishing off the Japanese. Then, in the words of General Collins, who was watching from the observation post atop Hill 52, "they suddenly came to life," and with a mighty rush pushed the last Japanese defenders from Sims Ridge. Company F swept out to the west, and Company E, with Davis in the lead of the assault, stormed a 45° slope in a sudden cloudburst to capture another small hill south of the ridge. By mid-morning the battalion had seized the southwest tip of Hill 53. And by noon the Wolfhounds were fully in command of the Galloping Horse.

"Captain Davis's action," General Collins stated flatly, "was the deciding factor."

"It was a brilliant attack," agreed Colonel McCulloch, "the more so because the odds were all against him."

The most unhappy face in the Wolfhounds' zone of action on that memorable day belonged to an Aussie cameraman who, during Davis's headlong fight, had been off to one flank in a perfect position to shoot the action as Davis vaulted into the enemy stronghold.

"What a moment," declared the photographer, with genuine grief in his voice, "to discover there was no more film in my camera!"

➵➵➵ ➷➷➷

TEN

SALERNO, D-PLUS 4

Charles E. Kelly

➵➵➵ ➷➷➷

NOT LONG ago, his neighbors in the Iroquois Homes housing development in Louisville, Kentucky, were startled to learn that the wavy-haired, slightly-built fellow, with the pretty brunette wife and five children, who lived in 1407 Manslick, was the famous "Commando" Kelly of World War II. They were surprised to learn his identity because nothing about him suggested a swashbuckling war hero. To them he was just a friendly, easy-going guy they called "Chuck," who worked hard all week and liked to fuss around with his kids on weekends.

This picture of "the new Kelly" would come as no real surprise to those who had known him when. Kelly always was a family man—what else would you expect of a fellow who was himself one of nine boys? The photos he carried overseas in his battered wallet were not girl friends or pin ups—they were pictures of his mother, his dad, and his brothers, seven of whom were in the Service.

"We Kellys have a simple motto," he once explained. "All for one and one for all."

It was this creed that Kelly took to war with him. And since he was no longer surrounded by family, he transferred his fierce loyalty to the men of the infantry rifle company with whom he campaigned from Salerno to the Rapido.

Pittsburgh's tough 23d Ward, where he had spent his life, became a dull place to Kelly after Pearl Harbor. Two of his brothers had quickly enlisted, and he, too, joined up, picking the infantry as his branch of service.

Kelly's war began at the infantry replacement training center at Camp Wheeler, Georgia. Here he breezed through basic training, learned to handle an M-1 rifle and got to like the heft of the 20-pound Browning Automatic Rifle—the BAR—which he was to use so effectively later on in Italy.

From Camp Wheeler he was sent to an infantry unit at Fort Benning. There his first contact with the proud men who wore jump boots and paratroop wings impelled him to request assignment to a parachute infantry outfit. But as the days went by, and more of his fellow trainees landed in hospital cots, their army days as good as over, Kelly became less and less enthusiastic about the prospects of jumping out of airplanes.

His problem was solved for him, however. He and a Pittsburgh buddy were in Atlanta on a short pass, when they had a sudden impulse to see the Smoky City once more. They flew home, stayed a few days, and then returned to Fort Benning, where they were promptly arrested as AWOL's—men absent without leave.

Kelly pleaded guilty before the Court Martial and drew 28 days' restriction to the post and a $28 fine.

"What's more," his C.O. told him, after the Court's verdict had been announced, "this finishes you as a paratrooper."

This last part of the sentence didn't exactly break Kelly's heart. His military affairs were soon straightened out, however, and he was returned to the ranks of the infantry. He was then sent to Camp Edwards, Massachusetts, which was both a staging area and an amphibious training center, and assigned to Company L, 143d Infantry, of the 36th (Texas) Infantry Division.

In April, 1943, the division sailed for North Africa, where

it resumed training, with emphasis on amphibious techniques. There were practice landings on the Arzew Beaches, and then the division was combat-loaded on ships of the fleet for its first wartime combat assignment.

The Texans' D-Day target, September 9, 1943, was a spot on the west coast of Italy that in the days following became known as the Salerno Beachhead. As the assault vessels neared the invasion beaches, the infantrymen were more fully briefed on their missions once they hit the shore. They were to push across the beach between the other regiments of the division and reorganize at the rail line east of Paestum. They were then to move on the road junction south of Hill 140, and capture the town of Capaccio, and Hill 386.

The 3d Battalion in which Kelly served, under the command of Lieutenant Colonel Joseph S. Barnett, Jr., climbed down the nets into the landing craft and began moving toward the dimly visible shore a few minutes before dawn. As their ungainly craft ploughed through the heavy seas, the Germans bombarded them with mortar and artillery fire.

Confusion reigned supreme on the beachhead. Mingled with milling infantrymen were harried engineers and sailors of the beach parties. A high-ranking U.S. officer was exhorting people to move quickly because the beach was under fire; and an English-speaking German voice (via a high-powered amplifier) urged the Americans to throw down their weapons "because we have you covered." Singly and in pairs the soldiers of the assault battalions ran across the beach toward the intended rendezvous points.

As Kelly loped forward he somehow made a wrong turn and headed inland in one direction while his comrades went in another. He became aware that machine gun fire was covering the sector into which he was advancing, and presently he reached a ditch in which seven or eight GI's were crouching for protection from gunfire.

"Jump in here!" they yelled. Kelly followed their advice

and plunged into slime up to his ears. To his additional disgust, his beautifully cared for BAR dropped from his hands and disappeared in the muck. In a silent rage, Kelly submerged in the muck and groped for it. When he had it in his grip he pushed it out on the ground before him and pulled himself out of the ditch by grabbing the low-hanging branch of a nearby tree.

Heavy machine gun fire kicked up dust all around him, and he dived for cover in a clump of bushes. He lay there panting and cleaned his mud-crusted automatic rifle, hoping it would work when he needed it.

Several hours passed before Kelly was finally able to get going again. He met a group of soldiers of another regiment, realized that he must have gone in the wrong direction, and decided it would be best to double back toward the beach and then head for the hill the company was supposed to attack after it reorganized.

Starting back toward the beach, he spotted several German Mark IV (medium) tanks clanking toward him. Kelly hit the ditch, sighted his BAR, and began hopelessly trying to hit the slits in the tank's armor. His fire had no effect, and the tanks ploughed right past him as if he didn't even exist. Pleased at still being alive, Kelly jumped back on the road and continued his solitary march to rejoin his company.

The next day he was with his company as it stumbled into the shadow of Hill 315. On the morning of September 13 (D-plus 4), Colonel William H. Martin, the regimental commander, ordered the main effort to be launched. The 2d and 3d Battalions were to move in the assault. Kelly was Company L's lead scout. According to plan, the company veered left as it approached Altavilla and entered a ravine, where it immediately came under enemy shellfire.

The attack slowed to a halt as the company was pinned down by machine gun fire. The merciless heat of the mid-morning sun beat down on the attacking troops, but no one seemed inclined to press the attack in view of the machine gun fire that was ahead.

"Captain," Kelly called softly to Marion P. Bowden, the company commander, "can I go out there and see what's doing?"

Bowden squinted at him and nodded his assent.

With four other volunteers, Kelly moved forward and crawled out what seemed like a long way. He studied the terrain in an effort to locate the well-hidden enemy machine gun.

"Over there!" he suddenly exclaimed. "Aren't those sandbags?"

One of the volunteers who had accompanied him was Milky Holland. He fired a rifle grenade behind the supposed sandbags. There was a muffled explosion, followed by a series of short angry bursts of machine gun fire.

Kelly swiftly adjusted the bipod on the barrel of his automatic rifle and pushed it out in front of him. The others squinted behind their rifle sights, and all five opened fire. But the enemy drove them back with a barrage of 80-mm. mortar fire.

Captain Bowden was encouraged by their success in locating the gun, and told Kelly he wanted him to return to the draw at once. "Just keep an eye on those people," Bowden told him, "and see if they're up to anything."

This time when Kelly moved out he was accompanied by First Lieutenant John C. Morrisey who lugged a light machine gun, Private Frank LaBue, and Sergeant Holt, who had been on the earlier expedition.

They worked their way down the draw as before, but when they were within sight of the machine gun nest they ran into a force of about 70 German soldiers who were on the prowl and spoiling for a fight. The Germans split up to take them from several sides, and at the same time the machine gun cut loose—but this trip Kelly was in a good firing position and he had its range. He pulled off a burst of ten rounds that silenced the gun, and killed its three man crew.

The German combat patrol swarmed down on them and Kelly brought his BAR around. They were less than fifty yards away when he opened up. He fired a full magazine and then the others took up the slack while he reloaded—except for Lieutenant Morrisey, whose machine gun had jammed. Kelly thrust a new magazine into the BAR, pulled the trigger, and more Germans tumbled to the ground. When he had wiped out more than half of their attacking force, about 40 men, the enemy fell back to let their mortars and artillery take over.

"We can't do any more good out here," declared Morrisey. "Let's get on back to the company."

Their withdrawal was accomplished only after considerable difficulty. Flying steel fell on the ground around them, rifle and machine gun fire sniped at them. They managed to run the gauntlet of fire, however, and make it back to Bowden at the command post. Here Morrisey and LaBue and Holt reported that Kelly had shot down forty Germans or more.

But this incident was a mere preliminary to the main event, which began later on the same day shortly after Kelly had been sent back to Altavilla for more ammunition. He found himself leading a force of about a hundred soldiers in the defense of a three story building in which the GI's had barricaded themselves when the Germans suddenly counterattacked. This building, formerly the mayor's house, soon became the only position in Altavilla held by U.S. forces. The building was turned into a fortress, an island of stubborn resistance in a German tidal wave.

The Americans who were barricaded in the house fought

back from every window, while the Germans raked them with
automatic weapons from nearby houses and from the command heights of Hill 315.

From his perch at a second-story window Kelly aimed his
BAR and cut loose a burst at four German soldiers setting up
a machine gun on Hill 315. Three toppled and lay still, but
the fourth was still alive and made the mistake of kicking
his foot. Kelly fired another burst and four lifeless forms
sprawled by the silent gun. After that he roamed from window to window, seeking targets no one else could hit.

It was a sniper's field day—but it wasn't any fun. When
the Germans cut loose, they aimed for the windows, and the
defenders too suffered heavy casualties. One of the men hauled
a machine gun over to the window where Kelly was blazing
away, and whenever Kelly paused to reload, the machine gun
slammed into action. This worked for a while. But eventually,
while Kelly was crouching to get a full magazine into the automatic rifle, a sudden burst of enemy fire killed the machine
gunner at his shoulder.

Finally his BAR got so hot it wouldn't work. Kelly tossed it
away and went off in search of a new one. He found one and
returned to the windows to fire until it, too, turned red and
purple from the heat and became so warped it was useless.
Once again he searched for a BAR, but this time he had to
settle for a tommy gun.

Night came and brought a little rest to the thinned ranks
of the defenders in the three-story fortress. The Germans continued to fire sporadically throughout the long night, while
the GI's peered into the darkness or slept fitfully.

Climbing to the third floor in the first rays of daylight,
Kelly located a rocket launcher (bazooka) and six shells.
Then he returned to his second-story vantage point and poked
the long tube out the window. He had a good deal of difficulty

firing the unfamiliar weapon; and when he finally did manage to trigger a round, the rear-blast was so terrific that the whole house shook.

Kelly aimed at the nearest enemy troops in view, and fired five more rounds. Then he found an incendiary, which he seized and hurled with all of his might to the roof of a nearby building which held a force of Germans. The incendiary worked like a charm and Kelly watched with satisfaction as the building began to blaze.

But still the Germans kept moving in, getting closer and closer to the fortress. Kelly could see one group working its way toward the mayor's house through a ravine at the rear of the building. His eye wandered speculatively over the ammunition supplies—the littered room was like an ordnance display room—and he had a sudden inspiration. He took a 60-mm. mortar shell from its cardboard container and studied it thoughtfully. The safety pin, he knew, controlled the pro-pelling charge and the cap which sets off the charge. But there was a second safety pin inside, and he didn't know how to get it out manually.

He tapped the shell gently on the window ledge, and the second pin dropped out.

At that point Kelly realized that he was holding a live shell in his hand, and, if his plan worked, it would become a bomb, or a sort of super hand-grenade. For, he figured if he could manage it so that the shell landed nose first, it might go off. Kelly considered the height, and decided that the weight of its fall would supply enough pressure to set the shell off.

To put his theory to the test, he took aim at the Germans who were moving down the ravine. He held the shell as if it were a football, and eyed the window opening warily. If so much as a vine or an overhanging board were to strike the shell, it would probably go off in his face and blow him, the room, and its occupants to smithereens.

After an instant's hesitation, he hurled the shell. Down it hurtled, toward the bottom of the ravine. There was a roaring explosion, and when the dust cleared away, Kelly and the others, now clustered around the window, could see dead Germans sprawled in the ditch.

As the morning ticked by, Kelly repeated this maneuver until he ran out of mortar shells. Then he ran downstairs and out into the bullet-swept courtyard, where he broke up an enemy attack by firing a 37-mm. anti-tank cannon at practically point-blank range until an officer ordered him back into the house.

As the day wore on he acquired, in order, a carbine, a World War I vintage Springfield '03 rifle, and another BAR. Toward evening he had run out of BAR magazines, so he had to pull cartridges out of a machine gun belt to reload. By the time it was dark, he had burned out his third BAR.

That night the handful of survivors were ordered to make a break for it and to attempt to rejoin their commands. During the darkness they broke out in groups of six. Kelly was among the last to leave, as he and several other crack shots remained behind to cover the withdrawal.

Finally it was their turn. They fled into the blackness and stumbled through unfriendly hills and woods, looking for the U.S. lines. It wasn't until two days later that Kelly and several others of the Company L contingent rejoined their outfit, which had by that time given them up for dead.

It was D-plus 6 by then. The Division had been in combat only a week, but already Kelly's name was a legend among the men who wore the T-Patch of the 36th.

❯❯❯ ❯❯❯ ❯❯❯ ❮❮❮ ❮❮❮ ❮❮❮

SAIPAN NIGHTMARE

Thomas A. Baker

❯❯❯ ❯❯❯ ❯❯❯ ❮❮❮ ❮❮❮ ❮❮❮

WHEN the final showdown came, Tom Baker was propped with his back against a telephone pole. A cigarette was in his left hand, a blazing .45 pistol in his right.

The *Gyokusai* was at the peak of its fury. *Gyokusai*. Far more than a mere *banzai* attack, it was a special and final devotion to the Emperor. Literally translated it means, "Die in honor."

Thomas A. Baker, Sergeant, 105th Infantry Regiment, too badly hurt to move, waited for them to get a mite closer. *Die in honor*. He would prove it worked both ways. After all, it was for this that he had come 8,000 miles.

Times had been hard when Tom Baker graduated from Troy (New York) High School in 1934. He was lucky to find a job at the YMCA. Someone reminded him they paid a dollar a drill down at the Armory. In the fall of 1935, when he was 19, he had enlisted in Company A, 105th Infantry Regiment, 27th Infantry Division, the company with which he was to cross the Pacific to fight on an island called Saipan.

As the months rolled by he grew to enjoy his night a week and the occasional week ends of part-time soldiering. He took pride in Company A's progress, and was as quick as any "long-timer" to insist it was the best company in the

regiment. When his enlistment was up in 1938, Tom re-
enlisted—and this time the dollar a drill was not what decided
him.

By the summer of 1940 it was evident that it was just a
matter of time until the Division would be called into federal
service for a year of training under the provisions of the new
Selective Service Act. Summer camp at DeKalb, New York,
was three weeks instead of the usual two. On October 15,
the long columns marched out of the armories and headed
for the trains that would carry them to Fort McClellan, Alabama. It was "just for a year."

"Just a year" turned into "the duration-plus six," when the
Japanese attacked Pearl Harbor. The New York division was
rushed to the west coast, and was the first full combat division
to leave the states for duty in the Pacific. It manned beach
defenses and garrisoned Hawaii for nine months.

Combat teams were sent to seize Makin Island and to take
part in the capture of the Eniwetok Atoll. But it was not until
the early summer of 1944 that the Division fought as a unit,
in one of the bloodiest and costliest of the campaigns in the
Pacific.

It was assigned to the V Amphibious Corps (Marines) for
the assault upon the enemy island bastion of Saipan.

This was the baptism of fire for the 1st Battalion 105th
Infantry, in which Tom Baker soldiered. Nearly every other
infantry battalion in the division had already seen some action,
but for one reason or another Lieutenant Colonel William J.
O'Brien's battalion had not yet heard a shot fired in anger.
And on Saipan it distinguished itself as one of the outstanding
combat infantry battalions in World War II. "Wherever it
appears in the narrative of battle," the division historian has
written, "it lights up the whole scene."

In the battalion's gallant march from Aslito Airfield, to
Nafutan Point, to Death Valley, to Flores Point, and to the

Tanapag Plain where the *Gyokusai* fell like a saber blow, two soldiers in particular inspired the outfit's fight. One was its peppery battalion commander, Colonel O'Brien; the other was the quiet Company A soldier, Tom Baker.

The regiment had come ashore on D-plus 2 (June 17). The next day it moved into position on the V Corps right flank along the south coast, with Colonel O'Brien's battalion on the left of the regimental zone of action. The intense heat and the vast cane fields slowed down the drive toward the objective, which was Nafutan Point.

On June 19 the attack continued. The battalion slugged its way forward until it was halted by an enemy strong point consisting of a 77-mm. dual purpose gun covered by mutually-supporting machine guns atop the high ground called Butter-fly Ridge.

Twice Company A attacked. Each time it was hurled back. Tom Baker was then an ammunition carrier in a mortar squad. Sergeant Joseph Farolino, the squad leader, sent him back to the company command post for a new supply of mortar ammo.

While he was waiting for ammo to reach the command post from the rear, Baker looked around restlessly. His gaze fell on a bazooka and four rounds of high explosive. He picked up the long tube and hurried forward.

Sergeant Joseph Bachrik who was with a mortar section at the edge of a cane field saw Baker moving far ahead of the company lines, out into the open where there was no cover of any kind. Lugging the bazooka tube and his four rounds of ammunition, Baker sprinted 50 yards up the ridge until he was close enough to fire point-blank into the enemy strong point. He fired all four rounds, wiped out the enemy position completely, and enabled the attack to continue.

Three days later the 27th Division was given a new zone of action. Colonel O'Brien's battalion was attached to the 165th

Infantry, then fighting with the 4th Marine Division. The battalion of Troy soldiers pushed into the horror of Death Valley as they drove northward.

On July 2 the battalion, by then back under its own regimental control, was ordered to pivot to the west and slice into the gap between the 165th Infantry and 106th Infantry. It was a tricky maneuver, but it went off without a hitch. Then the battalion encountered heavy fire near Papako.

Company A, advancing slowly across an open field flanked by numerous, well-concealed enemy dugouts, was in a dilemma. It was already 5 p.m., and they had less than an hour in which to reach the objective and dig in for the night. To delay meant the possibility of a gap in the lines; even more important, it meant that there might not be enough daylight left to organize defensive positions for the night. Captain Louis Ackerman motioned for his company to cross the field and get going.

Sergeant Tom Baker lingered as the platoons started forward. Someone asked why he wasn't moving out.

"Maybe they're planning a surprise for us," Baker murmured, as his eyes swept the edges of the cane field.

The company was moving through the rubble of what had once been a fine cane field when Baker, who was still prowling around the periphery, froze and held his breath for an instant. He had stumbled upon an enemy strong point manned, as it turned out, by two officers and 12 Japanese soldiers. They were baiting a trap, letting the vanguard of Company A pass their gunsights.

Baker didn't need to have the rest of the picture filled in— he knew what would inevitably occur in a few seconds unless swift action was taken. And he was the only Company A soldier in position to do anything about it.

With a shout he bounded into the enemy position firing as fast as he could, and dropping behind a packing case to reload when his M-1 rifle was empty. He killed all of the Japanese and destroyed their machine guns with grenades before he moved on.

In moving forward, he ran into a six-man enemy group hiding in a clump of bushes. He opened fire and killed all six of them. Then he raced up to rejoin the company as it continued to push across Tanapag Plain.

In the four days that followed, the battalion moved forward at an unbelievable pace. "They've broken through," a Marine Corps observer radioed back to his superiors. "They're going a mile a minute!"

On D-plus 21, the drama on Saipan was near its climax. The advance guard had pushed to within a few hundred yards of the village of Makunsha on the northwest coast of Saipan. Victory and the end of a bitter campaign seemed clearly in sight. But the night brought one of the most devastating Japanese counterattacks of the war in the Pacific, the *Gyokusai.*

Its full fury descended upon the 1st and 2d Battalion, 105th Infantry. As these two battalions pushed north on July 6, Japanese General Yoshitsugu Saito gathered his officers in the cave that served as his command post; after a hate-filled diatribe against the "American devils," he called for a final all out effort.

"I will advance with those who remain," he declared, "to deliver still another blow to the American devils, and leave my bones on Saipan as a bulwark of the Pacific . . . I will never suffer the disgrace of being taken alive . . . I advance to seek out the enemy. Follow me."

That night, O'Brien was faced with the prospect of being forced to dig in his battalion on the beach, in the midst of thick woods. If he did this, however, his riflemen and machine gunners would have no fields of fire if the enemy attacked. Therefore he decided to pull back off the beach and organize defenses to the east of the railroad tracks. It was not until ten minutes after dark that the battalion began to dig its positions. Company A was on the north leg of the perimeter—its left flank on the railroad track and its zone of action about one hundred yards across. Captain Ackerman placed his two light machine guns facing north, one covering the railroad track, and the other set up in a little concrete building along the front of the perimeter. Sergeant Tom Baker was in command of a squad on the front line of the perimeter near the railroad.

While O'Brien's battalion was moving around in the dark getting its defensive perimeter organized, the Japs were massing for the attack to the north.

The attacking column began to assemble soon after dark. The force gathered slowly at Marpi Point to the north, and added naval personnel and civilian laborers as it neared Makunsha. When it was seen that there weren't enough rifles to go around, officers gave away their pistols and kept only their prized swords. Some of the Japs were armed with daggers and hunting knives. Others fashioned crude spears out of bamboo poles. The head of the enemy column reached Makunsha, less than half a mile north of the battalion perimeter, about the same time that Captain Ackerman returned from a conference with Colonel O'Brien.

While Ackerman was briefing First Sergeant Mario Occhionero, they suddenly heard a strange buzz. It got louder and louder; then several Japs crashed through the bushes and dashed into the company area. Someone shot them, which was a signal for numerous isolated attacks, all of which were hurled back.

Division artillery responded with a mighty roar. Interdicting fire was placed along the railroad and on the highway north of Makunsha. Between midnight and 7 o'clock the next morning, division artillery hurled 2,666 rounds of high explosive.

Although this fire caused no great casualties among the Japs after the first few rounds, according to enemy soldiers later taken prisoner, it did largely succeed in disorganizing the attacking advancing column. It frightened and harried the Japs, but it did not deter them from going through with the *Gyokusai*. Inch by inch they worked toward the perimeter—and at 3:37 a.m. the full weight of their attack was hurled upon O'Brien's battalion.

In the thick of the fight, the picturesque O'Brien stood waving a pistol in each hand, roaring, "We'll slug it out with 'em. We won't give 'em one inch!" He emptied his pistols at the oncoming enemy until he ran out of ammunition. Then he hurled the guns at them, and fought with a sword he had picked up until he was overwhelmed. The courageous O'Brien was posthumously awarded the Medal of Honor.

In the initial stages of the attack, a Japanese grenade had dropped into Baker's foxhole, badly mangling one of his legs. Tom nonetheless picked off enemy soldiers with his rifle as they tried to storm his position and roll back the company's left flank.

The sheer weight of the attack forced him to drag himself out of the foxhole. Immediately he was almost engulfed by a wave of attackers. He clubbed at them with his rifle and managed to break away. By then his weapon was so misshapen from this hand-to-hand fight that it would not fire. Baker crawled around looking for another weapon and some ammunition.

He had gone about ten yards when he was seen by Private First Class Frank P. Zielinski, who also was wounded. Zielinski, nevertheless, picked him up and hauled him about 150 yards toward the rear of the perimeter. Then Zielinski was hit and could not continue any further with the helpless Baker.

As he set the sergeant on the ground, Baker was hit again, through the chest this time. The violence of the enemy attack reached a new high in frenzy, and the front line of the perimeter began to crumble.

Captain Bernard A. Toft, an artillery forward observer, was moving toward the railroad when he saw Baker sprawled on the ground and went to him. He carried the wounded noncom back along the railroad tracks about 30 yards. Then he was hit.

Again someone stopped to help Baker, but this time Baker snarled, "Get away from me. I've caused enough trouble."

About 6 a.m. Corporal Carl V. Patricelli of 1st Battalion Headquarters Company was helping to form a line about a hundred yards to the rear of the abandoned battalion command post, when he heard someone weakly call out his name. He turned and saw Baker, propped against a telephone pole. Patricelli ran to him and tried to help him.

"It's no use, Pat. I'm finished," Baker said flatly. "Just give me a cigarette."

Patricelli lighted a cigarette and placed it between Baker's lips. The wounded man thanked him and took a couple of deep puffs.

His friend—Patricelli was one of the old crowd from Troy —looked Baker over and noticed that he wasn't armed. He mentioned this and Baker explained that he'd given a pistol he'd found to someone else who wasn't armed.

Patricelli had, a few minutes earlier, picked up an extra .45 pistol. He slipped it out of his belt, loaded it with a clip of seven rounds and inserted an eighth round in the chamber. Silently he handed it over to Baker.

"Thanks," Baker replied. "I'll take care of some of them before I go."

Just then there was a rattle of gunfire and a series of savage shrieks as the Japanese launched another attack.

"You get out of here, Pat," Baker said firmly. "Thanks for everything and give my regards to all the guys."

That was the last time Thomas A. Baker was seen alive by

any of his buddies. When the handful of survivors of the battered battalion were reinforced, they launched a counter-attack and swept back into the area that had been overrun by the Japanese.

Staff Sergeant Joe Farolino, First Sergeant Occhionero, and Staff Sergeant Carmen J. Ancona found Tom Baker still propped with his back against the telephone pole. In his lifeless grasp was the empty pistol.

True to his promise to Patricelli, he had fought until his last breath. Sprawled at his feet were eight Japanese, all of them dead.

※»-※»-※»-※«-※«-※«

ONE MAN ARMY AT ANZIO

Alton W. Knappenberger

※»-※»-※»-※«-※«-※«

THE NEW replacement was a friendly kid with a
Pennsylvania Dutch name and a ready grin. He was
only a little more than nineteen and had been in the
Army less than ten months when he reached the 3d Infantry
Division in Italy via an African replacement depot. Shortly
before the division embarked upon an amphibious operation
code-named "Shingle," he was assigned as an automatic rifle-
man in Company C, 30th Infantry Regiment.

Private First Class Alton W. Knappenberger was not entirely pleased with becoming a BARman—the automatic rifle
weighed close to twenty pounds when it was loaded and fully
equipped. He himself weighed only one-twenty, and he often
thought wistfully of the sleek hunting rifle he had used in
the hills around Green Lane, Pennsylvania, where he had
grown up. But he kept his thoughts to himself.

Most of the company he had joined had fought with the
division in the breaching of the German Winter Line; many
were still on hand who had made the beachhead landing at
Salerno the previous September; a few were veterans of the
Sicily campaign, and there were even some who had made
the landing at Casablanca on November 8, 1942—when
Knappie was not yet old enough to join the Army.

There had been strong parental opposition to his going

into the service in March, 1943. His mother, Mrs. Harvey
Seibert, was a Mennonite, and greatly opposed his taking part
in the war. As a Mennonite—Alton had actually drifted away
from the church as a teen-ager—he should, his mother felt,
declare himself a pacifist—a conscientious objector.

Only eighteen years old, with just a seventh-grade education, Alton was not awfully good with words. As best as he
could, though, he explained that he could not sit out the war
as a conscientious objector. Soon afterward he volunteered
at his draft board and was sent to the infantry replacement
training center at Camp Jackson, South Carolina.

Then came the boat ride to North Africa, the truck ride to
a dusty replacement center, weeks of waiting, and another
boat ride—to Italy, where the 3d Division had been pulled out
of the line on the approaches to Cassino, so that it might train
for an amphibious assault against an important beachhead
north of Rome.

The target was an obscure Italian village, an ancient seaside
resort where Nero had vacationed and where Benito Mussolini also liked to frolic in the gentle surf. Its name was Anzio.

January 22, 1944, was D-Day—and the initial landing was
a deceivingly mild operation. It wasn't nearly the terrible
ordeal that Knappenberger and the other replacements had
anticipated.

The regiment attacked enemy positions along the Mussolini
Canal. The 1st Battalion engaged in a bitter fight to seize an
important road junction, thereafter named "Kinney's Corner"
for Major Oliver G. Kinney, the battalion commander. In
the waning hours of the January day, the battalion attacked
up the Ponte Rotto-Cisterna axis and slugged its way a distance of 1,500 yards through a violent rainstorm.

The storm eventually washed away; but another sort of
violence launched itself against the 3d Division—and the full

brunt of its fury was hurled against the 1st Battalion, 30th Infantry Regiment.

It came early on February 1. After a promising start, in which it advanced another 1,000 yards and pushed across the Pantano Ditch less than a mile west of Cisterna, the battalion was checked by strong artillery fire. There was a pause and then the forward movement came to a full halt. The mud-caked infantrymen of the famous old Rock of the Marne Division had advanced as near to Cisterna as the U.S. forces were destined to get until the city finally fell in May.

Suddenly, the battalion was attacked by a strong German task force—a battalion of infantry with artillery and armor attached. In the savage counterattack which struck the 1st Battalion, 30th Infantry, at around 0830, all of the battalion officers in the area, and nearly all of the noncoms in the rifle companies, were killed or captured. The battered survivors pulled back to safer ground, behind the ditch. But even as the retreat commenced, a stubborn strong point of resistance developed around an exposed knoll on the right flank of Company C's zone of action on the battalion left.

The strong point of the resistance to the German attack was a BAR in the hands of the new kid—Knappenberger. He settled himself on the knoll in full view of the enemy and simply refused to be intimidated.

He evidently upset someone's timetable, for suddenly an entire German platoon hurled itself upon him. All of the Germans were armed with automatic weapons, chiefly machine pistols. The racket made by the machine pistols got Knappie all worked up. He fired long savage bursts with the BAR, and it seemed to Private First Class Charles McGregor, who was close enough to witness the action, that German gunners went down like tenpins.

Then a German machine gun went into action about 65

yards off to Knappenberger's flank. Bullets kicked up all around the knoll. It was clear that the enemy gunner had Knappie's range.

To draw a bead on this new source of danger, it was necessary for Knappenberger to get up on one knee to aim the BAR. He tucked the heavy automatic rifle against his chin and began to shoot. After a few well-aimed bursts, two of the enemy lay dead, one was wounded, and the fourth member of the crew was running in terror.

But while he was absorbed in wiping out the machine gun crew, Knappenberger didn't notice a new menace until it was almost too late. Two Germans armed with "potato masher" hand grenades slipped around the knoll to attack.

Private First Class Ralph W. Moody saw Knappenberger glance up just as the grenades started toward him—a distance of about 30 yards. The busy BARman turned his fire upon the pair who had thrown the grenades and killed both of them. But it was too late to duck away from the grenade explosions. Both missiles hit the ground in front of him and kicked buckets of dirt and rock into his face. The only damage he suffered was a dent in his helmet.

A second machine gun now opened up on him from a distance of about 100 yards. Knappenberger took this gun and its crew under fire and pumped lead steadily until he knocked it out. Then the enemy turned a high-velocity 20-mm. *flakswagon*, normally an anti-aircraft weapon, on him. The kid soldier just ignored the flak whirring around his ears and aimed for the crew.

When the push began that morning, Knappenberger had had thirteen magazines, each containing twenty rounds of ammunition for his BAR. His supply of cartridges now was dwindling fast, and he knew he wouldn't last five seconds if he ever ran out. He sized up the situation—and knew that if he was to have more ammunition, he'd have to get it himself. So, with the flak gun peppering away, he crawled 20 yards through heavy fire until he found a fallen U.S. BAR-man whose cartridge pouches were full.

His logistics problem was solved and he was back in business. The BAR crashed back into action and Knappie's shooting wiped out the entire crew of the flak gun. Then he was again assailed by an enemy platoon—and more Germans tumbled to the ground.

During his fantastic one-man stand Knappenberger fired 600 rounds of ammunition, and according to McGregor, Moody, and Private First Class Daniel P. Vasian, he killed at least 60 enemy soldiers in the engagement on the road toward Cisterna.

Lieutenant Colonel Edgar Doleman, regimental executive officer, paid high tribute to Knappenberger and the others who refused to pull out. "But for this small group, of which Knappenberger was the most outstanding, much more serious losses would probably have been suffered. Had the enemy's attack not been disrupted for approximately two hours, it could have become very serious. . . ."

After his two-hour holding action, Knappie deemed it prudent to rejoin his company—and found only 23 left of the 240 who had gone into battle. All of the officers and non-coms were gone. Someone suggested that he was in line for a promotion to corporal.

"Nope," Knappie declared earnestly, "not me. They make you a corporal or a sergeant, and then you have to work."

Reminded that he had done a pretty good day's work out in that open field on the road to Cisterna, Knappenberger replied, "Oh, that was different."

The war correspondents who surrounded Knappie in Rome when he was awarded his Medal found out that he loved to hunt. One of the interviewers asked, half-jokingly, if he were a pretty good shot.

"I dunno," replied the young man who had killed 60 enemy soldiers and held up the advance of a German battalion for two hours. "I think that doggone BAR has ruined my shootin'."

THIRTEEN

CHIP OFF THE OLD BLOCK

Theodore Roosevelt, Jr.

WHEN he was a young boy, Theodore Roosevelt, Jr., eldest son of the man who was then Governor of New York and later twenty-sixth President of the United States, would steal into his father's bedroom, slip into a pair of his father's shoes, and stamp clumsily around the room.

There are those who claim that, although he spent his whole life trying, he was never able to fill those big shoes; and there are those who say he filled them as Old Teddy never would have been able to.

Like his famous father, young Teddy got his start in life as a wealthy, sickly, and nearsighted boy; and he had to strive mightily to overcome the defects in his physical make-up. He graduated from Harvard, served in the New York State legislature, and was appointed an assistant Secretary of the Navy. He also became a prominent big game hunter, and led safaris in both Africa and Asia. Like his father before him, he was both soldier and politician.

But there was an essential difference between father and son, which was explained by a friend of the Roosevelt family this way:

"Old Teddy was a dilettante soldier and a first-class politician; Young Teddy was a dilettante politician and a first-class soldier."

He was more than a first-class soldier. He was one of the genuinely great combat leaders in the history of the United States Army. This was the opinion of both General Dwight D. Eisenhower and General Omar N. Bradley, and it is a tremendous tribute to a man who was a reserve officer—a citizen soldier rather than a member of the regular military establishment.

Some six weeks after the D-Day landings on the coast of France, Eisenhower and Bradley were worried over the failure of a particular division to move as aggressively as it should. Eisenhower therefore asked Bradley to nominate a new commanding general, who might breathe some fire into the division. Bradley scanned the list of brigadier generals, and without a moment's hesitation asked for permission to appoint Ted Roosevelt.

On the following morning he received Eisenhower's approval, but by then it was too late. Shortly after sending his message off to Eisenhower, Bradley was advised that Roosevelt had died in his sleep of a heart attack.

It seemed incredible to Bradley, and to a lot of other soldiers, also, that Ted Roosevelt should die in bed after having lived through more hair-raising front line escapes than any other U.S. general officer in World War II.

When had he decided that he wanted to be a soldier? Maybe when he saw his father march off as lieutenant colonel of the Rough Riders during the war with Spain. In any event, World War I found him a field officer in the 26th Infantry Regiment of the 1st (Big Red One) Infantry Division, where he served gallantly throughout the conflict, being gassed, wounded twice, and decorated fifteen times.

The end of the war found him in command of the 26th Infantry Regiment which was nearing Sedan in the waning days of the struggle. It had been agreed that the French should have the honor of being the first into Sedan; but the 1st Division had other ideas. It was supposed to have halted in its tracks shortly before the Armistice. Instead it marched across the front of another U.S. division and into a sector that the French were about to attack with artillery.

The French commander angrily demanded that the Americans move out at once. But Colonel Ted, in command of the "invaders," refused to quit the sector, saying that he was moving on Sedan in accordance with orders. It became a prize fiasco, with the French threatening to turn their guns on the Americans; and General Pershing nearly exploded when he learned of the 1st Division's audacity. Roosevelt's patrols, which were nearing Sedan, were hastily withdrawn, and the French then entered the historic city.

In a sense Ted Roosevelt picked up where he had left off when he answered the call to arms just before the U.S. entry into World War II. Early 1940 found him a full colonel, once again commanding the 26th Infantry Regiment of the 1st Division.

The years between the wars had been a period of marking time for Ted. In politics he turned out to be thoroughly unlike his father or his cousin Franklin. He had no "feel" for the way of the politico—and never once did he succeed in winning an important election. The magnetic personality which inspired troops in the field failed utterly to attract voters at the polls.

Appointed Assistant Secretary of the Navy in 1921, he resigned this post to run as Republican candidate for Governor of New York in 1924, but was soundly beaten by Alfred E. Smith, who rolled up a 109,000 vote plurality—and in a year when Calvin Coolidge, the Republican presidental candidate, carried the state by 870,000 votes. It was a stunning blow to Ted's political hopes, and he soon plunged into other activities, among which were the James Simpson–Roosevelt Expedition to Asia in behalf of the Field Museum of Natural History, big game hunting in Africa, and a continuing interest in the American Legion, which he helped to found in France in 1919.

At the request of Coolidge he once again entered government service, first as Governor of Puerto Rico (1929–32) and then as Governor-General of the Philippines (1932–33). When his cousin Franklin became President in 1932, Ted, now 45, settled down as a member of a New York business firm, commuting between the city and his Oyster Bay home.

This arrangement came to an end in 1940, when he once again found himself working at the soldier's trade. It was, clearly, the trade he was best cut out for. He believed in rugged realistic training, and he was an officer of the old school, who did everything himself that he expected his men to do.

In 1942 he became a brigadier general and assistant division commander of the 1st Division. Later that year Terry de la Mesa Allen joined the Red One as commanding general; and in Allen and Roosevelt the famous 1st had an unbeatable combination.

It was soon apparent that their devotion to the division probably outweighed their devotion to the army itself. To them the 1st Division wasn't just the embodiment of the United States Army; it *was* the United States Army!

"Allen and Roosevelt," another general once complained, "seem to think that the United States Army consists of the 1st Infantry Division and eleven million replacements."

And Allen and Roosevelt agreed happily that this was so.

They fought their division through North Africa. Together they led the Red One through the *djebels* and *wadis* of North Africa to final victory in Tunisia.

Swinging the swagger stick that was his trademark, Ted

Roosevelt campaigned in the field with his men. He had a personality that made men respond to him. If he asked a mess sergeant if he were getting enough baking powder, the answer was always "No"; but from the way Roosevelt asked the question it was evident to the sergeant that something was finally going to be done about *that*, at least.

He once boasted to Ernie Pyle that every man in the division knew him by the sound of his voice. To put the boast to a test, he had the driver of his jeep pull off on the side of a road as a column of Red One Infantry tramped by.

After standing in the dark for a few moments, he called out, "What outfit is this?"

"Company F, 26th Infantry, General Roosevelt," came the cheery reply. "The best company in the division."

There were cheers, jeers, and catcalls all the way up and down the column as Roosevelt, with a look that clearly said "I told you so," motioned for Pyle to get back in the jeep.

Nevertheless, events were building up that were to lead to the downfall of both Roosevelt and Allen. For instance, there was a frightful ruckus in Oran when the 1st Division returned there for a rest after the conclusion of the North African campaign. Rear echelon troops were beaten up, and feelings ran high. Ted Roosevelt was said to have promised his men, "Beat hell out of the Germans and Italians, and we'll go back to Oran and beat up every MP in town!"

This story may be apocryphal—but the fact remains that when the 1st Division returned to Oran it did go out and did do a job on the soldiers who had the misfortune to wear the braid and brassard of the Corps of Military Police.

Oran sighed with relief when Allen, Roosevelt, and the 1st Division sailed for the invasion of Sicily.

The Division crashed ashore on Sicily, fought off a staggering German panzer attack (with Ted Roosevelt in the front lines, calling the fight, and relaying word back to Terry

Allen), and sliced up Sicily's spine toward the important enemy communications center at Nicosia. It was on the road to Nicosia that Teddy Roosevelt's "Rough Riders" rode again. These "Rough Riders" were a special task force organized by Ted Roosevelt—Major Frank Adams' 1st Cavalry Reconnaissance Troop, reinforced—and led by him in a slashing attack through the enemy's outpost line to a critical road junction five miles out of Barrafanca, a typical cavalry maneuver.

Nicosia fell and then Troina. When Troina was taken, the Red One had captured 18 cities in less than a month of determined fighting. On August 7, the Division was relieved by the 9th Infantry Division, and a message was received at Headquarters ordering Generals Allen and Roosevelt to report to General Bradley at once.

Wondering what was in the wind—but scarcely anticipating the shock they were due for—the two set off in a jeep for Bradley's command post at Nicosia.

On the way back to Corps they were flagged down by an MP who wrote out a ticket because Allen was not wearing the required steel helmet.

"Why, don't you *understand*," fumed Roosevelt, "this officer is General Allen of the 1st Division?"

"Sir, *I* understand perfectly," the MP replied courteously. "But my captain wouldn't understand if I let Julius Caesar himself ride by without a helmet. And by the way, sir," he added respectfully, "I'm going to have to give *you* a ticket for wearing that stocking cap!"

Allen clamped his steel pot on his head and roared with glee at Roosevelt's discomfiture.

In his book, *A Soldier's Story*, General Bradley has adequately explained the reason he took the course that he did during that August 7 interview at Nicosia. It needs little comment:

". . . the 1st Division had become increasingly temperamental, disdainful of both regulations and senior commands. It thought itself exempted from the need for discipline by virtue of its months on the line. And it believed itself to be the only division carrying its fair share of the war."

Bradley was convinced that he had to break up the combination of Terry Allen, Teddy Roosevelt, and the 1st Division. It was, he felt, necessary to insure the success of future operations in which the 1st Division was to be used.

". . . to save the division from the heady effects of too much success, I decided to separate them. Allen . . . would feel deeply hurt if he were to leave the division and Roosevelt were to remain. He might have considered himself a failure instead of the victim of too much success. By the same token, Roosevelt's claim to the affections of the 1st Division would present any new commander with an impossible situation from the start. Roosevelt had to go with Allen for he, too, had sinned by loving the division too much."

Not only Allen and Roosevelt, but the rank and file of the 1st Division were shocked and upset by Bradley's action.

Nonetheless, the reign of Allen and Roosevelt had come to an end. Allen returned to the States, and took over another division which he later fought across France; while Roosevelt was assigned to the staff of the French general, Henri Giraud. His only solace was that when the attack against Corsica was unleashed he was able (at the age of 56) to go in with the first waves—his third combat amphibious landing of the war!

Meanwhile, in London, plans were hatched for the great cross-channel invasion—and Ted Roosevelt was determined to be in on it. Twice he wrote to General Eisenhower, pleading for a D-Day assignment with troops, but each time he was turned down. It was common knowledge among the officers of the general staff that he frequently suffered from attacks of arthritis, and Ike felt that he had been through enough.

In desperation Roosevelt, then in Italy, wrote to General Bradley: "I must be in on the Invasion . . . if it is only to swim across the channel with a 105 [105-mm. howitzer] strapped to my back. Help me get out of this rat's nest down here."

A third letter to Eisenhower finally brought the desired result, and Roosevelt was ordered to England for duty as a spare brigadier general with the newly-arrived 4th Infantry Division, which would see combat for the first time on the D-Day invasion beaches.

"Because the 4th Division was green to fire," Bradley later explained, "Roosevelt would go in with the landing wave. He could steady it as no other man could, for Ted was immune to fear."

The events of D-Day more than supported Bradley's confidence in Roosevelt. As someone who was on that bullet-raked beachhead with him later remarked, "You had to see him fight to believe it."

Stricken by an attack of arthritis just before the assault, he mentioned his pain to no one, and hobbled ashore with the first wave, which touched down on the shore of France about 2,000 yards south of its planned landing place. This was potentially a serious error, as it might have resulted in large-scale confusion.

That it did not is due largely to Ted Roosevelt's presence.

As soon as he realized that the first landing team had come ashore at the wrong spot, the general made a personal reconnaissance of the area behind the beach, in search of the causeway that was to be used for the drive inland. After reconnoitering, he returned to the beachhead landing point, and worked out details with the commanders of the assault battalions for an attack on enemy positions between them and the causeway.

Roosevelt thus exploited the error to the landing team's favor. The defenses behind the beach were knocked out as Roosevelt, waving his swagger stick, led the attack on the German strong points and secured an exit from the beaches over a lagoon-like body of water that had given the D-Day planners much anxiety.

By nightfall practically the entire 4th Division was ashore, and many elements had already fanned inland and made contact with the 101st Airborne Division. The 4th then helped pinch out Carentan, and moved in for the capture of Cherbourg. Ted Roosevelt continually roamed the front lines, inspiring his men to fight, just as he had inspired the soldiers of the 1st Division in World War I and in North Africa and Sicily. He died of a heart attack on July 13, on the very day that Bradley and Eisenhower were making the decision to reward his vigor and valor by fulfilling one of his cherished ambitions—to have a division of his own to command.

For his exploits on the D-Day beachhead, June 6, 1944, he was posthumously awarded the Medal of Honor on September 28, 1944. The last sentences of his Citation are worth quoting here:

"Although the enemy had the beach under constant direct fire, Brigadier General Roosevelt moved from one locality to another, rallying men around him, and directed and personally led them against the enemy. Under his seasoned, precise, calm, and unfaltering leadership, assault troops reduced beach strong points and rapidly moved inland with minimum casualties. He thus contributed substantially to the successful establishment of the beachhead in France."

❯❯❯ ❮❮❮

INTO THE DARK FOREST

John W. Minick

❯❯❯ ❮❮❮

BEYOND the terrible battleground lay the Cologne plain and the gateway to the Rhine. But for nearly three weeks the soldiers of Lieutenant General Courtney H. Hodges' First Army had been locked in mortal combat with crack *Wehrmacht* divisions in the thickets of the Huertgen Forest. Like a great primeval fortress, fifty square miles of dark fir trees stymied their attempt to advance into Germany.

As the danger to his homeland grew with each yard of the American offensive, the German soldier fought with ever-increasing ferocity. It is quite probable that in the Huertgen the German's cunning and his mastery of the most awful weapons of ground warfare were utilized to the greatest advantage. His defensive devices included the sniper's rifle, devilishly-constructed mine fields, booby traps, barbed-wire entanglements, narrow firebreaks covered by multiple machine guns, and countless abatis—road blocks formed by giant felled trees. The German even attached land mines to low branches, so that a protruding bayonet or the extended muzzle of a rifle was apt to detonate the explosive and blow the intruder to Kingdom Come.

Into the horror of this ancient forest, during a spell of the harshest, coldest weather that Europe had experienced in many years, a U.S. division rushed from the Luxembourg sector to relieve an outfit spent from hurling itself against the apparently impregnable German stronghold. One of the regiments of this division, 24 hours after moving into its new zone of action, became embroiled in one of the most sanguine combat actions of World War II. Out of the valor of its arms came a Distinguished Unit Citation, the highest award for gallantry in action that may be bestowed upon an entire unit.

The battle for which the regiment earned the DUC lasted for more than five days. But, in a sense, the factors which spelled out the difference between success and failure were decided in the minutes that followed the launching of the attack.

On the morning of November 21, 1944, the lead company in the assault found itself stymied at the edge of a German mine field. Artillery and mortar fire greeted the attacking column, and its commander was faced with the choice of being destroyed by shellfire or plunging into an uncharted mine field. It was a dismal prospect. Waiting for their commander's decision, the men peered miserably and uneasily into the swirling fog. Ahead of them, through the gloom, the enemy was waiting.

They were halted thus, near a clearing in the woods, when Staff Sergeant John W. Minick, a squad leader who had been scouting out in advance of the attack, worked his way to the company commander's side. He stared bleakly at the mine field and glanced at the billowing fog for a moment. Then he said in a quiet voice, "Skipper, you just follow old Minick . . ."

Four months earlier, eleven months after he had been drafted into the army at Carlisle, Pennsylvania, John W. Minick—somewhat over-age for an infantry private at 36— set down his belongings in a command post near a French farmhouse and reported for duty as a soldier in Company I, 121st Infantry Regiment, 8th Division.

It was during a little lull just before the Battle of St. Malo, and one of the officers of the company recalls his arrival. He was a swarthy fellow, about 5′8″, and weighing 150 lbs., with a scraggly mustache on a worried face. He was fresh from a training camp in the States, and seemed bewildered at finding himself in a bivouac area on the very fringe of the battlefield. He cried bitterly at the prospect of being in the infantry and having to kill or be killed.

There was nothing very heroic in the new man's deportment, and, considering his rather advanced age and unhappy state of mind, it was with some misgivings that First Lieutenant Stanley Schwartz of New York City, and Technical Sergeant Fred B. Hays of Mansfield, Georgia, welcomed him to the 1st Platoon of Company I.

But they and the other members of the platoon soon learned that the new man was a surprisingly good soldier in the field. They watched him carefully and noticed with some astonishment that he showed less signs of strain and even seemed to take on an air of confidence as the regiment marched again toward the sound of the guns—toward his baptism of fire. He definitely did not react to combat like a normally scared replacement.

Combat Team 121 was temporarily assigned to the 83d Infantry Division for the sweep of Brittany. The "Old Gray Bonnet" Regiment, formerly of the Georgia National Guard, engaged in the bloody battle for Dinard. Minick's performance in his first combat was so startlingly valiant that he was awarded the Bronze Star; and shortly afterward he earned an oak-leaf cluster for another gallant action.

Then, at St. Malo, the 3d Battalion, 121st Infantry, pushing boldly ahead, outstripped its support. It was very nearly cut off and annihilated when the Germans launched a savage counterattack. There was a moment when a handful of Company I soldiers, Lieutenant Schwartz and Sergeant Hays among them, had their backs to the wall.

Suddenly the attacking Germans were thrown off stride by a stream of deadly rifle fire. They paused in momentary confusion, the unseen marksman cut loose again, and more Germans fell. The others drew back. The astonished Schwartz and Hays were then joined by Minick who had remained behind above to fight when most of the others in the platoon had been forced to withdraw.

From then on, Minick, Schwartz, and Hays formed a partnership that endured until the Huertgen. They seemed to be an indestructible trio and distinguished themselves in the fighting time after time. They made a specialty of patrols behind enemy lines, both with and without the knowledge of Captain Jack R. Melton, the company commander.

Melton had already discerned Minick's worth as a fighting man, had put him in for a Distinguished Service Cross for the action at St. Malo, and had promoted him to staff sergeant. He quickly learned, though, that Minick was no model soldier. Minick's indifference to normal army protocol was monumental. For example, Minick never addressed him as Captain, but always called him "Cowboy," presumably because Melton hailed from Texas.

Minick keenly hated what is commonly called "garrison soldiering." When the regiment was in a rear area or an inactive sector he gave Melton and First Sergeant Howard C. Redding gray hairs by the thousands. Captain Melton twice busted him back to private for "hell raising," but always promoted him back to sergeant when Company I went into battle. Minick understood this arrangement and found it perfectly agreeable.

For his own part, Minick wasn't much on discipline, but he always insisted on what he considered "a full day's work" from every man in his squad. He didn't tolerate nonsense or carelessness and his good judgment as a field soldier earned him widespread renown. He never had any trouble getting volunteers for one of his patrols—and he was always the first to volunteer himself when Melton needed to dispatch a scouting party.

"Long before we reached the Huertgen," Captain Melton later declared in his report to the War Department, "Sergeant Minick's name had become synonymous with the gallantry of the infantry soldier of the 8th Division."

"He was the only man I ever knew," says Fred Hays, "who enjoyed it when the going was the toughest."

The savagery in the Huertgen was reaching its climax when the 8th Infantry Division was suddenly ordered to take over a sector in the gloomy, dripping forest. Its mission was to seize the vital Huertgen-Kleinhau ridge, which was considered the key to Duren and the enemy's defenses west of the Cologne plain. On the night of November 20, 1944, the 3d Battalion of the 121st Infantry was in an assembly area roughly 800 yards to the rear of the 3d Battalion, 12th Infantry Regiment, 4th Division. Major Roy Hogan, the battalion commander, conferred with his regimental commander, and then sought out Jack Melton. Company I was ordered to pass through the positions of Company K, 12th Infantry, to capture the ridge that lay about a thousand yards beyond the front lines.

In briefing his own officers and noncoms Melton stressed the point that they were to *pass through* the lines of friendly forces. There could be no stopping or withdrawing without dire consequence; there was only one direction, *forward!*

The battalion's order of march placed Company I in the lead. Melton decided to attack in columns of platoons, since he knew it would be necessary to penetrate mine fields and the only demolitions equipment available consisted of a few bangalore torpedoes.

The line of departure was crossed at 6:15 a.m. on November 21. Company I moved out under cover of a thick fog, having been told by 4th Division officers that a full enemy battalion was opposing them. The dense fog hovered over the attackers like a protective shroud, and Company I pushed into the woodline of the forest without a shot having been fired. But after they had advanced about 200 yards, the troops reached a concertina wire that was covered by two German machine gun nests. Beyond the concertina was an enemy mine field.

The arrival of Company I at the concertina wire provoked the enemy machine guns to action, and their fire was a signal for the opening of a prearranged barrage of artillery and heavy (120-mm.) mortar fire. It was a bad moment and every one knew it. Then Minick turned to Captain Melton.

"Just follow old Minick, Skipper," he said in a quiet voice. "And when I stop, you'd better stop, because you ain't going no further."

Melton nodded to him and Minick knifed through a place where the wire was breached and headed for the machine guns. Several others followed him. All but one or two were immediately pinned down by heavy machine gun fire. Minick, singlehanded, attacked the gun on the left flank, while Lieutenant Schwartz and a soldier named Trusty tackled the other one. Relentlessly firing his submachine gun, Minick killed two members of the German crew and took three others prisoner. He gestured violently with the tommy gun and made the Germans understand that they were to move out in front, and lead him through the mine field. They reluctantly picked their way toward their own lines, while Minick urged them on with an occasional prod. The mine field was breached—and then they were once more in dense woods, where the fir forest was like an impenetrable wall and where the fog was so thick there was no more than ten yards visibility in any direction.

Suddenly a German voice hailed the three prisoners who were still marching directly in front of Minick. A German trooper stepped out on the path and was considerably disconcerted to find that his countrymen were accompanied by a fierce American vigorously brandishing a submachine gun. He reached for a pistol and Minick shot him. Then the woods came alive with rifle fire. Minick didn't know it, but in rolling up the enemy's left flank he had stumbled upon an important enemy security outpost. He emptied the magazine of his tommy gun and swiftly reloaded as bullets crackled around him. Before help reached him Minick had killed 20 enemies and captured 20. The prisoners were sent to the rear and Minick once again moved out in advance of the company's attack. What he could not and did not know was that his action had already broken down the left flank of the German battalion on the ridge.

He pushed on boldly and as it turned out was within 30 yards of the enemy battalion command post and the objective when suddenly there was a rattle of gunfire. As Minick alerted himself for action, a machine gun chattered.

Fred Hays, who was about ten yards away, heard Minick yell, "Come on out! Come on out and fight!" Then there was a ground-shaking roar, the ugly noise of an exploding land mine. When the dust cleared, Minick lay in a heap on the ground.

With an angry yell Company I surged forward, past the dying Minick, and into the enemy positions on the ridge. For five days Company I held grimly to its foothold on the objective, far in advance of the rest of the regiment. At the end of that time Captain Melton marched out of the forest with eleven men. All, including himself, were wounded, although they were still on their feet. The company's casualties numbered 141—Minick among them.

The brave soldier's name, already a byword in the 8th Division, became in a short time a widespread legend. Even the busy division commander called Melton to express his regrets over the loss of so fine a fighting man.

"There is no doubt in my mind whatsoever," Captain Melton wrote in his report to the War Department, "that the actions of Staff Sergeant John W. Minick in that attack saved the entire company from complete annihilation. Only by his aggressive action was I able to get two-thirds of my company in the German dugouts."

He was a strange sort of hero—John W. Minick. The officers and his fellow soldiers of Company I of the Old Gray Bonnet Regiment will always remember how he cried the first time he went into battle—and how he turned out to be the perfect infantry soldier when the chips were down.

FROM D-DAY (June 6, 1944) to V-E DAY (May 7, 1945), the expeditionary forces under the command of General of the Army Dwight D. Eisenhower fought their way across France, through the Lowlands, and into Germany. By the war's end 129 Medal of Honor actions [1] had taken place on the Continent—the alphabetical roll of honor starts with Staff Sergeant Lucian Adams of the 3d Infantry Division and runs to Second Lieutenant Raymond Zussman of the 756th Tank Battalion. Adams was killed in action in the course of a one-man attack on enemy machine gun positions in the Mortagne Forest of France; Zussman was a tank commander turned foot soldier who led a small detachment in a fight at Noroy le Bourg, France, that resulted in the capture of 92 prisoners.

[1] This figure does not include awards to personnel of U.S. Army Air Forces. In the Aerial Offensive against Europe, 22 Medals were won. The largest aggregate number—five—went to airmen who participated in the August, 1943, strike on the Ploesti oilfields.

By far the greatest number of Medal-winning actions took place during the battle of France, in which 61 soldiers earned the award—among them Second Lieutenant Audie L. Murphy, 3d Division, the most-decorated soldier of World War II; Lieutenant Colonel Robert G. Cole, who led his paratroopers of the 101st Airborne Division in one of the most daring bayonet attacks in U.S. military history; and Technical Sergeant Charles F. Carey, Jr., whose antitank platoon of the 100th Division was overrun by a force of 200 Germans accompanied by 12 tanks. Carey organized his men as riflemen, moved back into the area, and fought from house to house. When he reached a house where the Germans had four of his men trapped, Carey found an old staircase, maneuvered it under an attic window and got his men out safely. Sergeant (later Second Lieutenant) Edward C. Dahlgren of the 36th Division saved an entire platoon that had been cut off when the Germans counterattacked at Oberhoffen, France. Then he went after an enemy stronghold in a wine cellar, smashed his way in with hand grenades, and marched out again with 26 prisoners.

There were 16 Medal actions in Belgium, three in Holland, two in Luxembourg, and 47 in Germany (including Staff Sergeant John W. Minick, and a 1st Division Huertgen hero, Technical Sergeant Jake W. Lindsey, the 100th winner of the medal in World War II).

The medals went to members of 31 infantry divisions, 4 airborne divisions, 7 armored divisions, and 6 separate battalions. A lion's share were cornered by infantrymen of the 1st Division (15) and the 3d Division (19).[2]

Most of those who earned the medal were infantrymen; others were members of the armored forces and the airborne

---

[2] The 3d Division, the only U.S. division which fought the Nazis on all fronts—North Africa, Sicily, Italy, France, and Germany—boasted a list of 35 Medal of Honor men by the end of World War II.

outfits. Among them was a medic (Private Harold A. Garman of the 5th Division), 2 engineers (Technician Fourth Grade Truman Kimbro of the 2d Division and Private First Class Herman C. Wallace of the 76th Division), and three artillerymen (Technician Fifth Grade Forrest E. Peden of the 2d Division, Private First Class George B. Turner of the 14th Armored Division, and First Lieutenant James E. Robinson, Jr., of the 63rd Division).

Chronologically, the story of the men who earned the Medal of Honor in the annihilation of Hitler's Fortress Europe starts with Private Carlton W. Barrett of the 1st Infantry Division and three others—First Lieutenant Jimmie W. Monteith, Jr., Technician Fifth Grade John W. Pinder, and Brigadier General Theodore Roosevelt, Jr.—who earned the medal in the heat and fury of D-Day. The story concludes with the spectacular bravery of Captain Michael Daly and Private Joseph F. Merrell, who fought into the outskirts of the Nazi shrine city of Nuremberg in the vanguard of the 3d Infantry Division, April 18, 1945.

In all of the campaigns of the E.T.O. (including North Africa, Sicily, and Italy), 209 Medals of Honor were awarded in tribute to the valor of army men of both the ground and air.

❯❯❯ ❯❯❯ ❯❯❯ ❮❮❮ ❮❮❮ ❮❮❮

A NOTE OF TRIUMPH

Melvin Mayfield

❯❯❯ ❯❯❯ ❯❯❯ ❮❮❮ ❮❮❮ ❮❮❮

SWEATING U.S. infantrymen in dust-stained green fatigues, the work clothes of the jungle fighters in the Pacific war, glumly sat out a seven-hour truce while psychological warfare teams went into action with loudspeakers and leaflets. It was D-plus 168 on Luzon, and it was twenty days since the campaign had officially been declared over.

Neither leaflets nor loudspeakers were able to convince the enemy troops in their mountain stronghold that the campaign had "ended." And so, when the seven hours were up, the U.S. regimental commander wearily issued orders for the attack to be resumed.

Two columns moved out—one to engage bypassed Japanese positions south of Kiangan village; the other to march northwest to seize Kiangkiang and the towering heights of Mount Puloy.

Corporal Melvin Mayfield, a 26-year-old Ohio farmer, was a soldier in the 1st Battalion, 20th Infantry Regiment, 6th Infantry Division. His battalion, the one that was to take Kiangkiang, pushed up the broken trail that led from Kiangan toward a *barrio* called Pacdan. It was a tedious march over rugged terrain deep in the central part of North Luzon; the mountain province had originally been inhabited only by the primitive Ifugaos, but it was now a hideout for more than 20,000 Japanese troops under General Tomoyuki Yamashita, the "Tiger of Malaya."

The 1st Battalion, 20th Infantry, with the 1st Battalion, Buena Vista Regiment of veteran Filipino guerrilla troops from southern Luzon attached to it, proceeded slowly but surely toward the objective. On July 26, two days after the drive got under way, the combined American-Filipino force was stopped in its tracks 400 yards short of Pacdan.

Before them loomed three hills forming a semicircular ridge. Company B, 20th Infantry, hurled itself at the ridge, only to be driven back by savage machine gun and rifle fire. Concealed in a labyrinth of connecting trenches and bunkers, deep caves and cleverly placed spider holes, Japanese gunners enjoyed a field day.

By the morning of July 29, the 1st Battalion was still stalled southwest of Pacdan. By now the battalion commander had become impatient; and after giving his company commanders final orders for a new attack, Colonel Paul H. Mahoney, the regimental commander, came to the battalion observation post to watch the attack. The plan of action called for Company A, 20th Infantry, to make a diversionary attack up the left slope and thus be in a position to furnish support fire for Companies A and C of the Buena Vista Regiment, which would make the main effort on the right.

Down to Company D, the heavy weapons company, came orders to set up a forward observation post for the 81-mm. mortars accompanying the Filipino assault companies. Better send someone who knows his business, the battalion exec warned.

The First Sergeant agreed that it was a job for the most dependable man he had. He chose Corporal Melvin Mayfield, a Muskingum County Ohioan who had seen a good deal of soldiering since he had been inducted into the army in the peacetime draft in February, 1941, ten months before Pearl Harbor. Mayfield had been in the 20th Infantry, which since the Civil War has been known as "Sykes Regulars," since he joined the 6th Division at Milne Bay, New Guinea, more than a year before.

He had taken part in the push toward Sarmi Village on the northern coast of Netherlands New Guinea, where the 20th Infantry fought the bloody battle of Lone Tree Hill. Then he had been in the D-Day landing on Lingayen Gulf, January 9, 1945—and now he was one of the few old-timers who had made the whole miserable Luzon campaign. In the regiment's fight for Munoz, and in the battle for San Mateo, Mayfield had already earned a reputation as a dependable and fearless soldier.

The tall hawk-faced corporal quickly assembled his communications equipment, rounded up the men who would accompany him, and started toward the front to meet the commander of the Filipino force which was to make the attack. He paused for a moment of banter with a mortar platoon sergeant.

"When I get on this thing," and he tapped the leather carrying case that held his field telephone, "I want to hear those eighty-ones singing."

"You got to get up there first," was the laconic reply.

An air strike was called and the bombers rained nine tons of high explosives and 26,000 gallons of napalm on the ridge. The artillery fired 4,000 shells of high explosives; the 4.2 inch mortars added another 4,000 rounds; and the 81-mm. mortars pumped more than 8,000 shells onto the fire-scorched ridge. The expenditure of ammunition was so vast that the GI's called the objective "Million Dollar Ridge."

The lush natural growth on the ridge, noted Captain Robert

E. Phelps, the Battalion S-3, was leveled until it was only "a sort of stubble."

High on an adjoining hill where the 1st Battalion observation post was located, Colonel Mahoney looked at his watch and saw that it was 1 p.m. The attack would get under way on schedule. The little group of staff officers peered through binoculars and took turns at a 20-power telescope to watch the course of the action.

Company A moved out boldly and began its planned deception, the feint that was to draw the enemy's fire while the two Filipino companies attacked on the right. But the company was unable to work its way up the steep terrain and was forced to fall back. The Filipino attack, meanwhile, moved out swiftly.

The Filipino companies had to do without supporting fire, since Company A had been unable to make its move. Nevertheless, the soldiers stormed up the hill, and by 2:30 p.m. they had won a shaky toe hold on the upper slope. Before they could reorganize and renew the attack on the crux of the strong point, they were pinned down by machine gun, rifle, and grenade fire. Those men who had ventured out on the hill were forced to seek refuge in the lee of a huge boulder.

"Even then," says Colonel Mahoney, who was following the fight from his vantage point, "I don't think they realized the danger they were in—that their front and left flank were particularly vulnerable to counterattack. And from our position we could see that the Japs were maneuvering around and getting ready to hit them."

The situation looked extremely critical. Then the viewers in the observation post were electrified at the sight of a lone figure who came up the slope by leaps and bounds, hurtling past the huddled forms of the guerrillas pinned down on the hillside. They watched transfixed as the soldier, who was the only human being in action on that battlefield, dashed from cover to cover, from fox hole to fox hole, in his advance up to the summit of the ridge. Firing his carbine from the hip, he moved steadily across the hilltop, apparently oblivious to the enemy fire.

Captain Phelps, who was squinting into the telescope, exclaimed, "That's Mayfield! The lineman from Dog Company."

As he came abreast of the Filipinos who were hugging the boulder, Mayfield shouted for them to cover him with rifle fire, then moved out again to attack four caves that seemed to be the strong point of the enemy defenses.

He reached the first cave and lobbed a phosphorus grenade into its yawning mouth. There were terrified shrieks, and then two Jap soldiers bolted into the open. Their pistols barked, but Mayfield was waiting with a finger on the trigger of his carbine, and had the drop on them. He cut them down with two shots. Then—as enemy machine gun fire spattered all around him—he coolly approached the second cave, where he again started proceedings with a phosphorus grenade. An instant after he threw it he was forced to hit the dirt behind a clump of bushes and rocks. His second grenade exploded, and there was no further sign of activity in or near the cave.

Mayfield gathered himself for a frontal attack on the two remaining caves. When he decided the time was right, he hurtled from cover and sped toward the mouth of the third cave. From the hilltop observation post it looked as though he were going to run right inside it. But he veered off like a quarterback being chased by an opposing lineman, and lobbed the grenade on the dead run. In the next instant he hit the dirt again as a stream of angry bullets buzzed a couple of inches away from his head.

Once again he rolled into the bushes and took stock of the

situation. Then he headed for the last cave. The hillside was alive with bullets as enemy riflemen tried to pick him off. But Mayfield hurled his grenade unerringly—and an instant later there was a mighty roar as an enemy ammunition cache blew up. The explosion rocked the hill and caused a rockslide that sealed the cave entrance.

Back at the battalion observation post, Captain Burt shouted a useless warning as Mayfield's carbine flew from his hand, shattered by a burst of machine gun fire. For a moment the former Ohio farmer stared at his right hand, all covered with blood.

Weaponless, wounded, and without any more grenades, Mayfield was stymied only for an instant. He wheeled about and went racing back across the hilltop toward the spot where the Filipinos were still waiting. He picked up a handful of grenades and stuffed them in his shirt. Then he grabbed another rifle, and barked out orders for the Filipinos to follow him. In an instant their indecision evaporated and they began to surge up and over the summit.

"C'mon! C'mon!" Mayfield urged them.

He picked out a light machine gun squad and told them to stick close to him. Then he raced swiftly across the hilltop toward the enemy stronghold for the second time. He moved past the shattered and deserted caves, over a small saddle that led to the main enemy observation post on the center hill. He signaled for the Filipino machine guns to go into action, then shifted their fire off to one side as he headed for the observation post, singlehandedly attacking and killing two Jap gunners who pumped heavy machine gun fire at him as he advanced. Then he called for his machine gun crew to move up to a better vantage point to fire into a row of enemy positions down the reverse slope.

By this time the Filipinos of the Buena Vista Regiment were charging fiercely, shouting their ancient war cries. As they swarmed down on the enemy Mayfield was still in the lead, waving wildly and urging them to press the attack. They routed the enemy from the three hills that formed the ridge— Mayfield alone killed more than thirty Japanese soldiers in the headlong dash—and soon the remainder of the 1st Battalion, 20th Infantry, moved up to consolidate the gain.

The next day the battalion was in Pacdan, poised for the push toward Kiangkiang.

An attack that had nearly been a disaster had been turned into a brilliant victory. "And we had Corporal Mayfield to thank for it," said Colonel Mahoney, who had seen the action from start to finish. "It was his fight every inch of the way. He cinched the taking of the ridge for us."

Although the infantry continued to attack Yamashita's crumbling mountain stronghold, the gigantic world war had just about run its course. Even as Corporal Melvin Mayfield was storming the ridge before Pacdan, a strange new weapon was being fitted into the bomb bay of a B-29 Superfort on the tiny island of Tinian. Seven days later the first combat A-Bomb would be dropped over Hiroshima, and in 35 days Japan would surrender unconditionally.

THE FINAL Medal of Honor action in World War II, Corporal Melvin Mayfield's one-man assault against Japanese positions in the Cordillera Mountains on July 29, 1945, came 1,327 days after Pearl Harbor—three years, two months and twenty-three days after the fall of Bataan. The locale of Mayfield's fight was roughly 200 miles northeast of Abucay, where Lieutenant Alexander R. Nininger, Jr., died in action on January 12, 1942 to earn the first Medal of Honor awarded in the second World War.

A total of 83 Army Medals of Honor were awarded for action in the Pacific—70 to ground force officers and men,

13 to members of the Army Air Force. The Air Force group included General James H. Doolittle (then Colonel), who was honored for leading the Tokyo Raiders against Japan's capital on June 9, 1942. Another was awarded to Staff Sergeant Henry E. Erwin, a radio operator in a B-29 that was engaged in combat over Koriyama, Japan. A defective phosphorus bomb which he discharged exploded in the launching chute and shot back into the interior of the plane; Erwin was struck full in the face, blinded, and severely burned. In a few seconds the cabin of the plane filled with smoke, making it impossible for the pilot to see. Erwin realized that the plane and crew were lost if the blazing bomb remained in the ship. He scooped it up in his bare hands and groped for the copilot's window. The navigator's table barred his way, so he held the burning bomb between his forearm and body as he released the spring lock and raised the table. Then he stumbled down the narrow passage that led into the smoke-filled pilot's compartment. With burning hands he found the window and hurled the bomb into the sky. Then, completely afire, he collapsed on the floor. The smoke cleared and the pilot was able to pull the big ship out of its dive at an altitude of 300 feet. Erwin lived to tell of his terrible ordeal.

New Guinea was responsible for eight Medal of Honor winners, Guadalcanal for three, Bougainville for one, and New Georgia for three, among them the fabled Private Rodger Young.

The battle for Attu in the Aleutians and the fight for Manus in the Admiralty Islands each produced one Medal of Honor man. Two medals, both posthumous, came out of the smoke of Saipan.

In the China-Burma-India theater of operations, one U.S. soldier was named for the Medal of Honor—First Lieutenant Jack L. Knight, commander of a troop in the 124th Cavalry

Regiment, the Mars Task Force. Lieutenant Knight bravely attacked a series of four pillboxes on a Japanese-held hill on the Burma road, north of Lashio. During the bitter fight he was wounded, and his brother, Curtis, a first sergeant, took command. Then Curtis was hit. Lieutenant Knight got someone to take his brother to the rear; then he propped himself up on an elbow to direct the attack, until only one of the pillboxes remained in action. Lieutenant Knight crawled toward it on his hands and knees, and was killed by rifle fire as he engaged it.

Nine soldiers were named for the Medal of Honor following the action on Okinawa. Among them was Private First Class Desmond T. Doss, a soft-spoken man and a dedicated and dauntless soldier when his regiment of the 77th Infantry Division was fighting for its life at The Escarpment. Another was Private First Class Clarence B. Craft, a new replacement assigned to the 96th Infantry Division, who boldly stood on top of a hill where his battalion had been stymied for 12 days and called for his buddies to toss hand grenades up to him so that he could hurl them at the enemy. Then he made a brilliant one-man attack that resulted in the capture of the hill—a hill that proved to be the key to the entire Japanese defense line, which, in the words of the citation, "rapidly crumbled after his utterly fearless and heroic attack."

The largest number of medals were awarded for combat valor in the Philippines. To begin with, five men earned the Medal of Honor during the Battle for Bataan, including Generals Douglas MacArthur and Jonathan M. Wainwright, the two highest-ranking officers ever to receive the medal.

In the return to the Philippines 36 more Army men earned the Medal of Honor. Twenty-two were awarded for action on Luzon, and the others were for incidents on Leyte, Mindanao, and Negros.

The completeness of the U.S. victory in the Pacific is underlined by the fact that the last Medal of Honor action (May-field's), like the first (Nininger's), took place on Luzon. It was the liberation of this island that more than any other action during the Pacific war foreshadowed what Franklin D. Roosevelt once called "the inevitable triumph."

❯❯❯ ❯❯❯ ❯❯❯ ❮❮❮ ❮❮❮ ❮❮❮

COLONEL HILLTOP
Lee R. Hartell

❯❯❯ ❯❯❯ ❯❯❯ ❮❮❮ ❮❮❮ ❮❮❮

THE 2d Infantry Division was recovering from the terror of the Kunu-ri gauntlet in December, 1950, when First Lieutenant Lee Ross Hartell reported to the command post of the 15th Field Artillery Battalion. The 15th was one of the battalions that had taken the full brunt of the Chinese Communist drive against the Chonchon River on November 27, and now it was mending and girding itself for a return to the fight.

Hartell, newly arrived in Korea, was unhappy at being assigned to the battalion which, he had heard, had the "bug out" fever so bad that, ". . . all they have to hear is a hint there's a Chinaman in the neighborhood and they're ready to run south."

In a letter to his younger brother, Chick, Lee wrote: "I realize the Kunu-ri thing couldn't be helped. But never having been in an outfit that was beat I am . . . sure disappointed."

Lee had fought through World War II as an artilleryman in the 43d Infantry Division—a Connecticut-Rhode Island National Guard outfit. He became a member of the battery's survey section, and not long after the 43d shipped out to the Pacific to fight at Rendova, Munda, Arundel, New Georgia, and in the Philippines, he was promoted to sergeant.

During the Arundel scrap he had earned the Purple Heart. His own job had been done, and he had gone back to the No. 1 gun position and offered to spell one of the weary gunners during a lengthy firing mission. He had just taken over when the gun was blown up. There were eight casualties; but Hartell had been lucky that time, and had suffered only minor cuts and abrasions.

After the war, Lee re-enlisted in the Guard and took examinations for a commission. He was made a second lieutenant in the field artillery around the same time that he got married.

He tried hard to make a go of civilian life. "But there's no use kidding about those things," one of his old Danbury buddies recalls. "Lee's heart was still in the Army. He had a long talk with Peggy and the outcome was he enlisted as a sergeant in the regular army."

Several months later he was recalled as an artillery second lieutenant, and sent off to train recruits at Fort Dix, New Jersey. He spent two years there. Then, Korea . . . and marching orders for Lieutenant Hartell.

Shortly before Christmas Lee became a member of the 15th Field Artillery Battalion, a 105-mm. howitzer outfit firing in support of the 9th Infantry Regiment. He was ordered to form a forward observer team and then join Company B.

Hartell studied the roster and found that all of the experienced recon sergeants and radiomen had already been commandeered. Then his eye caught the name of a corporal who, he knew, had been cited for bravery.

"You want to come up front as my recon sergeant?" he asked the corporal. "I'm not promising you any promotion— just hard work and fighting."

"Sir, they never made the Chinaman that can scare me."

Hartell looked at the corporal thoughtfully and said, "Okay, Belmore, you're on the team." He selected a soldier called

Shrapnel Williams as his radioman, and a driver-mechanic named Terlin to round out the crew.

With their quarter-ton trailer bouncing crazily behind the jeep, "Easy 8 FO Team" reported to Captain Wallace, the commander of Company B, 9th Infantry. A couple of weeks after their first meeting, Hartell wrote home to tell the family about Wallace. "I think," he said, "I have really made a life-long friend."

Mid-January found the Division battling in the bitter, 25° below zero Korean winter. The 9th Infantry was fencing with the enemy near the key communications center of Wonju. Baker Company, with Easy 8 FO Team attached, marched down the railroad tracks January 14, swept into a broad valley, and stopped for noon chow.

Something about a hill that lay ahead of them troubled Hartell, and he whipped out his binoculars. He thought he detected movement and a glint of steel and reported this to Wallace. The company commander looked through the glasses, but saw nothing suspicious. He handed Hartell a can of beans and grinned, "It's just your imagination, Lee. You're a man looking for trouble."

Hartell took the can of beans, walked back 15 or 20 yards, and propped his binoculars up in front of him on the hood of a wrecked jeep. He swallowed—hard—as he saw a head pop up over a pile of rocks on the hillside.

He called for Wallace and pointed to the binoculars. "Take a squint at my imagination."

The company commander looked, whistled softly, and raced back to his radio man. He called the Battalion command post and reported activity on the skyline. About fifteen figures were now plainly visible.

Battalion replied, "Go get 'em!"

"How about softening them up with some artillery, Lee?" Wallace asked.

"Sure thing," Hartell answered, and called in his Fire Direction Center. The answer was: "Unsafe to fire. People on hill believed friendly."

Wallace issued a "hold fire" order to the company, and they all moved out up the hill to meet their "friends."

They were 50 yards from the top when a definitely unfriendly soldier stood up in his fox hole and fired. He didn't hit any one, but Baker Company went into action—fast.

They started pumping lead as they rushed up the hill in assault order. The enemy hurled grenades down on them as they climbed, but the GI's kept moving in. Then it was hand-to-hand for a few minutes until the Reds broke and started to run down the far side of the hill.

In the little village at the base of the far side of the hill the retreating enemy alerted about 120 soldiers, and a general exodus from the area got under way. Wallace halted his men at the top of the hill and took stock of the situation.

They counted 22 enemy dead, four enemy wounded—and none of the Baker Company men had suffered even a scratch!

Hartell had his radio at the crest of the hill and was reporting in as he watched the Reds run. They had to go two miles on a winding uphill road before they would be lost to view in the next hill mass.

In a moment or two Hartell got his Fire Direction Center and called in a fire mission. The company meanwhile was vastly unhappy as it watched the enemy "escape." Wallace sat quietly next to Hartell. They both knew that most of the men in the company had never really seen artillery in action before.

Hartell fired far over the enemy, and continued to adjust with one gun ahead into the area at the gap on the horizon. The kids in the infantry company looked back at him, and sneered at the waste of ammo. Wallace just smiled and didn't say anything. He knew what Hartell had in mind.

Then the artillery lieutenant called "cease fire," and ordered a battery to fire three VT (proximity fuse) when he gave the command.

The troops muttered, "Shoot 'em up before they get away." Hartell leaned against a rock and paid no attention. Soon ten of the Reds dashed into the gap, and Hartell yelled, "Fire!"

The effect in the gap was both devastating—to the enemy—and awe inspiring—to Baker Company. Enemy bodies flew in all directions.

Hartell dropped his fire 400 yards to catch stragglers. Then he moved up 200, and the main group jumped off the road into the rice paddies. That's what he'd been waiting for, and he called for fire left and right of the road, ranging up and down toward the gap.

The infantry soldiers were so impressed with Hartell, that they nicknamed him "Colonel Hilltop" for the way he'd slaughtered the enemy while calmly standing on the hill.

Several days later Hartell and his FO team accompanied an armored assault patrol, a platoon strength foray ordered to make contact with the enemy, probe his strength, and return to U.S. lines.

The destination was a small town two miles southeast of Hoengsong. The force consisted of four tanks, two half tracks mounting quad-fifties, two self-propelled M-19s (dual forties), and two jeeps being used by the patrol leaders and Hartell.

Easy 8 FO team had orders to proceed only to maximum artillery range and then pull back into the nearest friendly perimeter. They moved along, but were slowed up when a tank bogged down. Another tank stayed behind to help it get free. They by-passed blown-out bridges, and finally reached a place where they had to use a bridge that was strong enough only for the half-tracks. A radioed message to the command post brought orders to continue on with just the half-tracks and jeeps.

When the patrol reached the maximum artillery range, the

patrol leader asked Hartell if he and the FO team were going to pull out. This was an academic question, however, for without the tanks the patrol had no radio capable of establishing radio contact with the command post.

Hartell's SCR 619, however, enabled them to get in contact with an artillery plane overhead which in turn had contact with the infantry command post through the artillery net. Lee asked the pilot to get permission to provide continuous cover, which was granted. This meant that the FO radio would be the patrol's only contact with the rest of the army. Hartell's Easy 8 FO team joined the Infantry.

Hartell and Chung were up with the point of the patrol, so that they would be able to interrogate any civilians who had information that was worth radioing back to Intelligence.

They moved along and presently stopped a bearded old *papa-san* who was traveling across country with a young boy. Chung questioned them and learned that two miles east and a half-mile south there was an enemy headquarters of some sort with several hundred troops.

If this were true, Hartell realized, their chance of being able to pull back at the end of the mission would be slim. But there wasn't much to go on. He radioed the plane the information he had received, and asked the pilot to look around. After a few minutes the pilot reported word of activity in two nearby villages, and Hartell asked him to set up a fire mission for the artillery back in Wonju.

Just then the lead scout, who had reached a knoll where the road made a sharp turn, signaled "Down!" The patrol leader was back with the half-tracks; so Hartell and his recon sergeant moved up to the scout.

The soldier pointed over the crest to the stretch of road that lay beyond. About 200 yards away, strolling nonchalantly toward them, were two enemy soldiers.

They were practically in a PW cage, Hartell told himself;

when they got so close that they couldn't possibly get away, he told Chung to call to them to halt and surrender.

The words were hardly out of Chung's mouth when one Red pulled a pistol, the other unslung his burp gun, and the pair went into action! The soldier with the burp gun was able to get off only a very short burst before he was cut down by Belmore's carbine and the scout's M-1. Hartell went for the soldier who had pulled the pistol and hit him above the knees.

Lee hollered "Cease fire!" when he realized that the soldier with the pistol had a brief case on him. He told himself there must be some very important information in the brief case to cause two men to fight against such hopeless odds. The soldier with the brief case lay wounded on the ground; the other man was dead.

By this time the patrol leader had worked his way to the front, and quickly gave orders for inner security on the surrounding hills. Then he moved a quad-forty up front to provide road safety.

They went over the crest toward the two bodies. The wounded man was a North Korean Lieutenant. He told Chung he was carrying top secret orders from Chinese Communist headquarters to a front line North Korean commander in Sugol.

Then Hartell remembered the information he had from the old *papa-san*, and called for an immediate air strike against Sugol. Soon the sky was swarming with swooping and diving F-80s. The artillery plane marked the target for them, and they went crashing in with napalm and rockets. The artillery plane reported enemy running in all directions. The jets strafed and rocketed the area until their ammo supplies were exhausted.

Meanwhile the North Korean officer died, despite first aid efforts to save his life. Chung looked through the brief case and told Hartell he thought the contents were highly important.

Hartell threw the brief case into his jeep, and the patrol moved forward. At Pyongjang-ni they found it was impossible to take the vehicles any further. The remnants of a wooden bridge were still smoking, evidence that an enemy rear guard had departed just before them. Local civilians told Hartell, through Chung, that for two days badly beaten Chinese and North Korean soldiers had been moving through their town toward the north.

A few enemy wounded, and some frostbite victims who had been left behind testified to this. Contact was made with the rear, and orders came: "Carry on to destination on foot. Contact imperative."

Leaving a small guard force for the vehicles, and the quad crews, the patrol moved out again, 26 men and 2 officers.

They walked on all afternoon, finally reaching the junction of the main supply route that led back to Hoengsong. Nothing of any note had taken place during this march, and so they kept on toward Saemal, their destination. It was getting toward dusk and the artillery plane was about to leave them. As soon as the patrol reached Saemal, Hartell assembled all the information Intelligence could use on road conditions, bridges, obstacles, probable mined areas, and fortifications. He added that civilians in Saemal reported heavy enemy troop concentrations in Hoengsong.

Then Hartell and the patrol leader agreed that it was high time they pulled out. Williams and Belmore traded off on the radio, and managed to stay out in front of the foot soldiers as they practically galloped back over hill and dale in the gathering darkness. At any moment, at every turn of the road, they expected to tumble into a Red ambush. But somehow they all made it back to Pyongjang-ni, where the vehicles waited for them.

Hartell pitched forward into his jeep too exhausted to think about anything, including the possibility of ambush. He slipped into a warm parka, and despite the bouncing ride over the rutted frozen roads he was soon sound asleep. When they reached the tanks, they found them getting ready to pull back alone, as they thought that the patrol must have been cut off.

Hartell roused himself and boarded the lead tank. They used their lights, because without them the tanks couldn't have maneuvered over the road. Two miles up the road they were met by nine tanks, two M-19s, and three half-tracks sent by the corps commander to aid them. Hartell remarked to one of the tankers that this was right neighborly of the corps commander. Then he learned that it was the *brief case* the General wanted.

It was nearly midnight when Lee brought the brief case to the Intelligence office south of Wonju, and the interpreters went right to work on it. Evidently the contents were hot, because within ten minutes the brief case was being sent up to Eighth Army Headquarters. That was the last Hartell heard of the incident until he was later awarded the Bronze Star Medal for his part in the day's activity.

On February 5, Lee was sent to the division air strip to report for duty as an aerial observer. Everything went fine on the first day up; but on the second day, the air was a little rough and Lee was glad that a colonel had forgotten his helmet in the ship. After that he knew enough to carry a pocketful of chewing gum.

Then the Chinese struck again—and hard. Three divisions smashed the ROK's and broke through to hit the U.S. artillery positions. Hartell's own battery was among those that was hardest hit.

Hartell and his pilot, Captain Valdez, were in the sky at dawn. They laid down fire on Reds that were attacking a group that had been cut off up the line. They called in continuous fire while the Yanks in the trap tried to run the gauntlet; but when hundreds and hundreds of Chinese swarmed all over them, the artillery had to be called off. They were only able to hover over them . . . helpless. It was a bitter pill.

Hartell and Valdez flew as many as twelve hours during the day, and spent spare time checking the evacuation tents hoping for some news of their outfit. On the morning of February 14 they were flying north of Wonju, when Hartell noticed something that seemed curious—a heavy tree line on a sand beach and a heavy growth of trees in a river bed. Only they weren't trees, he quickly realized—but thousands of men and pack animals, moving down all the trails from the north to an assembly point. There were two or three divisions of Chinese gathering for an assault on the Wonju-Yogu main supply route.

Lee grabbed his map and flashed a quick alert call. The G3 sounded dubious, but finally Hartell's excitement got some action. One round of white phosphorus was fired!

Hartell screamed into the microphone: "Drop 400! Fire for effect! Request battalion continuous fire. Request give me everything, there's thousands of 'em!"

A voice came on the air. "Let's watch our ammo expenditures."

This was too much for Pilot Valdez, and he blew up. Grabbing the mike he gave out the general's call sign. Another voice cut in. "Give that plane all the fire power he wants—division artillery at your disposal—fighter jets on the way!"

Battalion after battalion opened up, firing on the data Hartell yelled into his microphone. Enemy ran in all directions. Finally, after three hours, what was later famous as the "Wonju Shoot" came to an end. The flight report sheets credit Hartell and Valdez for having "fired" artillery rounds which caused nearly 3,500 casualties in the two enemy divisions.

Hartell had obtained some measure of revenge for the battered 15th Field Artillery.

During the weeks and months that followed, Lee flew more than 200 aerial missions. In the first month alone he logged more than 160 hours in the air, and by June 13, when he was relieved from aerial observation, he had earned the Air Medal with six oak-leaf Clusters.

He had a chance to go home. But then an FO up front was killed, and Baker Company of the 9th Infantry—Smiley Wallace's old outfit—needed help. Lee Hartell responded; he'd take the job.

Lee re-joined Baker Company, now under Captain Ed Krzyzowski,[1] on the night of August 26 near Kobansan-ni. That evening the company was ordered to occupy Hill 700, out in front of the main line of resistance.

They moved in—and the enemy moved out. Hartell went about his business like the old pro that he was by now. He started adjusting artillery fire on the retreating enemy. Then he adjusted in defensive fire to cover the likely approaches of attack.

The Chinese counterattacked at four in the morning. The first warning was an attack on the company's perimeter from the rear. Almost at the same instant an attack came on the company's right flank. Within a few minutes the enemy was trying to crash the perimeter on all sides.

Squatting on the exposed knoll in the immediate area of one of the attacks, Hartell used a soundpowered phone to

[1] Captain Edward C. Krzyzowski, commanding officer of Company B, 9th Infantry at the time of Lieutenant Hartell's action, himself earned the posthumous award of a Medal of Honor by dint of his valorous actions several days later from August 31 through September 3, 1951.

maintain contact with Lieutenant Joe Burkett at the Baker
Company Command Post.

Burkett called for artillery flares, and Hartell quickly got
them adjusted for him. Burkett then asked for defensive fire
and Hartell told him it was already on the way. Within a few
short moments shells were falling where they were needed.

Out on the slope of Bloody Ridge a large enemy force
came charging up the hill to within ten yards of Hartell's
position. Lee was wounded in the hand, but kept calling fire
instructions back to the FDC, maneuvering the artillery fire
so that a wall of withering high explosive ringed the company's front and left flank, which were most seriously threatened. For a moment the enemy dispersed and fell back; but
they stormed up in a few minutes, overran the outpost, and
then closed in on the spot where Hartell was standing. A
bullet crashed into his chest, and at 6:30 a.m. Hartell's phone
went dead.

SEVENTEEN

❯❯❯ ❯❯ ❯❯ ❰❰ ❰❰ ❰❰

BAYONET ATTACK
Lewis L. Millett

❯❯❯ ❯❯ ❯❯ ❰❰ ❰❰ ❰❰

EASY Company of the 27th (Wolfhound) Infantry Regiment waited curiously for the time when battle would reveal to them the abilities of their new commanding officer. Captain Lewis L. Millett had come into his assignment with his eyes wide open—he knew it was going to take a lot of doing to convince the men that anyone could replace their old C.O.

Even the greenest replacements in the company knew of Dusty Desiderio's fight on the Chongchon during the terror-filled night of November 27, 1950, when only Easy Company stood between screaming Chinese Communist assault troops and the headquarters of a U.S. task force that was operating considerably in front of the main battle line in North Korea. The company had been encircled, and had endured a night of bone-jarring artillery and searing machine gun and rifle fire. Its tanks had panicked and the drivers wanted to run—but Desiderio had pounded on the armored hulls with his rifle butt and bare fists and bullied them back into firing positions.

He was seriously wounded by the fragments of an exploding shell, but gave no thought to himself as he hobbled from man to man, leading the fight against the intruders with every ounce of his fast-ebbing energy. The Chinese hurled maddened attacks against the Company, and when it seemed that they must succeed by sheer weight of numbers and superior firepower, the men heard Desiderio crying above the sounds of battle, "Hold until daylight and we've got it made; hold until dawn!"

The tempo of the fight increased; the Reds surged into the positions of the spent and weary company. Desiderio was in the forefront of the fight, firing his rifle until he ran out of ammunition; then he fired an abandoned carbine until its ammunition, too, was gone, at which point he hurled it at the enemy, and drew his pistol.

Suddenly a burp gun cut loose and Desiderio crumpled to the ground. Instantly several men dashed out to drag him to cover—but it was too late.

The Easy Company soldiers grimly leveled their weapons and blazed away at the enemy as word of the captain's death made the rounds. The perimeter spit death into the shadows and held the enemy at bay until it was light enough for the big guns of the task force to swing into action. They had obeyed Dusty Desiderio's final command and had held until the dawn.

For its gallant fight, Easy Company was awarded a Distinguished Unit Citation. For Desiderio there was the posthumous award of the Medal of Honor, and the soldiers of Easy Company solemnly told each other, "There'll never be another one like him."

Against this background, Lew Millett arrived on the scene to take command. Millett wasn't a complete stranger to the Wolfhounds of Easy Company. They had seen him around as a forward observer for the artillery battalion that had fired in their support—now he had come to take Dusty Desiderio's place.

They had to admit he was an imposing military figure—six feet tall, with the build of an athlete, and straight as a birch. His long stride set a rough pace on the route march.

The shapeless green field cap hid short-cropped white-blond hair—but nothing under the sun could hide his flaming red mustache, his pride and joy.

Millett was also proud of his tough physical condition, and he tried to transmit this pride to his men. He would pause during a march and point to a hill a half a mile high.

"We're going up there at a full run," he would tell them. "And we'll come down the same way! Let's go!"

Driven by this dynamo who seemed never to move except "on the double," the company tumbled, slipped, and slid over the treacherous ice-crusted hills of Korea, until they eventually mastered the knack of running down hill full-tilt like a pack of mountain goats.

Millett strove to make his men more conscious of two weapons. He urged them to carry grenades at all times; and he especially preached to his infantrymen the gospel of the bayonet.

He was shocked to learn how few of his men still carried bayonets. When he called for a show-down inspection in his entire outfit, he didn't find enough bayonets to equip a platoon. He requisitioned, scrounged, and horse-traded, until by January, he had enough to go around.

The other companies in the battalion heard and laughed openly. Even his own battalion commander ventured a comment that Millett was just wasting his time.

But the tall New Englander stubbornly devoted a few hours every day to teaching his men a simplified drill, one that involved only the basic strokes used in close combat fighting.

His regiment, in the meanwhile, had withdrawn with its division to Osan and then back to Pyongtaek, as the Reds exerted tremendous pressure and made little secret of the fact that they hoped soon to drive the Americans into the sea. Then the Eighth Army stiffened and could be pushed back no more. The Reds had come as close as they ever would to duplicating the perilous conditions of July and August, 1950, when the United Nations position consisted of the Pusan perimeter.

All through Eighth Army the word "attack" was in the air. Divisions adjusted their boundaries and readied themselves for the push.

In Easy Company of the 27th Infantry Regiment, Lew Millett admitted to himself that he was pleased with the way his men had taken to the bayonet. It was not uncommon for Easy Company to practice its bayonet drill during a break in a march. Then came the day when the new company commander told his men they looked good and they were ready.

"From now on," he said, "bayonets will be fixed whenever Easy Company attacks. And," he promised, "you're going to use them."

By this time the company had become aware of the fact that Millett was not a run-of-the-mill officer. They heard stories about his colorful past, they watched him go through his paces, and they sensed something of the air of destiny that surrounded him.

His fellow graduates of the class of 1940 at Dartmouth, Massachusetts, High School had nominated him in the year book for a likely career as a "soldier of fortune." That summer Lew enlisted in the Army Air Corps; but at that time President Roosevelt had just announced his policy of "all aid short of war," and Millett wanted to make sure that the war wasn't going to be fought without him. He therefore headed for a Canadian Army recruiting depot.

"You're from—?" he was asked.

"Massachusetts."

"Delightful place, Ontario," the recruiter murmured as he made out Millett's papers.

Lew Millett became a tanker with the 8th Princess Louise

Regiment. He was taken out of this outfit for special radar training and shipped to England in time to get in on some of the excitement of the Battle of Britain.

Pearl Harbor and the invasion of the Philippines brought America into the war, and by early 1942 Millett wanted to get back into a U.S. outfit. He turned himself in at the Embassy in London and was told to await orders. While he was waiting, Millett received permission to attend the British Army Commando School—and came through the course with flying colors. He was then ordered to join the 1st Armored Division of the United States Army.

He joined the "Old Ironsides" division in Northern Ireland —a fully qualified tank jockey, a radar expert, and a graduate of the Commandos. After basic training therefore, he was assigned to the 27th Armored Field Artillery Battalion as a driver.

Soon his division was involved in the North African campaign. In Tunisia Millett acquired the first of his many combat decorations, when he earned the Silver Star for fearlessly driving two half-tracks loaded with ammunition out of haystack camouflage that had been set afire by enemy shellfire.

At bloody Kasserine Pass he shot down a Messerschmitt 109 with a caliber .50 machine gun on a truck mount, and was thereupon advanced to the rank of private first class. At Salerno he earned a second stripe, and added a third at Cassino. By this time he was an artillery forward observer, manning a front-line post with the infantry to spot targets and adjust fire for his outfit's guns.

He was taken off the line south of Bologna in November, 1944, and ordered to report to General Mark Clark, commander of the Fifth Army. Clark grinned at Millett's serious expression—and pinned the shiny gold bars of a second lieutenant to his field jacket.

Lieutenant Millett then immediately hurried back to the

front. During a battle south of Leghorn the Germans unleashed a massive attack that seemed certain to overrun the U.S. infantry—so Millett called artillery fire down on his own observation post to chase the Jerries back.

He returned home to New England after World War II and for three years attended Bates College. Three years of college served mainly to convince him he was cut out to be a soldier.

His request for active duty was approved in Washington, and he was ordered to the 25th Infantry Division stationed in peacetime garrison in Japan. He was assigned by Division Artillery to the 8th Field Artillery, the support battalion of the 27th Infantry.

The peaceful routine of garrison life was shattered by the warfare in Korea and soon the 25th Division was ordered into the fight.

Rugged and unhappy days were ahead for the U.S. forces, who were initially overwhelmed by superior enemy manpower and firepower. The artillery gun positions were the enemy's favorite targets for after dark infiltration. Nerves grew ragged as artillery redlegs manned their guns all day, then had to fight to keep them at night. Millett organized a 50-man volunteer security platoon of artillery-men to patrol the perimeters at night.

Brigadier General George B. Barth, artillery commander of the division, later remarked, "I am convinced Millett does not know what it means to be afraid. I know of no other man in whose behalf I can make such an unequivocal statement."

On the afternoon of November 27, 1950, Millett was serving as FO for Easy Company when the Chinese uncorked the attack in which Dusty Desiderio was mortally wounded. Toward twilight Millett's observation post came under fire of enemy mortar gunners. Millett watched fascinated as a shell burst fifteen feet from him.

"I knew I was going to get it," he explained later, "but I had to watch."

Two fellow FO's were killed. Millett's leg was ripped by flying steel, and he was ordered out to an aid station. On the way he passed Desiderio, who told him about the desperate fight being waged by Easy Company. Millett let the medics go to work on his leg, but before he passed out from the pain he had an argument with a medic who wanted to take his rifle from him. When he came to he was in an ambulance convoy—and still clutching the M-1.

The convoy didn't get very far before it was jumped by the Reds, and Millett was glad he had a weapon. He fought clear of the ambush and led a group of survivors to a perimeter held by Lieutenant Colonel Gordon E. Murch and his 2d Battalion of the 27th Infantry.

Millett's leg needed time to heal, and he wasn't strong enough to serve as an FO. He was therefore assigned as an aerial observer with Captain Jim Lawrence of the division air section.

Flying a spotting mission one day, the pair saw an F-51 crash in a rice paddy far behind enemy lines. From aloft they could see enemy foot troops start to move in on the pilot. Lawrence streaked in over the wreckage and Millett yelled that the pilot was on the ground. They looked around the sky and saw that the flier's squadron had vanished.

"Put 'er down, Jim," Millett yelled to his pilot. Lawrence nodded and set the light plane down on a road that ran close by the rice paddy. Millett jumped out and introduced himself to Captain John Davis of the 27th South African Fighter Squadron.

Millett guided the dazed pilot toward the L-19 and told Lawrence, "Better get him out of here."

Lawrence looked quizzically at Millett's stiff leg.

"Don't worry, I'll wait for you!"

The small plane buzzed off and Millett cradled a carbine in his arms as he sat back to wait. Soon it would be dark—and he knew Lawrence had to get back before dark or not at all. The better part of an hour passed and then he heard shouted orders and a crackle of small arms fire coming from the far side of the rice paddy. The Reds were closing in—fast.

Dusk was beginning to settle over the hills that ringed the rice fields, and Millett started to think about clearing out. Then he heard the sweet sounds of the L-19's single engine being pushed to the limit by Jim Lawrence. Lawrence skillfully dropped his plane on to the road, Millett scrambled aboard, and the small ship wheeled around and took off into the night just as a Red patrol penetrated the outer edges of the rice paddy.

But this wasn't the kind of combat action Lew Millett wanted.

The man he went to with his problem was Colonel Murch, who knew Millett's record of occupation duty in Japan and as Forward Observer for the 2d Battalion in Korea. He liked Millett, but shook his head when Millett mentioned a transfer to his outfit.

"There's nothing here at headquarters," he explained. "The only thing I could offer you would be one of the line companies."

Millett smiled happily.

"I'll take Easy Company, sir."

But it wasn't quite that simple. First there was Millett's own battalion commander to consult, and this gentleman made no secret of the fact that he considered Millett completely crazy. Nonetheless, he arranged for Millett to put his request before Brigadier General George B. Barth, the Artillery Commander. If the Old Man approved, the project would have his blessing, he said.

To Barth—a one-time infantryman—it was like losing one

of his family. But he listened until Millett finished making his request, then extended his hand. "Congratulations, Captain Millett. Good luck to you—and Easy Company!"

And that's how Lew Millett swapped his crossed artillery cannon for infantry muskets.

Operation Punch was launched by Eighth Army in the early hours of February, 1951. Lew Millett was at last leading Easy Company in the attack. The company was spearheading north atop the mud-spattered Pershing tanks of the 64th Tank Battalion.

They had been moving steadily, and without opposition through all the morning, but after midday the column drew fire from the heights which lay ahead of them. Easy Company got its orders from battalion: *Dismount, form as skirmishers, attack!*

Millett got his platoon leaders together and indicated how they would attack the hill.

"Pass the word along to fix bayonets," he ordered. "Move out in three minutes. Keep your eye on me."

The platoons wheeled into position and moved up the slope. It was a beautifully executed maneuver—but after storming the hill, Easy Company found empty holes, abandoned packs, and weapons. The enemy had not stayed to fight.

Operation Punch continued to roll north.

On February 5, Easy Company was moving through a frozen rice paddy, when suddenly its 1st Platoon was pinned down as it moved in against a low, plateau-like ridge. Automatic weapons from the hill forced tanks and troops off the road, but to Millett it didn't appear that much of a scrap was at hand.

The Chinese held two strong points on twin peaks straddling the road. As the lead element of Easy approached a draw which would have afforded some cover, all hell broke loose.

"Second Platoon!" Millett hollered. "Fix bayonets—move in on the left flank of the 1st."

Then he ordered the 3d Platoon to support the attack with rifle, BAR, and machine gun fire. They had drawn in-coming artillery by this time, but Millett abandoned his fox hole command post, shouting, "C'mon with me!"

He dashed for a defilade position at the base of the hill and paused there for two minutes, while the 2d Platoon formed to the left of the 1st.

The Captain led the two-platoon attacking force.

"We'll get 'em with the bayonet! Let's go!" he yelled, as he started out.

Now that the Americans had left the "protection" at the base of the hill the enemy could bring his fire to bear. But the men had picked up Millett's yell, and they surged up the hill after the Captain.

The 1st Platoon, which had followed Millett to the base of the hill, had taken casualties as it stormed across an open paddy in full view of Red marksmen. Now it found its upward climb aided by a bulging rock formation on the ridge-line.

The 2d Platoon, which had moved into the base easily, now found itself a target of enemy gunners, entrenched on a high ridge 150 yards away in Fox Company's area.

To the rear, on a hill, the 3d Platoon still was laying down covering fire, but they were sweating. Having lost sight of the line of Easy Company riflemen, they were afraid that their bullets might be striking too close to their buddies.

As though to reassure them—and tell them it was okay to lift their fire—Captain Millett suddenly appeared on the sky-line, rifle in one hand, waving with the other, calling his men forward. Even as he did so, Chinese Communist Force soldiers could be seen streaming out of fox holes, skittering down the reverse slope helter-skelter. Some bolted toward the right flank, to the enemy position in Fox Company's front. Easy's two assault platoons followed, bayonets flashing.

Up on a hillside to the rear, observers with the battalion command post gasped as they watched the audacity of Millett's attack. Colonel Murch later congratulated the captain and headquarters prepared a recommendation that the Distinguished Service Cross, the nation's second highest military decoration, be awarded to Captain Lewis Millett for his bold bayonet attack against the heavily entrenched foe.

Easy Company reached the approaches to Hill 180 about noon two days later. This hill—later to be known as Bayonet Hill—was actually one of a series of three knobs overlooking the I Corps route of march.

With his 3d Platoon in reserve, Millett moved up with the rest of the company, anticipating little or no action. He came abreast of the ridge fully intending to bypass it completely, since he was satisfied that the Chinese had once again pulled out.

Back in the 3d Platoon—dug in on top of a hill to the rear and right of the company—Private Victor Cozares scanned the ridge. There was something he didn't like about it—but he didn't know what it was. He lay there with the others in the platoon, ready to deliver covering fire should the company meet with any opposition. Cozares kept his eyes glued to his binoculars, scanning the ridge as Millett's party came abreast of it.

Suddenly he realized what was troubling him—there was too much foliage for the crest of an otherwise barren hill. He had to be sure. So he checked with the others in the platoon, and they all peered anxiously at the point now under suspicion. They called for the radioman to stand by to alert Captain

Millett, when suddenly an enemy soldier showed himself on the ridgeline. Cozares hissed at the men near him to hold fire, but a nervous soldier fired wildly, and the enemy soldier disappeared.

Now the enemy knew his ruse had been detected—but he still held good cards. Part of Easy Company was now directly under his guns.

Lieutenant John T. Lammond radioed Millett and briefed him. Millett ordered Lammond to keep the 3d Platoon where it was, in position to provide hill-to-hill covering fire. He got his tanks off the road and told them to singe the hill up to the halfway mark until he told them to stop.

From here on, Millett told himself, it was all in the timing. He consulted his watch and gave himself ten minutes to get his attack underway.

Leaping aboard one of the tanks, he swung a .50 caliber machine gun right on the target he wanted covered and cut loose a long burst.

"Keep it going there!" he told the gunner as he dropped off the tank and moved on.

Quickly he wheeled and dashed out to the 1st Platoon which was in position behind a dike-like defilade on the roadside. He called to platoon leader Lieutenant Raimund Schulz to get the platoon ready to move up.

By this time the enemy had directed heavy fire toward Easy's attacking forces. Seventy-five yards away was a ditch that offered some protection—but the Reds were covering the field too thoroughly to take advantage of it. It was evident the 1st Platoon couldn't stay where they were. They were taking casualties at an alarming rate. First the light machine gun went dead—ruptured cartridge. Then the center of the platoon's line became silent, and Millett saw his attack crumbling away before it was even launched.

He sized up the situation, then scrambled out of his own

position, and plunged into the 1st Platoon's thin, wavering line.

Spotting Sergeant First Class Floyd E. Cockrell, Millett yelled, "Get ready to move out! We're going up the hill! Fix bayonets! Charge! Everyone goes with me!"

He gestured with his own rifle and plunged out across the open field, hurdling the small rises and avoiding the furrows, miraculously never losing his feet. Cockrell and thirteen men followed. They hadn't left the dike a minute too soon. Enemy rifle and machine gun fire from Hill 180 suddenly zeroed-in on the spot they'd evacuated, and those who hadn't followed the captain immediately were cut down left and right as they spilled out in a vain attempt to catch up with Millett's group.

The base of the hill protected them from Red gunfire and artillery, and flinging himself against the slope, Millett paused there to give Schulz, Cockrell, and the rest of the men a chance to catch up.

The lowest of the three knobs was directly over them, part of its rim rounded off to form a conventional Korean burial mound. The center knob and the last rise were some twenty yards higher.

Millett started up the first knob. As he reached the skyline, he spotted an enemy machine gun to his left on a ridge of somewhat higher elevation. Standing erect on the skyline he bellowed for an automatic rifle. Ray Velarde, one of Easy's BARmen raced up, and the Captain pointed out several key targets.

Private Jim Chung, one of Easy's ROK's, pointed to a position less than ten yards from Millett where eight enemy were squatting in their foxholes.

"Go ahead, Chung," Millett yelled, as he swung his M-1 in the direction indicated by the South Korean soldier. Millett got two, Chung the others in a quick tattoo of fire. Then

Millett uncorked the pins from a couple of grenades and heaved them in for good measure.

Millett got back to his radio and ordered Lammond to bring the 3d Platoon off its hill to join in the attack. Lammond's men responded quickly. They hadn't realized just how slippery the terrain to their front was—it was, in fact, a tremendous sheet of ice, and they came slithering down mostly on their rumps, somehow managing to cling to their weapons. Despite a withering hail of enemy fire, it took only five minutes until Lammond and Sergeant Donald Brockmeier had the platoon assembled on the left flank of the 1st Platoon at the base of Hill 180.

The company commander met the platoon as it moved into position. He told Lammond: "Attack straight up the hill!" Before the words were out of his mouth, part of the platoon under Sergeant Brockmeier had already started its assault, hoping to circle behind the enemy positions in the heights.

The Reds seemed to sense that this attacking force meant to dig them out, and not one enemy soldier made a move to surrender during the bloodletting that followed.

From the saddle that Jim Chung had raked with automatic rifle fire, two grenades came sailing down. Millett, out in front of the others, ducked away and continued to move straight up. More grenades came—in clusters. Millett had to perform a dance to keep from being splattered.

As he moved back and forth, he came to within fifteen feet of a Red buffalo gun—normally an antitank weapon. It was strictly antipersonnel now, firing point-blank at one of Millett's soldiers who dodged the five rounds aimed at him. Each shell whistled by Millett's ear, but he never even noticed, he was so intent on trying to locate the tier of fox holes which hid the defenders from his view.

His own men, who were in a sort of gully, couldn't see

him any longer, and grenades came at him from both sides. Twenty yards away one of his sergeants saw what was happening, but he was unable to get contact with the men in the gully to tell them that their grenades were endangering their own captain.

A cluster of grenades came from the Reds. Millett went into his dancing and dodging act again. Eight detonations nicked the terrain around him—then a ninth exploded behind him and some of its steel found a target in his back and legs. He could feel the blood coursing down his back, drenching his shirt and jacket.

Abandoning his plan for a straight-up assault, he circled to his right, passing by a series of empty fox holes as he moved. Suddenly he was looking the buffalo gun right in the teeth as he rounded the ridge. It was the first time he realized it was there, although its fire had whistled by his ear a few minutes earlier.

"Let's go!" he screamed. "Use grenades and cold steel! Kill 'em with the bayonet!" As the men hesitated, for an instant, he cursed them bitterly, and howling unprintable epithets— some of them in Chinese—he raced alone into the gun position. Stunned at first by his display of temper the men took up his cry as they followed.

But he was yards ahead of them. He tossed three hand grenades rapidly, and then, all alone, he rushed the V-shaped gun position, bayonet gleaming in the glare of ice and sun.

He attacked the inner right wing of the V, and with a savage thrust jammed the bayonet into the enemy soldier's face. He had to fire a round to get the rifle free—but nothing could have stopped him. The Red soldier at the apex of the V had been stunned by the grenade concussion, but now he reached for a grenade. Before he could turn it loose, Millett was at him like a wildcat, driving his bayonet into his throat, ripping him open. The third man—at the left wing of the

V—brought his rifle to bear, but too late. Millett slashed his chest with the bayonet. While Millett was finishing off the third man in the gun emplacement, his men entered headlong into a cold-steel charge against the Chinese who came up out of their holes to meet them. Urged on by their captain, who waved his rifle aloft as he vaulted out of the gun emplacement, Easy Company charged, bellowing and screaming, firing from the hip, ripping with the bayonet—until the ridge was cleared of the enemy.

It was later determined that there had been 200 enemy troops on the hill when the fight began. Forty-seven of them sprawled dead—18 killed by bayonets in the first company-strength bayonet charge since the first World War.

A U.S. army observer, Brigadier General S. L. A. Marshall, former Historian of the ETO, termed Millett's action the "greatest bayonet attack by U.S. soldiers since Cold Harbor in the Civil War."

>>> >>> >>> <<< <<< <<<

FIGHT UP THE RIDGE

Cornelius H. Charlton

>>> >>> >>> <<< <<< <<<

TEN THOUSAND miles separate the Governor's Island ferry named *Sergeant Cornelius H. Charlton* from the rocky peak that was known to soldiers of the now non-existent 24th Infantry Regiment as Charlton Hill. Casual passengers, idly reading the name lettered on the boat's wheelhouse, may perhaps wonder why the boat was named for Sergeant Charlton. Who was he? A hero of some forgotten battle? The charge up San Juan Hill? The Meuse-Argonne? Kwajalein? The Huertgen? It is quite likely that none of them has ever heard of Charlton Hill.

Perhaps they know that it was in Korea—but how could they know how it looked that morning of the second day of June, 1951? How can they possibly conjure up an adequate picture of the craggy, razorback ridges flooded with sunlight —beautiful, rugged, and at the same time ominous and malevolent.

"In the hours before dawn," someone recalled later on, "it looked like a medieval castle."

The map called it Hill 543.

In the darkness of the night that preceded the final attack, platoon sergeant Charlton pulled his blanket around him and leaned back against the stump of a tree. Corporal Willie Hayes looked at him. "Tomorrow?" Charlton nodded. It would be a day for some real soldiering. Not that he liked the dirty business, but he was a regular.

He was, in fact, working on his second hitch in the army. He'd enlisted first at the age of 17. He'd have joined up sooner, but his mother had firmly refused to allow him to enlist at 15.

The eighth and biggest of the Charlton's 17 children, "Connie" Charlton grew to young manhood in a series of West Virginia coal mining towns where his father worked through the days of depression and well into World War II. Then, in 1944, the Charltons moved north to New York City.

With six of their children, Esther and Van Charlton moved into a small apartment building, where Van worked as a superintendent. Connie enrolled at James Monroe High School, but he was already pestering his mother to let him join the army.

"He was always a good kid," a neighbor recalled some years later. "But his heart was set on being a soldier, and when he was 17 his mother gave him the okay to join up."

After basic training, Connie went to Germany. He re-enlisted while he was in Germany, because he knew he would be going home on leave and he didn't want anyone talking him out of staying in the army. After a leave at home, he was sent to Aberdeen Proving Grounds in Maryland, and then, early in 1950, he was ordered to the Far East Command.

For Connie Charlton that meant Okinawa, at first; when war flared in Korea his engineer outfit was shipped there, and during that autumn in the war zone Charlton became sergeant major of his battalion. It was a position that called for a master sergeant, but even though Connie didn't have the zebra stripes, his battalion C.O. said he was the man for the job and that the "rockers" for his stripes would soon be forthcoming.

But as the autumn turned to winter, Connie began to lose

interest in a job that kept him chained to an outfit destined to spend the war many miles behind the front lines, and he requested a transfer.

In March of 1951, the 24th Infantry Regiment, under the command of Colonel Henry Chesnutt Britt, a battle-experienced West Pointer from Tifton, Georgia, was defending a sector on "Line Lincoln" a dozen or so miles northeast of Seoul. It was to this regiment that Charlton asked to be assigned. Upon reaching regimental headquarters, he was ordered to report to Captain Gordon E. Gullikson of Beloit, Wisconsin, commander of Company G.

All of the other replacements who reached Gullikson that day were privates fresh off the "banana boat"—from Japan or the States. The captain was therefore surprised to see this big, confident sergeant standing among them.

That night, at the battalion command post, he managed to find out a little more about his new noncom. He learned of Charlton's prior service with the engineers.

"Why'd they send him here? Trouble maker?" he asked.

"Nope—he's supposed to be a fine soldier. Guess he just wants to fight."

In the weeks that followed Charlton's arrival at Gullikson's command post, the regiment saw only limited action. Nonetheless, the commander of Company G had observed enough; and when the platoon sergeant of the 3d Platoon was rotated home, he gave the job to Charlton.

A big attack was launched May 22, 1951, as the entire Eighth Army began to surge toward the north. During the first week of the offensive, Charlton's battalion led the regiment's assault. Barring the battalion's advance was Hill 438, from whose heights the Reds were pouring mortar fire into the U.S. lines. Charlton roused his platoon and led them in an assault which went straight to the top of the hill, where they learned that the Reds had fled, leaving their dead and wounded behind.

The advance was resumed. But on the next day, the tenth of the offensive, the Chinese finally decided to make their stand. The choice of terrain was theirs, and they made the most of it by entrenching themselves in a series of razorback ridges dominated by Hills 1147 and 543.

The 1st Battalion was in reserve. The 2d and 3d Battalions of Britt's regiment swarmed over Hill 1147 and engulfed the enemy—then got their noses bloodied at Hill 543.

With his company tactically deployed in what is described as a "blocking position," Connie Charlton decided he didn't like the looks of the nearby woods, moved into them swiftly, and captured 5 Chinese who were hiding out with a brand-new truck.

Nightfall brought word to Gullikson that the 3d Battalion had been unable to fight its way to the top of 543. It was his turn to try, and in the morning Charlton's platoon made its way up the path the 3d Battalion had taken. Charlton and his platoon leader decided to split their force. Each would take half of the men; one group would provide covering fire, while the other advanced into the gunfire coming from two well-placed enemy machine guns.

The lieutenant was the first to fall; Charlton, who had several days earlier been recommended for a battlefield commission, took over. He pulled the men together and moved out in front of them to spearhead the assault. Machine gun fire and hand grenades halted them, and it looked as if there were no way to go but back.

"All right! All right!" Charlton then called out, "Let's keep going!"

"The platoon was pinned down by intense fire," Captain Gullikson reported, "but three or four men followed Sergeant

Charlton as he made a frontal attack on the first of the two enemy positions that were causing all the trouble."

A concussion grenade landed almost at Charlton's feet, and the blast knocked him down. He picked himself up and threw a grenade that landed short of the mark; so he moved nearer and tossed another grenade. This one fell into the enemy hole, and when the survivors charged out, Charlton met them and finished them off.

Leaping into the hole that held the now silent machine gun, the sergeant looked around and saw that only Willie Hayes and three others were still with him.

"Be right back!" he hollered to Hayes, and sprinted down the hill, regrouped the remainder of the platoon, and led them back up toward the crest of Hill 543.

The last machine gun nest was ahead of them now, half-hidden in a tower-like rock formation.

With Charlton leading the way, the platoon started to scramble up the rocks. The Chinese showered them with grenades, and the blasts sent most of the men crashing down the ridge. Charlton was hit and had a hole torn in his chest.

He shook off those who wanted to help him, got his wounded readied for evacuation, and again regrouped the surviving members of his platoon for a final all out effort. Again they began the climb—and this time they waded through the hail of fire to reach the top.

With rifles and carbines chattering, they fought over the top of the hill and confronted the second machine gun. Connie Charlton yelled orders to his men, and flung himself at the gun emplacement. Another grenade struck him, wounding him mortally, but his rifle took its toll and the enemy machine gun went out of action.

The platoon surged over the crest and joined the rest of the company in driving the Reds off Hill 543. A vicious Chinese counterattack struck after dark, and at midnight the hill had to be abandoned.

But Charlton and his men had broken the enemy's back in this vital spot. When another unit arrived the next day, it was able to walk up Charlton Hill without encountering a living enemy soldier. On its blood-splattered slopes were the bodies of more than 600 Chinese soldiers.

Abraham Lincoln's birthday in 1952 was chosen as the day for President Harry S. Truman to make the award of Connie's Medal of Honor to Van and Esther Charlton. Several weeks later it was announced that the U.S. Army Ferryboat No. 84 would become the *Sergeant Cornelius H. Charlton*.

There was a solemn ceremony in the shadow of the old San Juan Dock on Governor's Island. When it was General Willis D. Crittenberger's turn to speak to Van Charlton, he said, gently, that "the foundations of democracy are built upon the bedrock of sacrifice."

These were words for the Charltons to cherish, just as they cherish the letter that they received from Colonel Britt, the Georgia officer who commanded the regiment in which Connie Charlton fought. "I feel honored," he wrote, "to have known a soldier like your boy. He was one of the best."

❯❯❯ ❯❯❯ ❯❯❯ ❮❮❮ ❮❮❮ ❮❮❮

GOOD LITTLE MAN

Lloyd L. Burke

❯❯❯ ❯❯❯ ❯❯❯ ❮❮❮ ❮❮❮ ❮❮❮

O N THE 25th day of Operation Commando, the battered 2d Battalion, 5th Cavalry Regiment, 1st Cavalry Division, found itself stymied at the approaches of Hill 200. This was a key spot, the kind of land military men sometimes call a "bargaining piece of terrain." Its heights commanded a view of the Imjin River and the surrounding landscape, and its capture would provide the division with important high ground in the outpost line of resistance.

For several days the dismounted troopers of the cavalry division had been hurling themselves against the heavily fortified hilltop, but the Red defenders had chosen to stand and slug it out.

The enemy fought back from behind his rock-reinforced bunkers and trenches. The 2d Battalion had a precarious toe-hold on a ridge about 30 feet wide, some 200 feet below the peak, with Company G nearest the enemy. Company G by this time, however, consisted of only 35 men, and the rest of the battalion was proportionately understrength.

The men in Company G stirred themselves and looked uneasily up at the hill still partially obscured in shadows. Soon it would be time . . .

While the foot soldiers clinging to the sides of 200 pondered their situation, a *chogi* party from the regimental ammunition point made its way across the floor of the 800-yard wide valley to the base of the hill.

Leading the ammunition bearers was First Lieutenant Lloyd Leslie Burke, the executive officer of Company G. Burke was the regiment's "old man" from the point of view of length of service in Korea. His replacement was expected momentarily, so he had been ordered out of combat and instructed to push supplies up toward the front. He regarded this assignment as a license to free lance his talents around.

He had already earned a DSC and Silver Star in thirteen months of combat in Korea, and seven or eight times during the progress of "Operation Commando," when he learned that a line company was bogged down or short of officers, Burke turned over the supply job to his second in command, grabbed a rifle, and took off for where the fighting was the heaviest.

"Scooter" Burke looks like anything but a rugged fighting man. Physically, it appears that nature has short changed him. He's on the runty side, and his eyeglasses give him an owlish look, more like a clerk's than a soldier's.

Back in Stuttgart, Arkansas, High School, he dreamed of excelling in sports. He tried out for every team, but never made the grade. He was too light for football, too small for basketball, not powerful enough for baseball. He became a drummer in the school band, and was so good that he won the State Drum Solo championship one year. His friends claim he could easily have become a drummer in a name band—and for quite a while that was his main ambition in life.

Burke entered Henderson State College, in Arkadelphia, Arkansas, when he was 18, to study business administration. In his freshman year, however, World War II hit its full stride, and the call went out for recruits. Two of Scooter's high school friends came down to Arkadelphia to talk things over, and the trio decided to enlist in the army. Burke served in Italy with the Engineers, was discharged in 1946, and returned to Henderson State where he resumed his interrupted business administration courses.

But somehow this didn't promise much future to him. He found what he wanted in a notice to ROTC enrollees that the school's most distinguished military graduate would be entitled to apply for a regular army commission.

This, Burke decided, was his slice of cake. He went about the business of completing his college courses and obtaining his degree. Along the way he met Virginia, who later became his wife. He was president of his fraternity, and also president of his class in his junior and senior years. Scooter had started to show his inborn qualities of leadership.

The 1942 High School Yearbook had said of Burke, "He ought to be a tin can, he rattles so. . . ." The 1950 Henderson State College Yearbook claimed he would be "a future general."

Burke finished college, was named distinguished military graduate, and was commissioned a second lieutenant of infantry in the regular army following his graduation on May 28, 1950.

With the ink on his papers hardly dry, Scooter reported to the Infantry School at Fort Benning. War flared in Korea, and toward the end of the summer Burke received his orders for the Far East Command. That meant only one destination —Korea.

He reached Korea on October 28, 1950, and one month later earned the DSC for blasting a path for his outfit through a Communist road block at Samso-ri. He was wounded for the first time on January 28, 1951—the date on which his first child, Gary Lee, was born. He was decorated again for his part in a five-day raid in August, 1951.

Thus, on October 28, 1951, he was leading his *chogi* party, lugging satchel charges, dynamite, and a flamethrower across the shell-packed valley floor toward the honeycombed defenses of Hill 200.

After he left the ammunition point, he found himself close to the battalion command post; so he put in a call to Lieutenant Colonel Richard L. Irby to let the battalion CO know he was in the area with ammunition.

"When you get up there," Irby told him in a tired voice, "see what you can do."

Burke led his group up the slope toward an outpost, where he ran into Captain Tom Giboney, the operations officer, who was running the show on the hill.

"How's it look, Tom?" asked Scooter in his soft Arkansas drawl.

Giboney shook his head and told Burke that Fox Company, woefully understrength, had jumped off in an effort to storm the top and had advanced only ten yards. Then Easy Company had tried and it, too, had been pinned down.

"The Old Man says to take it with George Company," Giboney told Burke, "and either they take it—or we've had it. There simply won't be enough men left for another attack."

The Scooter listened quietly.

"Who's gonna take 'em up that hill?" he asked.

"Sergeant Foster, the senior noncom. Officers are all gone," Giboney replied.

"I'll take 'em, Tom," Burke answered. "Not that Foster isn't a good noncom. But it's my place to take 'em up there."

Giboney didn't say anything, so Burke gave a few short orders to his carrying party and started off to find George Company—or what was left of it.

"Okay, Foster," he told the noncom. "We'll take it this time. Let's move out!"

He picked up an abandoned 57-mm. recoilless rifle, moved into the forward portion of the company's trench, and fired three rounds point-blank into the nearest enemy-held bunker. No damage was done, however, and enemy grenades continued to sail at them every time they tried advancing toward the Chinese defenses.

Burke, who was armed only with a pistol, borrowed someone's M-1 rifle, and moved into the forward portion of the trench, from which point he intently studied the enemy bunker. He noticed that the enemy grenadier exposed himself for a fraction of a second every time he came up into throwing position.

Bringing the M-1 up to his shoulder, Scooter held his breath, waited for the split-second when the grenade thrower would appear—and instantly pulled off his shot. But several seconds later, grenades were again being thrown. He didn't know if the thrower was a replacement or if he had missed the first time. Once again he took careful aim and fired, convinced he had a bead on the Chinese. He finally fired a whole clip—but the grenades kept coming. Burke was disgusted with himself; he'd always thought he had a pretty good eye.

He handed the rifle back to one of his soldiers, crouched at the edge of the trench, then catapulted into the open and dashed for the base of the enemy position some 25 yards away. He went careening into it, grateful for a low stone and dirt wall which protected him from the enemy. Hugging the wall, he could see the enemy grenades arching over his head, aimed at the trench he had just left.

Then the Chinese realized where he was and changed their tactics. They started dropping grenades from directly overhead. But Scooter wasn't caught napping. As fast as they came, he snatched them in midair and hurled them up and back into the Red trench. He handled three in this manner, then decided that sooner or later this game of give-and-take would have to go against him. So, he pulled his pistol from its holster, clicked off the safety, vaulted the low mud wall, and flung himself into the enemy trench, determined to take them by surprise.

Two Chinese soldiers looked up and started toward him. He killed them with two quick shots. The trench showed the results of his earlier efforts with the borrowed M-1: five dead Chinese. Another four or five lay dead, victims of the grenades he'd caught and tossed back into their midst.

He noticed a connecting communications trench leading to the next line of bunkers, lobbed several grenades in front of him, and cleared out the enemy force there. But he realized that most of the Reds had pulled back into a third, and more formidable, fortification. He tossed his last two grenades, then retraced his steps, intending to return to the trench where his men were waiting for him.

He was aware of the fact that his troopers were still engaged in a grenade-tossing fight with the Reds in the third bunker, and he swerved to his right to avoid getting in their line of fire. Out of the corner of his eye he spotted a Korean grave and decided that its rounded rim offered better cover. He edged over to it and started working his way around the upper part of the rim.

Concerned mainly with getting back to his men and keeping out of the line of fire, he hugged the ground and tried to move fast at the same time. Scurrying quickly over the burial mound, he was totally unprepared for the staggering sight that met his eyes as he plunged around the rim and prepared to dash for his own trench.

From the height he now occupied, his startled gaze took in the unbelievable sight of a long enemy-filled trench winding around below him and all the way up to the peak of Hill 200. The well-entrenched enemy soldiers were laughing and chattering as they dropped shells into mortar tubes and sent them whooshing off into the shattered ranks of the 2d Battalion.

At first his eyes refused to believe what they saw. But

Scooter didn't waste more than a few seconds marveling at the opportunity that lay before him.

Tearing back to George Company's trench, Burke told Sergeant Foster, "Get 'em ready to attack when I give you a signal!" He took the machine gun, the only one on the hill still in working order, its tripod, and three cans of ammunition, and ran out of the trench again.

Now he was sweating—and for good reason. What he had seen was enough to tell him this much: if the enemy sent a few heavily armed platoons down that hill, the battalion's lines would be smashed beyond repair. He had seen the enemy's strength—and he already knew the weakened condition of the 2d Battalion.

Hoping against hope that they wouldn't spot him, Scooter safely made the return trip to the top of the rim. Breathing hard, he set up the light machine gun, and slapped in the first belt. He eased himself behind the gunsights, turned the screw to keep the gun on free traverse, and spent another half-minute staring past the sights. It was a scene he knew he would never forget.

Then he pulled the bolt and leaned back on the trigger. He started spraying lead at the forward part of the trench, then moved up along the trench to knock out the mortar crew which had been tormenting his men back on the slope—and the Chinese in the bunker were so stunned by this unexpected turn of events that they did not return even a token fire.

The enemy commenced shrieking and waving their hands. Scooter peered at them, anxiously wondering why they didn't break and run. Actually, they were too stunned. Then finally it happened. A few started to run, and suddenly a mass exodus from the bunker line was under way. In their anxiety to get away from the ripping lead, they climbed over one another and poured pell-mell down the reverse slope.

Burke's machine gun jammed a couple of times and he had

to work the bolt by hand until it cleared. In one pause, as he
sweated to get the gun working, a Red soldier sighted him
and started throwing grenades. They broke all around him,
but the only damage he suffered was a cut on the back of his
left hand. He called for Foster and the others to come up
and add their rifle fire, which evidently convinced the enemy
that a full-scale attack had been mounted, and the Reds, far
outnumbering the weakened attacking company, continued to
pour out of the bunkers down the reverse slope.

Scooter still had nearly 250 rounds left in the gun. Stopping
only long enough to take off his field jacket, he wrapped the
bloody garment around the blazing-hot gun barrel, jerked the
gun from the tripod, and stalked down toward the enemy,
firing from the hip.

With Arthur Foster at his side, Burke moved relentlessly
down the bunker, spraying machine gun fire before him.
When his ammunition was gone, he tossed the machine gun
aside, pulled his empty pistol from its holster, and gripped it
tightly by the barrel to use as a club if he had to.

Someone handed him grenades. He yelled for his men to
watch out, then tossed two grenades into an opening off to one
side of the bunker. The smoke cleared. He was positive that
nothing could have survived, but he kept the men back, waiting for the dust to settle. As it did, five Chinese stumbled out,
hands up, without a mark on them!

Subsequent investigation showed that the underground corridors off the main bunker reached far back into the interior
of Hill 200 and that there were tunnels off the individual corridors, too. The Chinese had figured on staying there a long
time. The corridors, the Americans found, were jammed with
crates of newly-arrived winter clothing, boots, and supplies.

Hollering and whooping, George Company swarmed all
over Hill 200 as the Reds fled in terror. More than 200 Chinese
dead lay sprawled on the hillside at the end of the fighting.

Burke's attack force suffered only two casualties—and the key to the link-up of the 8th Army's front had been seized.

For years to come, troopers of the 5th Cavalry who were in Korea during Operation Commando will tell the story of the skinny, freckle-faced lieutenant who, fighting with pistol, M-1 rifle, grenades, and machine gun, blasted to bits three machine gun nests, and two mortar emplacements, and personally killed more than one hundred of the enemy on the high hill that overlooks the Imjin. Only the 5th Cavalry troopers won't remember it as Hill 200. They'll always call it Scooter Burke's Peak.

TWENTY

❯❯❯ ❮❮❮

OUTPOST INCIDENT

Ola L. Mize

❯❯❯ ❮❮❮

KING Company's march to the outpost wasn't a long one as the crow flies. But the infantrymen, laden with their rifles, packs, heavy weapons, and cases of ammunition, could not follow the path of the crow. Moving cautiously, because there was never any telling where enemy intruders might have set up an ambush, they made their way across the valley floor, into the humpbacked hills, around winding ridges, through thickets and dense underbrush until at last they reached the approaches to the finger-shaped hill that was their objective.

This was Outpost Harry—one of three important outposts along the 3d Division zone of action on the central front, about two miles in front of the main line of resistance. The other two were, of course, named Tom and Dick. Outpost Harry was situated on the right flank, overlooking Chorwon, hub of the old Iron Triangle.

King Company—more precisely Company K, 15th Infantry Regiment, 3d Division—took over the observation post on the afternoon of June 4, 1953. The outfit it relieved reported little or no action had taken place during the week just passed.

The 2d Platoon moved into the bunkers around the peak of the hill as the remainder of the company deployed in secondary positions on the slopes. Sergeant First Class Donovan B. Dobbs, platoon sergeant of the 2d Platoon, placed the squads and issued orders to his second in command, Sergeant Ola L. Mize, a soft-spoken Alabaman. Mize had been with the company only since Easter, but he had already earned a reputation as a first-class fighting man.

Although there was little activity at OP Harry in the week that followed, there was considerable activity at the village of Panmunjom where the drawn out "peace talks" were still in progress. On June 8, the UN and Red delegates signed the long-debated prisoner of war agreement; it seemed likely that a cease-fire might come at almost any moment.

But less than 48 hours after putting its signature to this document, the Red command launched a series of smashing thrusts against the UN line. One of the strongest of these sallies came on the night of June 10, and the brunt of the attack fell upon Outpost Harry where Company K was, ironically, spending its final night. It had been scheduled to pull back to the main line of resistance on June 11.

The first part of the attack came at 9:30 p.m., when a deafening roar of artillery fire enveloped the hill. Tons of steel and high explosives rocked the outpost. Before all communications were knocked out, Sergeant Mize, who was in a forward position, learned that one of the men at a listening post had been wounded by shell fragments. He found a medic and set off to find the wounded man.

Some enemy troops had already infiltrated the trenches, and Mize had to fight his way through them as he headed toward the listening post, oblivious to the roar of mortar and artillery fire.

Corporal Charles E. Lack saw him kill several Chinese in close range fighting as he covered the 150 yards to the wounded man's side. With the aid man's help, Mize pulled the badly-hurt soldier back to a friendly position in a bunker. Then he left the medic in charge of the casualty and turned his attention to organizing a defense in this important bunker position, which had already been knocked out of action from the pounding it had taken.

Mize saw that the place was a shambles and that only a handful of men were still alive. It was a ghastly sight. Even the living were half-buried in splintered rocks and dirt.

"How's it look out there, sergeant?" Private Allan K. England wanted to know.

"Not too good," Mize conceded. "They'll be coming in 'most any time now." He looked around as he heard the nervous voices of the Chinese closing in toward the bunker. They were in the trenches already.

"How many weapons in here still working?" he asked England.

England pointed to Mize's carbine.

"That's it," he said. All of the others were too full of dirt from the cave-ins to be used.

Mize went to the bunker door and posted himself in the shadows at the entrance—and not a moment too soon. He had scarcely taken up his position when the first of the enemy soldiers came down the trench, double-timing toward the doorway to the bunker.

He hesitated an instant, calculating a grenade's effective range, and then he tossed one into the oncoming Reds. It shook them up, and one or two didn't move further. But the rest gathered themselves together, moved in on the bunker, and were suddenly reinforced by a fresh wave of troops, who dropped over the parapet.

England, who was at Mize's shoulder, thought there were at least a hundred Chinese troops coming at them. Mize pulled his carbine off his shoulder and blazed away, using the weapon's automatic fire power to check the Reds' assault. England and another soldier, who was also without a weapon, crouched near Mize, caught the empty clips as fast as the carbine ejected them, expertly refilled them with new cartridges, and passed them back to the sergeant.

Enemy artillery continued to rock the outpost—even while the Reds were fighting in the trenches. Twice within ten minutes shells exploded so close to the bunker door that Mize was blown backwards into the rear of the position. But each time he quickly sprang to his feet again and managed to scramble back to his doorway position before the Reds could reorganize their forces for an all out assault.

At one point, several of the Reds made a rush for Mize as he was reloading. He slammed home the clip and ripped back on the operating slide with furious haste—just in time to drop one of the Chinese at his feet. The others ducked for cover.

Out of the lifeless man's hand rolled a concussion grenade. Before Mize could move out of the way of the blast, it went off with a roar and knocked him down. He was stunned, but he struggled to his feet and groped for his carbine—and not a moment too soon. He fired the clip in a long burst and the Reds fell back out of range.

By this time more than an hour and a half had passed since the beginning of the attack, and England warned Mize that they were practically out of ammunition.

"Come on," Mize told the others. "We'll head for the platoon command post."

The survivors of the bunker fight followed Mize as he sped up the trench. Corporal James J. Kelly counted the number of enemy bodies strewn around the bunker doorway—more than 40. As they pushed down the trench toward the platoon command post, they were attacked by fresh Chinese troops, and Mize, still the only one with a weapon, racked up five more enemy casualties.

They found the command post battered and out of action.

But there was ammunition there, and a few weapons. Mize passed around the carbines and rifles, and organized a barricade against which the enemy attacked time after time, only to be hurled back by the fire laid down by Mize, England, Corporal Kelly, and Sergeant James N. Holcomb. They were the only members of the platoon still in the fight.

Mize was the man who kept them going. He moved from one to the other, offering encouragement and handing out ammunition, begging them to keep up the fire. After two hours of constant attack, the enemy fire slackened off.

Mize decided not to sit tight—dawn was still three hours away. He led the others in a probing patrol to find out where the enemy was on the hill and to learn in what numbers he was there. They slipped down the trench toward the forward slope of the hill.

As they passed a bunker door, a Chinese Communist soldier stepped out and swung his burp gun on Sergeant Holcomb. Luckily, Mize was just a yard or so to the rear, and he bounded up instantly to cut the enemy soldier down.

After their probing patrol, they encountered a lieutenant with a radio set on his shoulder, staggering down the trench.

"If this thing works," Mize told the others, "we're going to give them fellas a bad time."

He called hoarsely into the set, sending out the code name for his outfit's supporting artillery. In a few moments he got an acknowledgment.

"Get this right, now," Mize said, firmly. "I need some artillery up here. You start shooting and I'll correct your fire." He described the enemy's deployment and the routes of attack that the Reds had used, and in a few moments U.S. artillery began to slam into enemy positions on the hill.

When it was nearly dawn Mize ordered the artillery to cease fire. He gathered the handful of men who were left—

England, Holcomb, and Kelly among them—and said he felt sure that a counterattack would surprise the enemy and might drive him off the hill entirely.

"At least," he added, "it's worth a try. Let's go."

Mize led them across the hill just as the first rays of dawn showed, firing rifles and carbines and tossing hand grenades before them. For nearly three hours the little band moved relentlessly against the enemy—until all opposition had been wiped out and there were no more Chinese Communists alive on the ground around Outpost Harry. All of the bunkers had been regained by eight in the morning, when a relief company started moving in.

"Well," Mize said to the eight who were left, "we might as well get started back to the battalion."

And so they limped back to the main line of resistance— all that was left of King Company after its harrowing fight in defense of the outpost.

From the other survivors the battalion commander learned the details of the incredible fight that Sergeant Ola L. Mize had waged up on Outpost Harry, how he had almost single-handedly held the strategically important outpost and personally killed more than 70 of the enemy in the savage, night-long fight.

"Well," said Mize uncomfortably, "there I was when the attack came. There just wasn't time to be scared or anything. We had to try and hold that position."

More than 36 years earlier, the 3d Division was being threatened with annihilation by a powerful German force headed for Paris. Major General Joe Dickman, who was then commander of the division, was asked by a French officer whether the 3d expected to withdraw in the face of superior forces. Dickman thereupon snapped the angry phrase that was to become the division's motto along the Marne in World War I, and at Anzio in World War II—*nous resterons là!*

At Outpost Harry, high over the Chorwon Valley in Korea, Sergeant Ola L. Mize breathed new meaning into those famous words . . . *We are staying there!*

NEAR THE end of the fourth week of fighting in Korea Sergeant George Libby of the 24th Infantry Division smashed a road block south of Taejon, where the division was fighting for its life. Libby pushed a number of wounded men on board an M-5 tractor from an artillery outfit and posted himself to ride "shotgun." The Reds poured a hail of merciless fire at the driver, and bullets splashed around him. A number of them ripped into his body, but they crashed the roadblock and got the wounded men to an aid station. By then it was too late for Libby, the first Medal of Honor man in Korea.

On the following day the division lost another soldier and gained its second Medal of Honor man with the disappearance of Major General William F. Dean. He was last seen in the outskirts of Taejon, where he exultantly told a junior officer, "I just got me a tank!" Later it was learned that he had been taken a prisoner of war; he was finally freed by the Communists in the course of operation Big Switch.

In the weeks after the 24th Division's fight at Taejon, other U.S. divisions followed the Taro Leaf to Korea. At the end —37 months later—the Eighth Army consisted of the 2d, 3d, 7th, 24th, 25th, 40th, and 45th Infantry Divisions, the 1st Cavalry Division, the 5th Regimental Combat Team, and the 187th Airborne Regimental Combat Team. Among them they produced 77 Medal of Honor men. The 2d (Indianhead) Infantry Division—the first division to reach Korea from the mainland of the United States—was foremost in the Eighth Army, with a total of 18 Medal awards. One of the soldiers who was with the 9th Infantry, first of the Indianhead regiments to land in Korea, remembers that Colonel Charles C.

Sloane, Jr. swiftly moved his command post ashore, took stock of the situation, and announced, "We've come looking for trouble!" In the space of about three weeks, mainly in the fight on the Naktong perimeter, his regiment earned five Medals of Honor.

The 77 men who earned the Medal in Korea ranged from buck private to two-star general. The youngest was eighteen, the oldest, fifty-one. Sixty of the Medal of Honor winners were enlisted men, 17 were officers. There were 19 privates, 18 corporals, and 23 in various grades of sergeant. Among the officers there were 3 second lieutenants, 8 first lieutenants, 4 captains, 1 lieutenant colonel, and 1 major general. Twenty-one Medal of Honor winners survived the conflict.

Among the privates there was Melvin L. Brown, an engineer in the 1st Cavalry Division from Mahaffey, Pennsylvania. Perched atop a 50-foot wall, he fought a swarm of North Koreans off with rifle and hand grenades. When he ran out of ammunition and had no more grenades, he killed twelve of them with a small shovel before he was overwhelmed.

During the Naktong River fight Private Luther Story, a 2d Division soldier from Americus, Georgia, broke up an enemy river crossing. He picked up an abandoned machine gun, moved it to a place that offered a good field of fire, and cut loose to kill more than 100 Reds. Later that day he attacked and destroyed a truck, full of North Korean troops, which was towing a trailer of ammunition. All of his company's officers had been hit, and when the senior noncom became a casualty, he gasped out an order for Story to take over.

The remnants of the badly battered company started to withdraw. Someone called to Story, who had posted himself facing the enemy.

"No!" he answered. "I'm staying!"

He gathered around him all the abandoned weapons he

could find, and until his last breath he fought off the North Koreans to cover the others as they scrambled to safety.

Following the Eighth Army's breakout from the perimeter, timed with the X Corps landing at Inchon on Korea's west coast, the Americans surged back to—and over—the 38th Parallel. Attacking in a heavy mist, a first lieutenant in the 1st Cavalry Division, Samuel S. Coursen, leaped unhesitatingly into a trench where one of his men was grappling with members of an enemy squad. Coursen wrenched the wounded man free, flung him to safety, and waded into the North Koreans, using his rifle like a club until he was overcome by sheer weight of numbers. Seven enemy dead were sprawled around his lifeless body when his platoon arrived on the scene.

A soldier who earned a battlefield commission, Carl H. Dodd, was a squirrel-shooting marksman from Kenvir, Kentucky, in the heart of uneasy Harlan County. Maybe that's why trouble never fazed Dodd, who, at the age of 25, was a veteran of two hitches as an enlisted man. In an attack up a savagely-defended hill, with night falling, Dodd heard one of his squad leaders order the men to take cover and return the enemy's fire.

"To blazes with that!" Lieutenant Dodd yelled at the top of his lungs. "Use marching fire and follow me! Let's go!"

His action marked the beginning of a 48-hour battle that won the vital heights of Hill 256.

The list of heroes is a long one—as long as more than a thousand days of combat in Korea, as long as one terrible night on the outpost line of resistance. Near comical-sounding Popsu-dong, a completely unfunny and bloody battle was being fought along the so-called "Kansas Line." All night the enemy attacked the U.S. 3d Division; in one of the key spots, Corporal Clair Goodblood, from Burnham, Maine, swore, "They'll take this gun over my dead body!" He kept his promise. The lines were overrun during the night; but when his battalion regained the terrain shortly after dawn, they found Goodblood slumped over the gun, surrounded by eleven empty ammunition boxes. All around his gun were piled the enemy's dead.

A private with less than seven months service, Joseph C. Rodriguez, led a 7th Division squad in an incredible attack against the enemy on a well-fortified ridge. When the others lagged, Rodriguez (who later earned a commission) went on alone, knocked out five Red machine gun emplacements, and killed 15 enemy soldiers.

In a determined enemy onslaught, two battalions attacked the Americans at Sobangsan. Fifty of them were killed by Private First Class Emory L. Bennett of Cocoa, Florida, before he succumbed to gunfire. Later his company commander said, "The Reds wanted Hill 717 at all costs. Bennett's stand stopped them in their tracks."

Ronald Rosser knew why he had come to fight. His motive stemmed from the day he had returned from his job in the Misco Mines in his home town of Crooksville, Ohio, to learn that his brother Dick had fallen in the Chinese winter offensive in 1951.

On the following day Ronald, a veteran, rejoined the Army, and shipped to Korea, where he became a corporal in the Heavy Mortar Company of the 38th Infantry, 2d Division.

As a forward observer, he carried a radio and moved with the forward elements of infantry, spotting target locations for the mortars. But one day they moved into the enemy, and Rosser knew that the time had come. He handed the radio to his buddy, Corporal Stan W. Smith, and slipped the safety off his carbine.

He charged through mortar and artillery fire, firing from the hip. Straddling a bunker, he riddled its occupants and moved ahead, only to find himself trapped by a pair of Chinese soldiers. Rosser drilled one through the head, then whirled and clubbed the other in the chest with the butt of the carbine. Then he jumped into the trench from which they had appeared, opened fire, and forced his way relentlessly down the length of the bunker. One of the Reds fled and Rosser uncorked a grenade. Another pair of Communist soldiers charged at him with bayonets fixed, but Rosser held his ground and drilled them.

Out of ammunition, the Ohio miner ran down the hill to pick up a new supply of bullets for his carbine and a shirtful of hand grenades. Then he attacked again . . . and again . . . roaming the hilltop like a terrible avenging angel.

The company to which he was attached got orders to move back to the battalion line, and Rosser at last came down the hill and took the radio back from Stan Smith. Although his wounds ached painfully, he scarcely noticed them on the march back. His expression was one of a man who had had a painful weight removed from his shoulders.

In the moments before dawn as Clifton T. Speicher and his buddies of Company F, 223d Infantry, 40th Division approached the jumping-off point for the attack on Hill 449, he remarked to Corporal Clarence Williams, "I'm going to kill a lot of them today."

He looked around at the skies that were fast turning light, and muttered, "How I hate to attack in the daylight." Then he led his men to their positions and sprinted out in the lead when the company commander gave the "Let's go!" signal.

Speicher was one of the first hit, but he kept going, vaulted into an enemy machine-gun nest, and engaged the four-man crew.

Firing his carbine from the hip he cut two of the crew

down quickly, and bayoneted the third. He wasn't fast enough to get the fourth, though, before a slug passed through his body armor and ripped into him.

He staggered out of the gun emplacement and attempted to join in the attack, but collapsed. The medics rolled him on to a litter and carried him down the hill. They were near the aid station when Speicher made a mighty effort to rise up as though to see where he was going. Then he slumped back, dead.

Nearly a month after the signing of the cease-fire at Panmunjom, repatriated U.S. soldiers were being processed through the big tents of Freedom City. A one-star general spoke to a clerk, who pointed out a skinny soldier who was waiting his turn.

The officer, Brigadier General Ralph Osborne, strode up to the former prisoner and asked, "Corporal Hiroshi Miyamura?" Startled, the ex-POW could only nod his head.

"Please step out here a moment," the General said. "Miyamura, I am honored to be the first to tell you that you have been awarded the Medal of Honor!"

Osborne then explained that the award, for the action in which Miyamura had been taken prisoner, had been kept secret so that the enemy would take no reprisals against him. "Had they known," he said to the sergeant, "you might not be alive today."

Two thousand one hundred and eighty-eight brave American soldiers have earned that special form of immortality represented by the Medal of Honor.

Who were they?

They were civilians who had turned soldier when their country needed them; they were "draftees" living up to a solemn obligation; they were "regulars" to whom soldiering was a way of life.

They came from the many states and territories, and a lot of them first saw the light of day on some foreign shore.

Who were they? *They were Americans.*

Some of them lived to tell about it—but more of them did not.

Their earthly rewards for having earned this high honor are truly inconsequential. Sometimes, it seems that even the honored dead have been forgotten; and we very often permit the honored living to walk among us unnoticed and unheralded.

This is only an illusion.

The bravery and dedication of these gallant men will never disappear from mind. Their heroism is already a part of the living history of our nation—a history whose strength is in large measure due to their indomitable spirits. Their deeds are apparent for all the future generations to see.

APPENDIX 1

❯❯❯ ❯❯❯ ❯❯❯ ❰❰❰ ❰❰❰ ❰❰❰

Summary of All Medals of Honor Awarded in the History of the Army

❯❯❯ ❯❯❯ ❯❯❯ ❰❰❰ ❰❰❰ ❰❰❰

Civil War 1861–1865	1,200
Indian Campaigns 1861–1898	416
War With Spain 1898	30
Philippine Insurrection 1899–1913	70
Boxer Rebellion 1900	4
Mexican Campaign 1911	1
World War I 1917–1918	95
Unknown Soldiers [1 U.S. and 5 Allies]	6
Greely and Lindbergh	2
World War II 1941–1945	292
Korean Conflict 1950–1953	77
Total	2,193

APPENDIX 2

⋙ ⋙ ⋙ ⋘ ⋘ ⋘

The Mitchel Raiders—April, 1862

⋙ ⋙ ⋙ ⋘ ⋘ ⋘

Pvt William Bensinger *Co G, 21st Ohio Infantry* (c)
Pvt Wilson W. Brown *Co F, 21st Ohio Infantry* (b)
Pvt Robert Buffum *Co H, 21st Ohio Infantry* (c)
Cpl Daniel A. Dorsey *Co H, 33d Ohio Infantry* (b)
Cpl Martin J. Hawkins *Co A, 33d Ohio Infantry* (b)
Pvt William Knight *Co E, 21st Ohio Infantry* (b)
Sgt Elihu H. Mason *Co K, 21st Ohio Infantry* (c)
Pvt Jacob Parrott *Co K, 33d Ohio Infantry* (c)
Sgt William Pittinger *Co G, 2d Ohio Infantry* (c)
Pvt John R. Porter *Co G, 21st Ohio Infantry* (b)
Cpl William H Reddick *Co B, 33d Ohio Infantry* (c)
Pvt Samuel Robertson[1] *Co G, 33d Ohio Infantry* (a)
Sgt Maj Marion A. Ross *21st Ohio Infantry* (a)
Sgt John M. Scott *Co F, 21st Ohio Infantry* (a)
Pvt Samuel Slavens *Co E, 33d Ohio Infantry* (a)
Pvt James Smith *Co I, 2d Ohio Infantry* (x)
Pvt John A. Wilson *Co C, 21st Ohio Infantry* (b)
Pvt John Wollam *Co C, 33d Ohio Infantry* (b)
Pvt Mark Wood *Co C, 21st Ohio Infantry* (b)

(a) *executed on 18 June 1862*
(b) *escaped on 16 October 1862*
(c) *exchanged on 18 March 1863*
(x) *no further information*

[1] Listed in most narratives as Robinson.

APPENDIX 3

✶✶✶ ✶✶✶ ✶✶✶ ✤✤✤ ✤✤✤ ✤✤✤

Awards—1898 to 1913

✶✶✶ ✶✶✶ ✶✶✶ ✤✤✤ ✤✤✤ ✤✤✤

KEY:

* = Posthumous award

Units:

1st No. Dakota Vol Inf = 1st North Dakota Volunteer Infantry Regiment (Militia)
4th U.S. Cavalry = 4th Cavalry Regiment (regular army)
9th U.S. Infantry = 9th Infantry Regiment (regular army)
36th Infantry, USV = 36th Infantry Regiment, United States Volunteers (emergency
  period troops mustered by the federal government)

Campaigns:

CRX = China Relief Expedition, the "Boxer Rebellion"
PI = Philippine Insurrection
PunX = Punitive Expedition, Mexico
WSp = War with Spain

Cpl Frank Anders   *1st No. Dakota Vol Inf (PI)*
Sgt Maj Edward L. Baker, Jr.   *10th U.S. Cavalry (WSp)*
1st Lt Matthew A. Batson   *4th U.S. Cavalry (PI)*
Pvt Dennis Bell   *10th U.S. Cavalry (WSp)*
Capt Harry Bell   *36th Infantry, USV (PI)*
Col J. Franklin Bell   *36th Infantry, USV (PI)*
Pvt George Berg   *17th U.S. Infantry (WSp)*
1st Lt Charles G. Bickham   *27th U.S. Infantry (PI)*
Capt George W. Biegler   *28th Infantry, USV (PI)*
Capt William E. Birkhimer   *3d U.S. Artillery (PI)*
Pvt Otto Boehler   *1st No. Dakota Vol Inf (PI)*
Capt Andre W. Brewster   *9th U.S. Infantry (CRX)*
Pvt Oscar Brookin   *17th U.S. Infantry (WSp)*
Pvt Ulysses G. Buzzard   *17th U.S. Infantry (WSp)*
Capt Bernard A. Byrne   *6th U.S. Infantry (PI)*
Pvt Charles P. Cantrell   *10th U.S. Infantry (WSp)*
Cpl Anthony J. Carson   *43d Infantry, USV (PI)*
Pvt Charles Cawetzka   *30th Infantry, USV (PI)*
1st Lt Josephus S. Cecil   *19th U.S. Infantry (PI)*
Asst Surg James R. Church   *1st U.S. Vol Cav (WSp)*
Sgt Clarence M. Condon   *3d U.S. Artillery (PI)*
Sgt Andrew J. Cummins   *10th U.S. Infantry (WSp)*
Pvt Charles P. Davis   *1st No. Dakota Vol Inf (PI)*

215

Pvt John F. DeSwan *21st U.S. Infantry (WSp)*
Cpl Thomas M. Doherty *21st U.S. Infantry (WSp)*
Pvt Willis H. Downs *1st No. Dakota Vol Inf (PI)*
Pvt Joseph L. Epps *33d Infantry, USV (PI)*
1st Lt Arthur M. Ferguson *36th Infantry, USV (PI)*
Pvt Frank O. Fournia *21st U.S. Infantry (WSp)*
Col Frederick Funston *20th Kans. Vol Inf (PI)*
Artificer Sterling A. Galt *36th Infantry, USV (PI)*
Cpl Antoine A. Gaujot *27th Infantry, USV (PI)*
Capt Julien E. Gaujot *1st U.S. Cavalry (PunX)*
Pvt Louis Gedeon *19th U.S. Infantry (PI)*
Sgt Edward H. Gibson *27th Infantry, USV (PI)*
Cpl James R. Gillenwater *36th Infantry, USV (PI)*
Pvt Thomas J. Graves *17th U.S. Infantry (WSp)*
2d Lt Allen J. Greer *4th U.S. Infantry (PI)*
Lt Col William R. Grove *36th Infantry, USV (PI)*
1st Lt Benjamin F. Hardaway *17th U.S. Infantry (WSp)*
Lt Col Webb C. Hayes *31st Infantry, USV (PI)*
1st Lt John W. Heard *3d U.S. Cavalry (WSp)*
Sgt Joseph Henderson *6th U.S. Cavalry (PI)*
Pvt Frank C. High *2d Oregon Vol Inf (PI)*
Sgt John A. Huntsman *36th Infantry, USV (PI)*
Pvt Gotfred Jensen *1st No. Dakota Vol Inf (PI)*
1st Lt Gordon Johnston *U.S. Signal Corps (PI)*
Pvt William Keller *10th U.S. Infantry (WSp)*
Pvt Thomas Kelly *21st U.S. Infantry (WSp)*
2d Lt John T. Kennedy *6th U.S. Cavalry (PI)*
1st Lt Charles E. Kilbourne *Signal Corps, USV (PI)*
Pvt John B. Kinne *1st No. Dakota Vol Inf (PI)*
1st Lt Louis B. Lawton *9th U.S Infantry (CRX)*
Pvt Cornelius J. Leahy *36th Infantry, USV (PI)*
Pvt Fitz Lee *10th U.S. Cavalry (WSp)*
*Maj John A. Logan *33d Infantry, USV (PI)*
Pvt Richard M. Longfellow *1st No. Dakota Vol Inf (PI)*
Pvt Edward E. Lyon *2d Oregon Vol Inf (PI)*
Pvt James McConnell *33d Infantry, USV (PI)*
Capt Hugh J. McGrath *4th U.S. Cavalry (PI)*
Pvt William P. Maclay *43d Infantry, USV (PI)*
Asst Surg George W. Mathews *36th Infantry, USV (PI)*
1st Lt Archie Miller *6th U.S. Cavalry (PI)*
Capt Albert L. Mills *AAG, USV (WSp)*
Capt John E. Moran *37th Infantry, USV (PI)*
2d Lt Louis C. Mosher *Philippine Scouts (PI)*
Pvt James J. Nash *10th U.S. Infantry (WSp)*
Pvt George H. Nee *21st U.S. Infantry (WSp)*
Pvt Jose B. Nisperos *Philippine Scouts (PI)*
Artificer Joseph A. Nolan *45th Infantry, USV (PI)*
Lt Col James Parker *45th Infantry, USV (PI)*
Musician Herman Pfisterer *21st U.S. Infantry (WSp)*
Pvt Charles H. Pierce *22d U.S. Infantry (PI)*
Pvt Alfred Polond *10th U.S. Infantry (WSp)*
Sgt Alexander M. Quinn *13th U.S. Infantry (WSp)*
Pvt Peter H. Quinn *4th U.S. Cavalry (PI)*
Sgt Charles W. Ray *22d U.S. Infantry (PI)*
Cpl Norman W. Ressler *17th U.S. Infantry (WSp)*

2d Lt Charles D. Roberts *17th U.S. Infantry (WSp)*
Pvt Marcus W. Robertson *2d Oregon Vol Inf (PI)*
Pvt Frank F. Ross *1st No. Dakota Vol Inf (PI)*
Capt William H. Sage *23d U.S. Infantry (PI)*
Sgt Henry F Schroeder *16th U.S. Infantry (PI)*
1st Lt George C. Shaw *27th U.S. Infantry (PI)*
Pvt George M Shelton *23d U.S. Infantry (PI)*
Cpl Warren J. Shepherd *17th U.S. Infantry (WSp)*
Surgeon George F. Shiels *USV (PI)*
Pvt Thomas Sletteland *1st No. Dakota Vol Inf (PI)*
2d Lt George E. Stewart *19th U.S. Infantry (PI)*
Surgeon Paul F. Straub *36th Infantry, USV (PI)*
Pvt William H. Thompkins *10th U.S. Cavalry (WSp)*
Musician Calvin P. Titus *14th U.S. Infantry (CRX)*
Pvt William B. Trembley *20th Kansas Vol Inf (PI)*
1st Lt Louis J. Van Schaick *4th U.S. Infantry (PI)*
Pvt Robert H. Von Schlick *9th U.S. Infantry (CRX)*
Pvt Frank O. Walker *46th Infantry, USV (PI)*
2d Lt George W. Wallace *9th U.S. Infantry (PI)*
Pvt George H. Wanton *10th U.S. Cavalry (WSp)*
Sgt Amos Weaver *36th Infantry, USV (PI)*
2d Lt Ira C. Welborn *9th U.S. Infantry (WSp)*
Cpl Seth L. Weld *8th U.S. Infantry (PI)*
Pvt Bruno Wende *17th U.S. Infantry (WSp)*
Pvt John C. Wetherby *4th U.S. Infantry (PI)*
Pvt Edward White *20th Kans. Vol Inf (PI)*
2d Lt Arthur H. Wilson *6th U.S. Cavalry (PI)*

APPENDIX 4

⋙ ⋙ ⋙ ⋘ ⋘ ⋘

World War I

American Expeditionary Force in France

6 April 1917 to 11 November 1918

⋙ ⋙ ⋙ ⋘ ⋘ ⋘

KEY:
* = Posthumous award
1 Engr, 1Div = 1st Engineer Regiment, 1st Division
2MGBn, 1Div = 2d Machine Gun Battalion, 1st Division
5 Mar, 2Div = 5th Marine Regiment, 2d Division, U.S. Army [1]
10 FA, 3Div = 10th Field Artillery Regiment, 3d Division
119 Inf, 30Div = 119th Infantry Regiment, 30th Division
(AS) = Air Service
(MC) = Marine Corps

Sgt Joseph B. Adkison *Atoka, Tenn.* 119 Inf, 30Div *29 Sep 18*
Cpl Jake Allex *Chicago, Ill.* 131 Inf, 33Div *9 Aug 18*
Capt Edward C. Allworth *Crawford, Wash.* 60 Inf, 5Div *5 Nov 18*
1st Sgt Johannes S. Anderson *Chicago, Ill.* 132 Inf, 33Div *8 Oct 18*
*2d Lt Albert Baesel *Berea, O.* 148 Inf, 37Div *27 Sep 18*
PFC Charles D. Barger *Mt. Vernon, Mo.* 354 Inf, 89Div *31 Oct 18*
*Pvt David B. Barkeley *Laredo, Tex.* 356 Inf, 89Div *9 Nov 18*
PFC John L. Barkley *Blairstown, Mo.* 4 Inf, 3Div *7 Oct 18*
Pvt Frank J. Bart *New York, N.Y.* 9 Inf, 2Div *3 Oct 18*
*Pvt Robert L. Blackwell *Person, N.D.* 119 Inf, 30Div *11 Oct 18*
*2d Lt Erwin R. Bleckley *Wichita, Kans.* 50 Aero Sqdn (AS) *6 Oct 18*
1st Lt Deming Bronson *Rhinelander, Wis.* 364 Inf, 91Div *26–27 Sep 18*
Cpl Donald M. Call *New York, N.Y.* 344 Tank Bn *26 Sep 18*
*Capt Marcellus H. Chiles *Eureka Springs, Ark.* 356 Inf, 89Div *3 Nov 18*
*Sgt Wilbur E. Colyer *Brooklyn, N.Y.* 1 Engr, 1Div *9 Oct 18*
*Pvt Henry G. Costin *Baltimore, Md.* 115 Inf, 29Div *8 Oct 18*
Sgt Louis Cukela *Minneapolis, Minn.* (MC) 5 Mar, 2Div *18 Jul 18*
PFC George Dilboy *Keene, N.H.* 103 Inf, 26Div *18 Jul 18*
Sgt Michael A. Donaldson *Haverstraw, N.Y.* 165 Inf, 42Div *14 Oct 18*
Lt Col William J. Donovan *Buffalo, N.Y.* 165 Inf, 42Div *14–15 Oct 18*
1st Lt James C. Dozier *Marion, S.C.* 118 Inf, 30Div *8 Oct 18*

[1] The 5th and 6th Marine Regiments were formed in the 4th Marine
Brigade, which was an organic part of the 2d Infantry Division, U.S. Army,
throughout World War I.

*PFC Parker F. Dunn *Albany, N.Y.* 312 Inf, 78Div 23 Oct 18

PFC Daniel R. Edwards *Moorville, Tex.* 2MGBn, 1Div 18 Jul 18

Sgt Alan L. Eggers *Saranac Lake, N.Y.* 107 Inf, 27Div 29 Sep 18

Sgt Michael B. Ellis *St. Louis, Mo.* 28 Inf, 1Div 5 Oct 18

Sgt Arthur J. Forrest *St. Louis, Mo.* 354 Inf, 89Div 1 Nov 18

Sgt Gary E. Foster *Spartanburg, S.C.* 118 Inf, 30Div 8 Oct 18

PFC Jesse N. Funk *New Hampton, Mo.* 354 Inf, 89Div 31 Oct 18

1st Lt Harold A. Furlong *Pontiac, Mich.* 353 Inf, 89Div 1 Nov 18

PFC Frank Gaffney *Buffalo, N.Y.* 108 Inf, 27Div 29 Sep 18

*1st Lt Harold E. Goettler *Chicago, Ill.* 50 Aero Sqdn (AS) 6 Oct 18

Sgt Earl D. Gregory *Chase City, Va.* 116 Inf, 29Div 8 Oct 18

1st Sgt Sydney G. Gumpertz *San Rafael, Cal.* 132 Inf, 33Div 29 Sep 18

*Sgt Thomas L. Hall *Ft. Mill, S.C.* 118 Inf, 30Div 8 Oct 18

Sgt M. Waldo Hatler *Bolivar, Mo.* 356 Inf, 89Div 8 Nov 18

1st Lt George P. Hays *Okarche, Okla.* 10 FA, 3Div 14-15 Jul 18

*Cpl James D. Heriot *Providence, S.C.* 118 Inf, 30Div 12 Oct 18

Cpl Ralyn Hill *Lindenwood, Ill.* 129 Inf, 33Div 7 Oct 18

Sgt Richmond H. Hilton *Westville, S.C.* 118 Inf, 30Div 11 Oct 18

Gy Sgt Charles F. Hoffman (Real name, Ernest Janson) *New York, N.Y.* **(MC)**
  5 Mar, 2Div 6 June 18

Capt Nelson M. Holderman *Trumbell, Nebr.* 307 Inf, 77Div 2-8 Oct 18

PFC Harold I. Johnston *Kendall, Kans.* 356 Inf, 89Div 9 Nov 18

Sgt James E. Karnes *Arlington, Tenn.* 117 Inf, 30Div 8 Oct 18

Sgt Phillip C. Katz *San Francisco, Cal.* 363 Inf, 91Div 26 Sep 18

1st Sgt Benjamin Kaufman *Buffalo, N.Y.* 308 Inf, 77Div 4 Oct 18

Pvt John J. Kelly *Chicago, Ill.* (MC) 6 Mar, 2Div 3 Oct 18

Sgt Matej Kocak *New York, N.Y.* (MC) 5 Mar, 2Div 18 Jul 18

Sgt John C. Latham *Rutherford, N.J.* 107 Inf, 27Div 29 Sep 18

1st Sgt Milo Lemert *Marshalltown, Ia.* 119 Inf, 30Div 29 Sep 18

Pvt Berger Loman *Chicago, Ill.* 132 Inf, 33Div 9 Oct 18

*2d Lt Frank Luke, Jr. *Phoenix, Ariz.* 27 Aero Sqdn, 1 Purs Gp (AS) 29 Sep 18

Capt George H. Mallon *Ogden, Kans.* 132 Inf, 33Div 26 Sep 18

Cpl Sydney E. Manning *Butler Co., Ala.* 167 Inf, 42Div 28 Jul 18

Sgt James I. Mestrovitch *Pittsburgh, Pa.* 111 Inf, 28Div 10 Aug 18

Capt L. Wardlaw Miles *Baltimore, Md.* 308 Inf, 77Div 14 Sep 18

*Maj Oscar F. Miller *Franklin County, Ark.* 361 Inf, 91Div 28 Sep 18

Pvt Sterling Morelock *Silver Run, Md.* 28 Inf, 1Div 4 Oct 18

Capt George G. McMurtry *Pittsburgh, Pa.* 308 Inf, 77Div 2-8 Oct 18

Pvt Thomas C. Neibaur *Sharon, Ida.* 167 Inf, 42Div 16 Oct 18

Sgt Richard W. O'Neil *New York, N.Y.* 165 Inf, 42Div 30 Jul 18

*Cpl Thomas E. O'Shea *New York, N.Y.* 107 Inf, 27Div 29 Sep 18

2d Lt Samuel I. Parker *Monroe, N.C.* 28 Inf, 1Div 18-19 Jul 18

Pvt Archie A. Peck *Tyrone, N.Y.* 307 Inf, 77Div 6 Oct 18

PFC Michael J. Perkins *Boston, Mass.* 101 Inf, 26Div 27 Oct 18

*Lt Col Emory J. Pike *Columbia City, Ia.* 321 MGBn, 82Div 15 Sep 18

Cpl Thomas A. Pope *Chicago, Ill.* 131 Inf, 33Div 4 Jul 18

*Cpl John H. Pruitt *Tucson, Ariz.* (MC) 6 Mar, 2Div 3 Oct 18

2d Lt Patrick Regan *Middleboro, Mass.* 115 Inf, 29Div 8 Oct 18

1st Lt Edward V. Rickenbacker *Columbus, O.* 94 Aero Sqdn (AS) 25 Sep 18

1st Lt George S. Robb *Assaria, Kans.* 369 Inf, 93Div 29-30 Sep 18

*Cpl Harold W. Roberts *San Francisco, Cal.* 344 Tank Bn 4 Oct 18

Cpl Samuel M. Sampler *Decatur, Tex.* 142 Inf, 36Div 8 Oct 18

Sgt Willie Sandlin *Jackson, Ky.* 132 Inf, 33Div 26 Sep 18

*Sgt William Sawelson *Newark, N.J.* 312 Inf, 78Div 26 Oct 18

1st Lt. Dwite H. Schaffner *Arroya, Pa.* 306 Inf, 77Div 28 Sep 18

Sgt Lloyd M. Seibert *Caledonia, Mich.* 364 Inf, 91Div *26 Sep 18*
*Capt Alexander R. Skinker *St. Louis, Mo.* 138 Inf, 35Div *26 Sep 18*
Pvt Clayton K. Slack *Plover, Wis.* 124 MGBn, 33Div *8 Oct 18*
*Lt Col Fred E. Smith *Rockford, Ill.* 308 Inf, 77Div *29 Sep 18*
*Gy Sgt Fred W. Stockham *New York, N.Y. (MC)* 6 Mar, 2Div *13–14 Jun 18*
Sgt Edward R. Talley *Russellville, Tenn.* 117 Inf, 30Div *7 Oct 18*
Maj Joseph H. Thompson *Beaver Falls, Pa.* 110 Inf, 28Div *1 Oct 18*
*Cpl Harold L. Turner *Aurora, Mo.* 142 Inf, 36Div *8 Oct 18*
1st Lt William B. Turner *Boston, Mass.* 105 Inf, 27Div *27 Sep 18*
Pvt Michael Valente *Ogdensburg, N.Y.* 107 Inf, 27Div *29 Sep 18*
Sgt Ludovicus M. Van Iersel *Glen Rock, N.J.* 9 Inf, 2Div *9 Nov 18*
Cpl John C. Villepigue *Camden, S.C.* 118 Inf, 30Div *15 Oct 18*
Sgt Reidar Waalar *New York, N.Y.* 105 MGBn, 27Div *27 Sep 18*
Pvt John C. Ward *Green County, Tex.* 117 Inf, 30Div *8 Oct 18*
1st Sgt Chester H. West *Fort Collins, Colo.* 363 Inf, 91Div *26 Sep 18*
Maj Charles W Whittlesey *Florence, Wis.* 308 Inf, 77Div *2–7 Oct 18*
*2d Lt J. Hunter Wickersham *New York, N.Y.* 353 Inf, 89Div *12 Sep 18*
*Pvt Nels Wold *Winger, Minn.* 138 Inf, 35Div *26 Sep 18*
1st Lt Samuel Woodfill *Bryantsburg, Ind.* 60 Inf, 5Div *12 Oct 18*
Cpl Alvin C. York *Pall Mall, Tenn.* 328 Inf, 82Div *8 Oct 18*

APPENDIX 5

❊❊❊❊❊❊

Awards between World War I and World War II

❊❊❊❊❊❊

Capt Charles A. Lindbergh Little Falls, Minn.	Air Corps Reserve; for nonstop flight from New York City to Paris, France, 20–21 May 1927
Maj Gen Adolphus W. Greely Newburyport, Mass.	U.S. Army, Retired; for outstanding public service, 1861–1906, including important Arctic explorations

APPENDIX 6

≫≫ ≫≫ ≫≫ ≪≪ ≪≪ ≪≪

World War II

The Far East

7 December 1941 to 2 September 1945

≫≫ ≫≫ ≫≫ ≪≪ ≪≪ ≪≪

KEY:
* = Posthumous award

Units:

45 Inf, P.S. = 45th Infantry Regiment, Philippine Scouts
112 Cav RCT = 112th Cavalry Regimental Combat Team
381 Inf, 96Div = 381st Infantry Regiment, 96th Infantry Division
503 ParInf = 503d Parachute Infantry
MTF = Mars Task Force (Burma)

Campaigns:

A.I. = Aleutian Islands
Admiral. = Admiralties
D.N.G. = Dutch New Guinea
Guad. = Guadalcanal
M.I. = Marianas Islands
N.G. = New Guinea
P.I. = Philippine Islands
R.I. = Ryukyus Islands
S.I. = Solomon Islands

S/Sgt Beauford T. Anderson *Eagle, Wis.* 381 Inf, 96Div *13 Apr 45,* R.I.
PFC Thomas E. Atkins *Campobello, S.C.* 127 Inf, 32Div *10 Mar 45,* P.I.
*Sgt Thomas A. Baker *Troy, N.Y.* 105 Inf, 27Div *19 Jun–7 Jul 44,* M.I.
*PFC George Benjamin, Jr. *Phila., Pa.* 306 Inf, 77Div *21 Dec 44,* P.I.
1st Lt Willibald C. Bianchi *New Ulm, Minn.* 45 Inf, P.S. *3 Feb 42,* P.I.
Maj Richard I. Bong *Poplar, Wis.* Air Corps *10 Oct–15 Nov 44*
*2d Lt George W. G. Boyce, Jr. *New York, N.Y.* 112 CavRCT *23 Jul 44,* N.G.
*PFC Leonard C. Brostrom *Preston, Ida.* 17 Inf, 7Div *28 Oct 44,* P.I.
*1st Sgt Elmer J. Burr *Nennah, Wis.* 127 Inf, 32Div *24 Dec 42,* N.G.
Sgt Jose Calugas *Iloiolo, P.I.* 88 FA, P.S. *16 Jan 42,* P.I.
*Maj Horace S. Carswell, Jr. *San Angelo, Tex.* Air Corps *26 Oct 44*
*Maj Ralph Cheli *New York, N.Y.* Air Corps *18 Aug 43*
*2d Lt Dale E. Christensen *Cameron Township, Ia.* 112 Cav RCT *16–19 Jul 44,* N.G.

*PFC Joseph J. Cicchetti   *Waynesburg, O.*   148 Inf, 37Div   9 Feb 45, P.I.
S/Sgt Raymond H. Cooley   *Dunlop, Tenn.*   27 Inf, 25Div   24 Feb 45, P.I.
PFC Clarence B. Craft   *San Bernardino, Cal.*   382 Inf, 96Div   31 May 45, R.I.
Maj Charles W. Davis   *Gordo, Ala.*   27 Inf, 25Div   12 Jan 43, Guad.
*PFC James H. Diamond   *New Orleans, La.*   21 Inf, 24Div   8–14 May 45, P.I.
Brig Gen James H. Doolittle   *Berkeley, Cal.*   Air Corps   9 Jun 42
PFC Desmond T. Doss   *Lynchburg, Va.*   307 Inf, 77Div   29 Apr–21 May 45, R.I.
S/Sgt Jessie R. Drowley   *St. Charles, Mich.*   132 Inf, AmDiv   30 Jan 44, Bgv.
*S/Sgt Gerald L. Endl   *Fort Atkinson, Wis.*   128 Inf, 32Div   11 Jul 44, N.G.
S/Sgt Henry E. Erwin   *Bessemer, Ala.*   Air Corps   12 Apr 45
*Sgt Ray E. Eubanks   *Snow Hill, N.C.*   503 ParInf   23 Jul 44, D.N.G.
*Sgt William G. Fournier   *Norwich, Conn.*   35 Inf, 25Div   10 Jan 43, Guad.
*Pvt Elmer E. Fryar   *Denver, Col.*   511 ParInf, 11ABDiv   8 Dec 44, P.I.
*PFC David M. Gonzales   *Pacoima, Wash.*   127 Inf, 32Div   25 Apr 45, P.I.
*PFC William J. Grabiarz   *Buffalo, N.Y.*   5 Cav, 1 CavDiv   23 Feb 45, P.I.
*Sgt Kenneth E. Gruennert   *Helenville, Wis.*   127 Inf, 32Div   24 Dec 42, N.G.
*T/5 Lewis Hall   *Bloom, O.*   35 Inf, 25Div   10 Jan 43, Guad.
*Cpl Harry R. Harr   *Pine Croft, Pa.*   124 Inf, 31Div   5 Jun 45, P.I.
*Sgt LeRoy Johnson   *Caney Creek, La.*   126 Inf, 32Div   15 Dec 44, P.I.
Col Neel E. Kearby   *Dallas, Tex.*   Air Corps   11 Oct 43
*Pvt Ova A. Kelley   *Norwood, Mo.*   382 Inf, 96Div   8 Dec 44, P.I.
PFC Dexter J. Kerstetter   *Centralia, Wash.*   130 Inf, 33Div   13 Apr 45, P.I.
*1st Lt Jack L. Knight   *Garner, Tex.*   124 Cav, MTF   2 Feb 45, Burma
*PFC Anthony L. Krotiak   *Chicago, Ill.*   148 Inf, 37Div   8 May 45, P.I.
S/Sgt Robert E. Laws   *Altoona, Pa.*   169 Inf, 43Div   12 Jan 45, P.I.
*Pvt Donald R. Lobaugh   *Freeport, Pa.*   127 Inf, 32Div   22 Jul 44, N.G.
G/A Douglas A. MacArthur   *Little Rock, Ark.*   Commander, U.S. Army, **Far East**   1 Apr 42
*Pvt Joe P. Martinez   *Taos, N.M.*   32 Inf, 7Div   26 May 43, A.I.
*PFC Martin O. May   *Phillipsburg, N.J.*   307 Inf, 77Div   19–21 Apr 45, R.I.
Cpl Melvin Mayfield   *Nashport, O.*   20 Inf, 6Div   29 Jul 45, P.I.
Pvt Lloyd G. McCarter   *St. Maries, Ida.*   503 ParInf   16–19 Feb 45, P.I.
M/Sgt Charles L. McGaha   *Crosby, Tenn.*   35 Inf, 25Div   7 Feb 45, P.I.
*Sgt Troy A. McGill   *Knoxville, Tenn.*   5 Cav, 1 CavDiv   4 Mar 44, **Admiral.**
*Maj Thomas B. McGuire, Jr.   *Sebring, Fla.*   Air Corps   25–26 Dec 44
Sgt John R. McKinney   *Woodcliff, Ga.*   123 Inf, 33Div   11 May 45, P.I.
*PFC William A. McWhorter   *Liberty, S.C.*   126 Inf, 32Div   5 Dec 44, P.I.
T/Sgt John Meagher   *Jersey City, N.J.*   305 Inf, 77Div   19 Jun 45, R.I.
*Pvt Harold H. Moon, Jr.   *Alberquerque, N.M.*   34 Inf, 24Div   21 Oct 44, P.I.
*PFC Edward J. Moskala   *Chicago, Ill.*   383 Inf, 96Div   9 Apr 45, R.I.
*Sgt Charles E. Mower   *Chippewa Falls, Wis.*   34 Inf, 24Div   3 Nov 44, P.I.
*Sgt Joseph E. Muller   *Holyoke, Mass.*   305 Inf, 77Div   15–16 May 45, R.I.
Capt Robert P. Nett   *New Haven, Conn.*   305 Inf, 77Div   14 Dec 44, P.I.
*1st Lt Alexander R. Nininger, Jr.   *Fort Lauderdale, Fla.*   57 Inf, P.S.   12 Jan 42, **P.I.**
*Lt Col William J. O'Brien   *Troy, N.Y.*   105 Inf, 27Div   20 Jun–7 Jul 44, M.I.
*T/4 Laverne Parrish   *Knox City, Mo.*   161 Inf, 25Div   18–21 Jan 45, P.I.
*Capt Harl Pease, Jr.   *Plymouth, N.H.*   Air Corps   6–7 Aug 42
PFC Manuel Perez, Jr.   *Chicago, Ill.*   511 ParInf, 11ABDiv   3 Feb 45, P.I.
*PFC Frank J. Petrarca   *Cleveland, O.*   145 Inf, 37Div   27 Jul 43, Bgv.
*PFC John N. Reese, Jr.   *Muskogee, Okla.*   148 Inf, 37Div   9 Feb 45, P.I.
PFC Cleto Rodriguez   *San Marcos, Tex.*   148 Inf, 37Div   9 Feb 45, P.I.
T/Sgt Donald E. Rudolph   *South Haven, Minn.*   20 Inf, 6Div   5 Feb 45, P.I.
Sgt Alejandro R. Ruiz   *Loving, N.M.*   165 Inf, 27Div   28 Apr 45, R.I.
*2d Lt Joseph R. Sarnoski   *Simpson, Pa.*   Air Corps   16 Jun 43
1st Lt Robert S. Scott   *Washington, D.C.*   172 Inf, 43Div   29 Jul 43, S.I.

*PFC William R. Shockley *Bokoshe, Okla.* 128 Inf, 32Div *31 Mar 45, P.I.*

Maj William A. Shomo *Westmoreland City, Pa.* Air Corps *11 Jan 45*

S/Sgt John C. Sjogren *Rockford, Ill.* 160 Inf, 40Div *23 May 45, P.I.*

Capt Seymour W. Terry *Little Rock, Ark.* 382 Inf, 96Div *11 May 45, R.I.*

*PFC William H. Thomas *Wynne, Ark.* 149 Inf, 38Div *22 Apr 45, P.I.*

*PFC John F. Thorson *Armstrong, Ia.* 17 Inf, 7Div *28 Oct 44, P.I.*

*Pvt Junior Van Noy *Preston, Ida.* 2ESB *17 Oct 43, N.G.*

*2d Lt Robert M. Viale *Bayside, Cal.* 148 Inf, 37Div *5 Feb 45, P.I.*

*S/Sgt Ysmael R. Villegas *Casa Blanca, Cal.* 127 Inf, 32Div *20 Mar 45, P.I.*

PFC Dirk J. Vlug *Maple Lake, Minn.* 126 Inf, 32Div *15 Dec 44, P.I.*

Gen Jonathan M. Wainwright *Walla Walla, Wash.* Comdr, U.S. Army in P.I. *12 Mar–7 May 45*

*Brig Gen Kenneth N. Walker *Col.* Air Corps *5 Jan 43*

*Maj Raymond H. Wilkins *Portsmouth, Va.* Air Corps *2 Nov 43*

*S/Sgt Howard E. Woodford *Barberton, O.* 130 Inf, 33Div *6 Jun 45, P.I.*

*Pvt Rodger W. Young *Tiffin, O.* 148 Inf, 37Div *31 Jul 43, S.I.*

Maj Jay Zeamer, Jr. *Orange, N.J.* Air Corps *16 Jun 43*

APPENDIX 7

>>> >>> >>> <<< <<< <<<

World War II
Mediterranean Front

>>> >>> >>> <<< <<< <<<

KEY:
* = Posthumous award
1 ArC = 1 Armored Corps
6ArInf, 1ArDiv = 6th Armored Infantry, 1st Armored Division

North African Campaign—October 1942 to May 1943

*Pvt Robert D. Booker *Callaway, Nebr.* Inf, 34Div *9 Apr 43*
*Col Demas T. Craw *Traverse City, Mich.* Air Corps [1] *8 Nov 42*
Maj Pierpont M. Hamilton *New York, N.Y.* Air Corps [1] *8 Nov 42*
*Pvt Nicholas Minue *Carteret, N.J.* 6ArInf, 1ArDiv *28 Apr 43*
*Sgt William L. Nelson *Dover, Del.* 60 Inf, 9Div *24 Apr 43*
Col William H. Wilbur *Palmer, Mass.* 1 ArC *8 Nov 42*

Sicily—July–August 1943

*2d Lt Robert Craig *Toledo, O.* 15 Inf, 3Div *11 Jul 43*
Sgt Gerry H. Kisters *Bloomington, Ind.* 82 Cav Rcn Sq, 2ArDiv *31 Jul 43*
*Pvt James W. Reese *Chester, Pa.* 26 Inf, 1Div *5 Aug 43*
1st Lt David C. Waybur *Piedmont, Cal.* 2 Rcn Tr, 3Div *17 Jul 43*

Italian Campaign—September 1943 to April 1945

*Sgt Sylvester Antolak *St. Clairsville, O.* 15 Inf, 3Div *24 May 44*
T/Sgt Van T. Barfoot *Carthage, Miss.* 157 Inf, 45Div *23 May 44*
1st Lt Arnold L. Bjorklund *Seattle, Wash.* 142 Inf, 36Div *13 Sep 43*
1st Lt Orville E. Bloch *Streeter, N.D.* 338 Inf, 85Div *22 Sep 44*
1st Lt Maurice L. Britt *Lonoke, Ark.* 30 Inf, 3Div *10 Nov 43*
2d Lt Ernest Childers *Tulsa, Okla.* 180 Inf, 45Div *22 Sep 43*
*Pvt Herbert F. Christian *Steubenville, O.* 15 Inf, 3Div *2–3 Jun 44*
Pvt William J. Crawford *Pueblo, Col.* 142 Inf, 36Div *13 Sep 43*

1 *Maj Hamilton and Col Craw voluntarily accompanied assault waves near Port Lyautey on a mission to pass through enemy lines to locate the French commander with a proposal for suspending hostilities. Craw was killed by machine gun fire at a roadblock; Hamilton was captured, but succeeded in accomplishing the mission.*

T/Sgt Ernest H. Dervishian *Richmond, Va.*   34Div *23 May 44*
*PFC John W. Dutko *Riverside, N.J.*   30 Inf, 3Div *23 May 44*
*2d Lt Thomas W. Fowler *Wichita Falls, Tex.*   1ArDiv *23 May 44*
*Capt William W. Galt *Stanford, Mont.*   168 Inf, 34Div *29 May 44*
*T/5 Eric G. Gibson *Chicago, Ill.*   30 Inf, 3Div *28 Jan 44*
S/Sgt George J. Hall *New York, N.Y.*   135 Inf, 34Div *23 May 44*
*Sgt Roy W. Harmon *Pixley, Cal.*   362 Inf, 91Div *12 Jul 44*
PFC Lloyd C. Hawks *Becker, Minn.*   30 Inf, 3Div *30 Jan 44*
Cpl Paul B. Huff *Cleveland, Tenn.*   509 Par Inf Bn *8 Feb 44*
*Pvt Elden H. Johnson *East Weymouth, Mass.*   15 Inf, 3Div *3 Jun 44*
Sgt Oscar G. Johnson, Jr. *Foster City, Mich.*   363 Inf, 91Div *16–18 Sep 44*
PFC William J. Johnston *Colchester, Conn.*   180 Inf, 45Div *17–19 Feb 44*
Sgt Christos H. Karaberis *Manchester, N.H.*   337 Inf, 85Div *1–2 Oct 44*
*S/Sgt George D. Keathley *Lamesa, Tex.*   85Div *14 Sep 44*
Cpl Charles E. Kelly *Pittsburgh, Pa.*   143 Inf, 36Div *13 Sep 43*
*PFC Patrick L. Kessler *Middletown, O.*   30 Inf, 3Div *23 May 44*
PFC Alton W. Knappenberger *Spring Mount, Pa.*   30 Inf, 3Div *1 Feb 44*
PFC Floyd K. Lindstrom *Colorado Spr., Col.*   7 Inf, 3Div *11 Nov 43*
Sgt James M. Logan *Lucinto, Tex.*   142 Inf, 36Div *9 Sep 43*
PFC John D. Magrath *East Norwalk, Conn.*   85 Inf, 10MtnDiv *14 Apr 45*
*S/Sgt Thomas E. McCall *Veedersburg, Ind.*   143 Inf, 36Div *22 Jan 44*
Pvt James H. Mills *Fort Meade, Fla.*   15 Inf, 3Div *24 May 44*
2d Lt Jack C. Montgomery *Sallisaw, Okla.*   180 Inf, 45Div *22 Feb 44*
*PFC Sadao S. Munemori *Los Angeles, Cal.*   100 Inf Bn, 442CT *5 Apr 45*
1st Lt Beryl R. Newman *Baraboo, Wis.*   133 Inf, 34Div *26 May 44*
*Capt Arlo L. Olson *Greenville, Ia.*   15 Inf, 3Div *13 Oct 43*
*Sgt Truman O. Olson *Cambridge, Wis.*   7 Inf, 3Div *30–31 Jun 44*
PFC Leo J. Powers *Clinton, Wash.*   133 Inf, 34Div *3 Feb 44*
*2d Lt Paul F. Riordan *Kansas City, Mo.*   34Div *3–8 Feb 44*
*Capt Robert E. Roeder *Summit Station, Pa.*   350 Inf, 88Div *27–28 Sep 44*
PFC Henry Schauer *Palouse, Wash.*   15 Inf, 3Div *23–4 May 44*
2d Lt Charles W. Shea *New York, N.Y.*   350 Inf, 88Div *12 May 44*
*Cpl James Slaton *Gulfport, Miss.*   157 Inf, 45Div *23 Sep 43*
*Pvt Furman L. Smith *Central, S.C.*   135 Inf, 34Div *31 May 44*
*Sgt Joe C. Specker *Odessa, Mo.*   48 Engr(C)Bn *7 Jan 44*
*Sgt John C. Squires *Louisville, Ky.*   30 Inf, 3Div *23–24 Apr 44*
*1st Lt Robert R. Waugh *Augusta, Me.*   339 Inf, 85Div *11–14 May 44*
*2d Lt Thomas W. Wigle *Detroit, Mich.*   135 Inf, 34Div *14 Sep 44*
S/Sgt Homer L. Wise *Baton Rouge, La.*   142 Inf, 36Div *14 Jun 44*

APPENDIX 8

❯❯❯ ❯❯❯ ❯❯❯ ❮❮❮ ❮❮❮ ❮❮❮

World War II

Aerial Offensive Against Europe, 1942–1945

❯❯❯ ❯❯❯ ❯❯❯ ❮❮❮ ❮❮❮ ❮❮❮

KEY:
* = Posthumous award
9AF = 9th Air Force
Bomb Gr = Bombardment Group
Ftr = Fighter
(H) = Heavy
TDY = Temporary Duty
Wg = Wing

*Lt Col Addison E. Baker *Akron, O.* 93 Bomb Gr (H), TDY 9AF *1 Aug 43*
*Brig Gen Frederick W Castle *New York, N.Y.* 4 Bomb Wg, 8AF *24 Dec 44*
*2d Lt Robert E. Femoyer *Jacksonville, Fla.* 447 Bomb Gr, 8AF *2 Nov 44*
*1st Lt Donald J. Gott *Arnett, Okla.* 42 Bomb Gr, 8AF *9 Nov 44*
Lt Col James H. Howard *St. Louis, Mo.* 354 Ftr Gr, 9AF *11 Jan 44*
*2d Lt Lloyd H. Hughes *Corpus Christi, Tex.* 389 Bomb Gr, 9AF *1 Aug 43*
*Maj John L. Jerstad *Racine, Wis.* 93 Bomb Gr (H), TDY 9AF *1 Aug 43*
Col Leon W. Johnson *Moline, Kans.* 44 Bomb Gr, 9AF *1 Aug 43*
Col John R. Kane *Shreveport, La.* 98 Bomb Gr, 9AF *1 Aug 43*
*2d Lt David R. Kingsley *Portland, Or.* 97 Bomb Gr, 15AF *23 Jun 44*
*1st Lt Raymond L. Knight *Houston, Tex.* 15th Air Force *24–25 Apr 45*
1st Lt William R. Lawley, Jr. *Birmingham, Ala.* 305 Bomb Gr, 8AF *20 Feb 44*
*Capt Darrell R. Lindsey *Fort Dodge, Ia.* 394 Bomb Gr, 9AF *9 Aug 44*
*Sgt Archibald Mathies *Finleyville, Pa.* 303 Bomb Gr, 8AF *20 Feb 44*
*1st Lt Jack W Mathis *San Angelo, Tex.* 303 Bomb Gr, 8AF *18 Mar 43*
*2d Lt William E. Metzger, Jr. *Lima, O.* 452 Bomb Gr, 8AF *9 Nov 44*
1st Lt Edward S. Michael *Chicago, Ill.* 305 Bomb Gr, 8AF *11 Apr 44*
F/O John C. Morgan *New York, N.Y.* 92 Bomb Gr, 8AF *28 Jul 43*
*1st Lt Donald D. Pucket *Boulder, Col.* 98 Bomb Gr (H), 15AF *9 Jul 44*
Sgt Maynard H. Smith *Caro, Mich.* 306 Bomb Gr, 8AF *1 May 43*
*2d Lt Walter E. Truemper *Aurora, Ill.* 351 Bomb Gr, 8AF *20 Feb 44*
*Lt Col Leon R. Vance, Jr. *Enid, Okla.* 489 Bomb Gr, 8AF *5 Jun 44*
T/Sgt Forrest L. Vosler *Livonia, N.Y.* 303 Bomb Gr, 8AF *20 Dec 43*

APPENDIX 9

※»→ »→ »→ «← «← «←

France–Belgium–Holland–Luxembourg–Germany

6 June 1944 to 7 May 1945

※»→ »→ »→ «← «← «←

KEY:
* = Posthumous award
† = Taken prisoner

Units:
30 Inf, 3 Div = 30th Infantry Regiment, 3d Infantry Division
ABDiv = Airborne Division
AFA = Armored Field Artillery Battalion
ArDiv = Armored Division
ArInf = Armored Infantry Battalion
ArRegt = Armored Regiment
CavRcnSq = Cavalry Reconnaissance Squadron
ECB = Engineer Combat Battalion
FA = Field Artillery Battalion
GliInf = Glider Infantry Regiment
MedBn = Medical Battalion
ParInf = Parachute Infantry Regiment
TDBn = Tank Destroyer Battalion
TkBn = Tank Battalion

Campaigns:
B = Belgium
F = France
G = Germany
H = Holland
L = Luxembourg

S/Sgt Lucian Adams *Port Arthur, Tex.* 30 Inf, 3Div (F) *28 Oct 44*
Pvt Carlton W. Barrett *Fulton, N.Y.* 18 Inf, 1Div (F) *6 Jun 44*
*1st Lt Raymond O Beaudoin *Holyoke, Mass.* 119 Inf, 30Div (G) *6 Apr 45*
T/Sgt Bernard P. Bell *Grantsville, W. Va.* 142 Inf, 36Div (F) *18 Dec 44*
S/Sgt Stanley Bender *Carlisle, W.Va.* 7 Inf, 3Div (F) *17 Aug 44*
Cpl Edward A. Bennett *Middleport, O.* 358 Inf, 90Div (G) *1 Feb 45*
M/Sgt Veto R. Bertoldo *Decatur, Ill.* 242 Inf, 42Div (F) *9–10 Jan 45*
Cpl Arthur O. Beyer *Mitchell City, Ia.* 603 TDBn (B) *14 Jan 45*
PFC Melvin E. Biddle *Daleville, Ind.* 517 ParInf, 13ABDiv (B) *23–24 Dec 44*
S/Sgt Paul L. Bolden *Hobbes Island, Ia.* 120 Inf, 30Div (B) *23 Dec 44*
1st Lt Cecil H. Bolton *Crawfordsville, Fla.* 413 Inf, 104Div (H) *2 Nov 44*

S/Sgt Hershel F. Briles *Colfax, Ia.* 899 TDBn (G) *20 Nov 44*

Capt Bobbie E. Brown *Columbus, Ga.* 18 Inf, 1Div (G) *8 Oct 44*

1st Lt Frank Burke *New York, N.Y.* 15 Inf, 3Div (G) *17 Apr 45*

PFC Herbert H. Burr *St. Joseph, Mo.* 41 TkBn, 11ArDiv (G) *19 Mar 45*

Capt James M. Burt *Hinsdale, Mass.* 66 ArRegt, 2ArDiv (G) *13 Oct 44*

*2d Lt John E. Butts *Medina, N.Y.* 60 Inf, 9Div (F) *14–16, 23 Jun 44*

*S/Sgt Alvin P. Carey *Lycippus, Pa.* 38 Inf, 2Div (F) *23 Aug 44*

*T/Sgt Charles F. Carey, Jr. *Canadien, Okla.* 397 Inf, 100Div (F) *8–9 Jan 45*

S/Sgt Clyde L. Choate *W. Frankfurt, Ill.* 601 TDBn (F) *25 Oct 44*

T/Sgt Francis J. Clark *Whitehall, N.Y.* 109 Inf, 28Div (L) *12 Sep 44*

PFC Mike Colalillo *Hibbing, Minn.* 398 Inf, 100Div (G) *7 Apr 45*

*Lt Col Robert G. Cole *San Antonio, Tex.* 502 ParInf, 101ABDiv (F) *11 Jun 44*

Sgt James P. Connor *Wilmington, Del.* 7 Inf, 3Div (F) *15 Aug 44*

T/Sgt Charles H. Coolidge *Signal Mountain, Tenn.* 141 Inf, 36Div (F) *24–27 Oct 44*

PFC Richard E. Cowan *Lincoln, Neb.* 23 Inf, 2Div (B) *17 Dec 44*

*T/Sgt Morris E. Crain *Bandana, Ky.* 141 Inf, 36Div (F) *13 Mar 45*

S/Sgt John R. Crews *Golden, Okla.* 253 Inf, 63Div (G) *8 Apr 45*

Sgt Francis S. Currey *Loch Sheldrake, N.Y.* 120 Inf, 30Div (B) *21 Dec 44*

2d Lt Edward C. Dahlgren *Perham, Me.* 142 Inf, 36Div (F) *11 Feb 45*

*T/Sgt Peter J. Dalessondro *Watervliet, Ky.* 39 Inf, 9Div (G) *22 Dec 44*

Capt Michael J. Daly *New York, N.Y.* 15 Inf, 3Div (G) *18 Apr 45*

S/Sgt Arthur F. DeFranzo *Saugus, Mass.* 18 Inf, 1Div (F) *10 Jun 44*

*PFC Charles N. DeGlopper *Grand Island, N.Y.* 325 GliInf, 82ABDiv (F) *9 Jun 44*

*Sgt Emile Deleau, Jr. *Lansing, O.* 142 Inf, 36Div (F) *1–2 Feb 45*

*S/Sgt Robert H. Dietz *Kingston, N.Y.* 38 ArIn, 7ArDiv (G) *29 Mar 45*

T/Sgt Russell E. Dunham *East Carondelet, Ill.* 30 Inf, 3Div (F) *8 Jan 45*

S/Sgt Walter D. Ehlers *Geary, Kan.* 18 Inf, 1Div (F) *9–10 Jun 44*

T/Sgt Forrest E. Everhart *Bainbridge, O.* 359 Inf, 90Div (F) *12 Nov 44*

1st Lt James H. Fields *Caddo, Tex.* 10 ArInf, 4ArDiv (F) *27 Sep 44*

2d Lt Almond E. Fisher *Hume, N.Y.* 157 Inf, 45Div (F) *12–13 Sep 44*

1st/Sgt Leonard A. Funk, Jr. *Braddock Township, Pa.* 508 ParInf, 82ABDiv (G) *29 Jan 45*

*S/Sgt Archer T. Gammon *Chatham, Ky.* 9 ArInf, 6ArDiv (B) *11 Jan 45*

S/Sgt Marcario Garcia *Sugar Land, Tex.* 22 Inf, 4Div (G) *27 Nov 44*

Pvt Harold A. Garman *Fairfield, Ill.* 5MedBn, 5Div (F) *25 Aug 44*

T/Sgt Robert E. Gerstung *Chicago, Ill.* 313 Inf, 79Div (G) *19 Dec 44*

*2d Lt Stephen R. Gregg *New York, N.Y.* 143 Inf, 36Div (F) *27 Aug 44*

S/Sgt Sherwood H. Hallman *Spring City, Pa.* 175 Inf, 29Div (F) *13 Sep 44*

*2d Lt James L. Harris *Hillsboro, Tex.* 756 TkBn (F) *7 Oct 44*

*PFC Joe R. Hastings *Malvern, O.* 386 Inf, 97Div (G) *12 Apr 45*

Sgt John D. Hawk *San Francisco, Cal.* 359 Inf, 90Div (F) *20 Aug 44*

*T/Sgt Clinton M. Hedrick *Riverton, W. Va.* 194 GliInf, 17ABDiv (G) *27–28 Mar 45*

S/Sgt James R. Hendrix *Lepanto, Ark.* 53 ArInf, 4ArDiv (B) *26 Dec 44*

*PFC Robert T. Henry *Greenville, Miss.* 16 Inf, 1Div(G) *3 Dec 44*

*PFC Silvestre S. Herrera *El Paso, Tex.* 142 Inf, 36Div (F) *15 Mar 45*

S/Sgt Freeman V. Horner *Mt. Carmel, Pa.* 119 Inf, 30Div (G) *16 Nov 44*

1st Lt Victor L. Kandle *Roy, Wash.* 15 Inf, 3Div (F) *9 Oct 44*

*S/Sgt Gus Kefurt *Greenville, Pa.* 15 Inf, 3Div (F) *23–24 Sep 44*

*S/Sgt Jonah E. Kelley *Roda, W.Va.* 311 Inf, 78Div (G) *30–31 Jan 45*

T/Sgt John D. Kelly *Venango Township, Pa.* 314 Inf, 79Div (F) *25 Jun 44*

Cpl Thomas J. Kelly *Brooklyn, N.Y.* 48 ArInf, 7ArDiv (G) *5 Apr 45*

*T/4 Truman Kimbro *Madisonville, Tex.* 2 ECB, 2Div (B) *19 Dec 44*

*Pvt Harold G. Kiner *Aline, Okla.* 117 Inf, 30Div (G) *2 Oct 44*

1st Lt Daniel W. Lee *Alma, Ga.* 117 CavRcnSq (F) *2 Sep 44*

1st Lt Turney W. Leonard *Dallas, Tex.* 893 TkBn (G) *4–6 Nov 44*
T/Sgt Jake W. Lindsey *Isney, Ala.* 16 Inf, 1Div (G) *16 Nov 44*
1st Lt Edgar H. Lloyd *Blytheville, Ark.* 319 Inf, 80Div (F) *14 Sep 44*
Sgt Jose M. Lopez *Mission, Tex.* 23 Inf, 2Div (B) *17 Dec 44*
Lt Col George L. Mabry, Jr. *Sumter, S.C.* 8 Inf, 4Div (G) *20 Nov 44*
Sgt Charles A. MacGillivary *Boston, Mass.* 71 Inf, 44Div (F) *1 Jan 45*
*PFC Joe E. Mann *Seattle, Wash.* 502 ParInf. 101ABDiv (H) *18 Sep 44*
T/5 Robert D. Maxwell *Boise, Ida.* 7 Inf, 3Div (F) *7 Sep 44*
†T/Sgt Vernon McGarity *Right, Tenn.* 393 Inf, 99Div (B) *16 Dec 44*
*Pvt William D. McGee *Indianapolis, Ind.* 304 Inf, 76Div (G) *18 Mar 45*
*PFC Francis X. McGraw *Philadelphia, Pa.* 26 Inf, 1Div (G) *19 Nov 44*
*Sgt John J. McVeigh *Philadelphia, Pa.* 23 Inf, 2Div (F) *29 Aug 44*
PFC Gino L. Merli *Scranton, Pa.* 18 Inf, 1Div (B) *4–5 Sep 44*
Pvt Joseph F. Merrell *Staten Island, N.Y.* 15 Inf, 3Div (G) *18 Apr 45*
*Sgt Harold O. Messerschmidt *Grier City, Pa.* 30 Inf, 3Div (F) *17 Sep 44*
*2d Lt Harry J. Michael *Milford, Ind.* 318 Inf, 80Div (G) *14 Mar 45*
*S/Sgt Andrew Miller *Manitowac, Wis.* 377 Inf, 95Div (F–G) *16–19 Nov 44*
*S/Sgt John W. Minick *Wall, Pa.* 121 Inf, 8Div (G) *21 Nov 44*
*1st Lt Jimmie W. Monteith, Jr. *Low Moor, Va.* 16 Inf, 1Div (F) *6 Jun 44*
2d Lt Audie L. Murphy *Farmersville, Tex.* 15 Inf, 3Div (F) *26 Jan 45*
*PFC Frederick C. Murphy *Boston, Mass.* 259 Inf, 65Div (G) *18 Mar 45*
1st Lt Charles P. Murray, Jr. *Baltimore, Md.* 30 Inf, 3Div (F) *16 Dec 44*
Sgt Ralph G. Neppel *Glidden, Ia.* 329 Inf, 83Div (G) *14 Dec 44*
1st Lt Carlos C. Ogden *Boston, Ill.* 314 Inf, 79Div (F) *25 Jun 44*
T/Sgt Nicholas Oresko *Bayonne, N.J.* 302 Inf, 94Div (G) *23 Jan 45*
*T/5 Forrest E. Peden *St. Joseph, Mo.* 10 FA, 3Div (F) *3 Feb 45*
*S/Sgt Jack L. Pendleton *Sentinel Butte, Mont.* 120 Inf, 30Div (G) *12 Oct 44*
T/Sgt Frank D. Peregory *Albemarle, Va.* 116 Inf, 29Div (F) *8 Jun 44*
*Pvt George J. Peters *Cranston, R.I.* 507 ParInf, 17ABDiv (G) *24 Mar 45*
*S/Sgt George Peterson *Brooklyn, N.Y.* 18 Inf, 1Div (G) *30 Mar 45*
*T/5 John J. Pinder, Jr. *McKees Rocks, Pa.* 16 Inf, 1Div (F) *6 Jun 44*
*PFC Ernest W. Prussman *Baltimore, Md.* 13 Inf, 8Div (F) *8 Sep 44*
*1st Lt Bernard J. Ray *Brooklyn, N.Y.* 8 Inf, 4Div (G) *17 Nov 44*
1st Lt James E. Robinson, Jr. *Toledo, O.* 861 FA, 63Div (G) *6 Apr 45*
*Brig Gen Theodore Roosevelt, Jr. *Oyster Bay, N.Y.* 4 Div (F) *6 Jun 44*
Pvt Wilburn K. Ross *Strunk, Ky.* 30 Inf, 3Div (F) *30 Oct 44*
*Sgt Joseph J. Sadowski *Perth Amboy, N.J.* 37 TkBn, 4ArDiv (F) *14 Sep 44*
*PFC Foster T. Sayers *Marsh Creek, Pa.* 357 Inf, 90Div (F) *12 Nov 44*
S/Sgt Joseph E. Schaefer *New York, N.Y.* 18 Inf, 1Div (G) *24 Sep 44*
*PFC Carl V. Sheridan *Baltimore, Md.* 47 Inf, 9Div (G) *26 Nov 44*
*S/Sgt Curtis F. Shoup *Napenoch, N.Y.* 346 Inf, 87Div (B) *7 Jan 45*
1st Lt Edward A. Silk *Johnston, Pa.* 398 Inf, 100Div (F) *23 Nov 44*
PFC William A. Soderman *West Haven, Conn.* 9 Inf, 2Div (B) *17 Dec 44*
S/Sgt Junior J. Spurrier *Russell County, Ky.* 134 Inf, 35Div (F) *13 Nov 44*
*PFC Stuart S. Stryker *Portland, Or.* 512 ParInf, 17ABDiv (G) *24 Mar 45*
Sgt Max Thompson *Bethel, N.C.* 18 Inf, 1Div (G) *18 Oct 44*
*Cpl Horace M. Thorne *Keansburg, N.J.* 89 CavRcnSq, 9 ArDiv (B) *21 Dec 44*
1st Lt John J. Tominac *Conemaugh, Pa.* 15 Inf, 3Div (F) *12 Sep 44*
*Pvt John R. Towle *Cleveland, O.* 504 ParInf, 82ABDiv (H) *21 Sep 44*
Capt Jack L. Treadwell *Snyder, Okla.* 180 Inf, 45Div (G) *18 Mar 45*
*Sgt Day G. Turner *Berwick, Pa.* 319 Inf, 80Div (L) *8 Jan 45*
PFC George B. Turner *Longview, Tex.* 499 AFA, 14ArDiv (F) *3 Jan 45*
*PFC Jose F. Valdez *Governador, N.M.* 7 Inf, 3Div (F) *25 Jan 45*
*PFC Herman C. Wallace *Marlow, Okla.* 301 ECB, 76Div (G) *27 Feb 45*
Lt Col Keith L. Ware *Denver, Col.* 15 Inf, 3Div (F) *26 Dec 44*

*Cpl Henry F. Warner *Troy, N.C.* 26 Inf, 1Div (B) *20–21 Dec 44*
*Sgt Ellis R. Weicht *Clearville, Pa.* 142 Inf, 36Div (F) *3 Dec 44*
*PFC Walter C. Wetzel *Huntington, W.Va.* 13 Inf, 8Div (G) *3 Apr 45*
1st Lt Eli Whitley *Florence, Tex.* 15 Inf, 3Div (F) *27 Dec 44*
Sgt Hulon B. Whittington *Bogalusa, La.* 41 ArInf, 2ArDiv (F) *29 Jul 44*
Pvt Paul J. Wiedorfer *Baltimore, Md.* 318 Inf, 80Div (B) *25 Dec 44*
*Cpl Edward G. Wilkin *Burlington, Vt.* 157 Inf, 45Div (G) *18 Mar 45*
*1st Lt Walter J. Will *Pittsburgh, Pa.* 18 Inf, 1Div (G) *30 Mar 45*
*T/5 Alfred L. Wilson *Fairchance, Pa.* 328 Inf, 26Div (F) *8 Nov 44*
2d Lt Raymond Zussman *Hamtramck, Mich.* 756 TkBn (F) *12 Sep 44*

APPENDIX 10

※※※ ※※※ ※※※ ◄◄◄ ◄◄◄ ◄◄◄

Korean Conflict

27 June 1950 to 27 July 1953

※※※ ※※※ ※※※ ◄◄◄ ◄◄◄ ◄◄◄

KEY:
* = Posthumous award
† = Former POW
‡ = Died in POW status
5 Cav = 5th Cavalry Regiment
5 RCT = 5th Regimental Combat Team
8 ECB = 8th Engineer Combat Battalion
15 FAB = 15th Field Artillery Battalion
16 Rcn = 16th Reconnaissance Company
19 Inf, 24Div = 19th Infantry Regiment, 24th Infantry Division
72 TB = 72d Tank Battalion
187 ABRCT = 187th Airborne Regimental Combat Team

M/Sgt Stanley T. Adams *Olathe, Kan.* 19 Inf, 24Div 4 Feb 51
*Pvt Charles H. Barker *Pickens, S.C.* 17 Inf, 7Div 4 Jun 53
*PFC Emory L. Bennett *Cocoa, Fla.* 15 Inf, 3Div 24 Jun 51
Sgt David B. Bleak *Shelley, Ida.* 223 Inf, 40Div 14 Jun 52
*SFC Nelson V. Brittin *Audubon, N.J.* 19 Inf, 24Div 7 Mar 51
*PFC Melvin L. Brown *Mahaffey, Pa.* 8 ECB, 1CavDiv 4 Sep 50
1st Lt Lloyd L. Burke *Stuttgart, Ark.* 5 Cav, 1CavDiv 28 Oct 51
*SFC Tony K. Burris *Blanchard, Okla.* 38 Inf, 2Div 8–9 Oct 51
*Sgt Cornelius H. Charlton *New York, N.Y.* 24 Inf, 25Div 2 Jun 51
*Cpl Gilbert G. Collier *Tichnor, Ark.* 223 Inf, 40Div 19–20 Jul 53
*Cpl John W. Collier *Worthington, Ky.* 27 Inf, 25Div 19 Sep 50
*1st Lt Samuel S. Coursen *Madison, N.J.* 5 Cav, 1CavDiv 12 Oct 50
*Cpl Gordon M. Craig *East Bridgewater, Mass.* 16 Rcn, 1CavDiv 10 Sep 50
Cpl Jerry K. Crump *Forest City, N.C.* 7 Inf, 3Div 6–7 Sep 51
†Maj Gen William F. Dean *Berkeley, Cal.* CG, 24Div 20–21 Jul 50
*Capt Reginald B. Desiderio *Gilroy, Cal.* 27 Inf, 25Div 27 Nov 50
1st Lt Carl H. Dodd *Kenvir, Ky.* 5 RCT, 24Div 30–31 Jan 51
‡SFC Ray E. Duke *Whitwell, Tenn.* 21 Inf, 24Div 26 Apr 51
*SFC Junior D. Edwards *Indianola, Ia.* 23 Inf, 2Div 2 Jan 51
*Cpl John Essebagger, Jr. *Holland, Mich.* 7 Inf, 3Div 25 Apr 51
*Lt Col. Don C. Faith, Jr. *Washington, D.C.* 32 Inf, 7Div 27 Nov–1 Dec 50
*PFC Charles George *Whittier, N.C.* 179 Inf, 45Div 30 Nov 52
*Cpl Charles L. Gilliland *Yellville, Ark.* 7 Inf, 3Div 25 Apr 51

232

*Cpl Clair Goodblood *Burnham, Me.* 7 Inf, 3Div 24-25 Apr 51
*Cpl Lester Hammond. Jr. *Quincy, Ill.* 187 ABRCT 14 Aug 52
*M/Sgt Melvin O. Handrich *Manawa, Wis.* 5 RCT, 24Div 25-26 Aug 50
*PFC Jack G. Hanson *Galveston, Tex.* 31 Inf, 7Div 7 Jun 51
*1st Lt Lee R. Hartell *Danbury, Conn.* 15 FAB, 2Div 27 Aug 51
Capt Raymond Harvey *Pasadena, Cal.* 17 Inf, 7Div 9 Mar 51
*1st Lt Frederick F. Henry *Clinton, Okla.* 38 Inf, 2Div 1 Sep 50
Cpl Rodolfo P. Hernandez *Fowler, Cal.* 187 ABRCT 31 May 51
Sgt Einar H. Ingman *Tomahawk, Wis.* 17 Inf, 7Div 26 Feb 51
*Sgt William R. Jocelin *Baltimore, Md.* 35 Inf, 25Div 19 Sep 50
*PFC Mack A. Jordan *Collins, Miss.* 21 Inf, 24Div 15 Nov 51
*Pvt Billie G. Kanell *Poplar Bluff, Mo.* 35 Inf, 25Div 7 Sep 51
*SFC Loren R. Kaufman *The Dalles, Or.* 9 Inf, 2Div 4-5 Sep 50
*PFC Noah O. Knight *Jefferson, S.C.* 7 Inf, 3Div 23-24 Nov 51
M/Sgt Ernest R. Kouma *Dwight, Neb.* 72 TB, 2Div 31 Aug-1 Sep 50
*Capt Edward C. Krzyzowski *Cicero, Ill.* 9 Inf, 2Div 31 Aug-3 Sep 51
*2d Lt Darwin K. Kyle *Racine, W.Va.* 7 Inf, 3Div 16 Feb 51
M/Sgt Hubert L. Lee *Leland, Miss.* 23 Inf, 2Div 1 Feb 51
*Sgt George D. Libby *Casco, Me.* 3 ECB, 24Div 20 Jul 50
*Sgt Charles R. Long *Kansas City, Mo.* 38 Inf, 2Div 12 Feb 51
*Cpl William F. Lyell *Old Hickory, Tenn.* 17 Inf, 7Div 31 Aug 51
*Cpl Benito Martinez *Ft. Hancock, Tex.* 27 Inf, 25Div 6 Sep 52
*1st Lt Robert M. McGovern *Washington, D.C.* 5 Cav, 1CavDiv 30 Jan 51
*Sgt LeRoy A. Mendonca *Honolulu, T.H.* 7 Inf, 3Div 4 Jul 51
Capt Lewis L. Millett *South Dartmouth, Mass.* 27 Inf, 25Div 7 Feb 51
†Cpl Hiroshi H. Miyamura *Gallup, N.M.* 7 Inf, 3Div 25 Apr 51
SFC Ola L. Mize *Gadsden, Ala.* 15 Inf, 3Div 10-11 Jun 53
*SFC Donald R. Moyer *Keego Harbor, Mich.* 35 Inf, 25Div 20 May 51
*PFC Joseph R. Ouellette *Lowell, Mass.* 9 Inf, 2Div 31 Aug-3 Sep 50
*Cpl Charles F. Pendleton *Ft. Worth, Tex.* 15 Inf, 3Div 16-17 Jul 53
*PFC Herbert K. Pililaau *Waianae, T.H.* 23 Inf, 2Div 17 Sep 51
Sgt John A. Pittman *Tallula, Miss.* 23 Inf, 2Div 26 Nov 50
*PFC Ralph E. Pomeroy *Quinwood, W.Va.* 31 Inf, 7Div 15 Oct 52
*Sgt Donn F. Porter *Ruxton, Md.* 14 Inf, 25Div 7 Sept 52
*Cpl Mitchell Red Cloud, Jr. *Friendship, Wis.* 19 Inf, 24Div 5 Nov 50
Sgt Joseph C. Rodriguez *San Bernardino, Cal.* 17 Inf, 7Div 21 May 51
Cpl Ronald E. Rosser *Crooksville, O.* 38 Inf, 2Div 16 Jan 52
*Cpl Dan D. Schoonover *Boise, Ida.* 13 ECB, 7Div 8-10 Jul 53
1st Lt Edward R. Schowalter, Jr. *Metairie, La.* 31 Inf, 7Div 14 Oct 52
*1st Lt Richard T. Shea, Jr. *Portsmouth, Va.* 17 Inf, 7Div 6-8 Jul 53
*SFC William S. Sitman *Bedford, Pa.* 23 Inf, 2Div 14 Feb 51
*PFC David M. Smith *Livingston, Ky.* 9 Inf, 2Div 1 Sep 50
*Cpl Clifton T. Speicher *Gray, Pa.* 223 Inf, 40Div 14 Jun 52
†1st Lt James L. Stone *Pine Bluff, Ark.* 8 Cav, 1CavDiv 21-22 Nov 51
*PFC Luther H. Story *Americus, Ga.* 9 Inf, 2Div 1 Sep 50
*2d Lt Jerome A. Sudut *Wausau, Wis.* 27 Inf, 25Div 15 Sep 51
*PFC William Thompson *New York, N.Y.* 24 Inf, 25Div 6 Aug 50
*SFC Charles W. Turner *Boston, Mass.* 2 Rcn, 2Div 1 Sep 50
*M/Sgt Travis E. Watkins *Gladewater, Tex.* 9 Inf, 2Div 31 Aug-3 Sep 50
PFC Ernest E. West *Wurtland, Ky.* 14 Inf, 25Div 12 Oct 52
1st Lt Benjamin F. Wilson *Vashon, Wash.* 31 Inf, 7Div 5 Jun 51
*PFC Richard G. Wilson *Cape Girardeau, Mo.* 187 ABRCT 21 Oct 50
*PFC Bryant H. Womack *Rutherfordton, N.C.* 14 Inf, 25Div 15 Mar 52
*PFC Robert H. Young *Vallejo, Cal.* 8 Cav, 1CavDiv 9 Oct 50

INDEX

238   HEROES OF THE ARMY